THE
PERILOUS
SEA

THE PERILOUS SEA

Salt-drenched tales of true adventure on the high seas from the pages of Yankee Magazine

Edited by Clarissa M. Silitch

a division of Yankee Publishing Incorporated,
Dublin, New Hampshire

PHOTO AND ILLUSTRATION CREDITS: 10, courtesy of Alan Murrell; 15, courtesy of Eric Murrell; 31, courtesy of Barbara Tallman Whitcomb; 35, 40, Austin Stevens; 48, 52, courtesy of William L. Bauhan; 58, Wide World Photos; 69, Herbert Balch Hewitt and the families of the *Can Do*; 77, Warren E. Patriquin; 83, U.S. Bureau of Ships, National Archives; 97, 101, 107, Peabody Museum of Salem; 114, Austin Stevens; 125, Jay Paris/courtesy of Hildy Paris; 138, Paul R. Turnbull; 145, Department of the Navy; 149, The National Archives; 152-153, U.S. Coast Guard; 166, 169, Bruce Hammond; 174, Wide World Photos; 180, 187, 191, The National Archives.

Designed by Jill Shaffer

Yankee Publishing Incorporated
Dublin, New Hampshire
First Edition

Library of Congress Catalogue Card Number: 84-51708
ISBN 0-89909-061-3 (hardcover)
0-89909-065-6 (softcover)

Contents

Foreword

Napoleon looked for more than competence, or even brilliance, in a general. He sought a general who was lucky. Luck, assuredly, can be a catalyst for victory. But the seafarers whose stories are so well told here . . . fishermen, yachtsmen, naval commanders . . . were, almost to a man, skilled and competent — and unlucky — seamen.

It is just this matter of luck, perhaps, that lends a touch of Greek tragedy, of predestined doom, to so many of the disasters and defeats recounted in *The Perilous Sea*. On shore, or in the air, luck seems less important; the causes of disaster can all too easily be traced to a pilot's error, a driver's carelessness, a railroad engineer's ignoring of a red signal.

But there is little carelessness evident in the yarns told in *The Perilous Sea*. What Captain Frank Quirk of the Gloucester pilot boat, *Can Do*, went out to do in a raging storm was precisely what he had often done before. Likewise, the commander of the USS *Indianapolis* was an officer of experience and dedication who took every precaution suggested by his years afloat. If his shortcut across shoal water was ill-advised, the captain of the *Argo Merchant*, also, was doing only what he had done before.

Raphael Semmes of the CSS *Alabama* could be faulted for taking out his sea-weary *Alabama* against the feisty Captain John Winslow and the USS *Kearsarge*. But Semmes had little real choice. Both he and his opponent knew that one lucky hit could — and often had — decided the outcome of many a naval engagement . . . as another defeated captain, Dacres of HMS *Guerrière* could attest when fire from "Old Ironsides" dropped his masts.

Few if any of the seafarers whom you will meet here can be fairly charged with taking unnecessary chances or with foolish or reckless conduct. They were doing precisely what they had always done. And there lies the irony. By doing what they had always done, they sealed their own fate. Once they set out on the course they chose, they could not turn back, they could not evade the disaster that awaited them. The unpredictable sea intervened — and neither the seamanship nor the courage mattered. The sea outweighed all else, and men and ship went down.

But *The Perilous Sea* is no grim, chill collection of unrelieved disasters and deaths. The sea does not triumph in all these stories. The passengers on board the sinking *Republic* and on the leaking *Danmark* were saved. Heroic action saved others on a disabled submarine and on an armored cruiser at the mercy of a storm.

What shines through every story, in fact, in *The Perilous Sea* is what a British poet, no doubt unfashionable these days, W.E. Henley, called "man's unconquerable soul." The sea does not triumph in any story here; the human spirit triumphs. Men may die, but the sea does not win. Instead, these stories affirm once again the courage and compassion of the human spirit at its best.

No one expected Captain Frank Quirk Jr. of the *Can Do* to risk his ship and his life because he was worried about young Coast Guardsmen in trouble in turbulent seas. Charles Willey's job description aboard a Navy armored cruiser did not include the task of getting as many of his comrades as he could out of a shattered boiler room filled with scalding steam.

Lovers of seafood have been known to raise their eyebrows over the high price of shellfish, lobsters and fish in their favorite restaurants. David Boeri's story in *The Perilous Sea*, recounting his days as a fisherman, may . . . and should . . . lower those eyebrows. Few if any foods are procured at greater cost than the seafood that adorns American tables. Folk in New Bedford and in Gloucester, wise in the ways of the sea, complain no less than their fellow Americans of such annoyances as high taxes. But they do not complain of the high price of seafood; they know its cost in ships and men.

And yet, the cost charged to seafarers by the ocean have never been so high, so terrible, so intimidating as to cause men to stay on shore. Greek legend tells of sailors aboard a doomed ship declaring stoically that though *their* ship is lost, other ships will sail on and make port. This attitude and their philosophy have been echoed by seafarers ever since.

John H. Ackerman
New Bedford Standard-Times
New Bedford, Massachusetts

"Those Huddled Masses"

"Am sinking — take off my people ..."

By Tim Clark

For five days, the cargo steamer *Missouri* had battled stiff westerly winds and high seas on its voyage from London to Philadelphia. Captain Hamilton Murrell of the Atlantic Transport Line was disgusted to learn that in the twenty-four hours preceding his noon sighting of April 5, 1889, the *Missouri* had covered only 134 miles — half a normal day's run. Murrell, though only twenty-three years old, was a veteran of twelve years in the merchant service, and the *Missouri* was his second command. But unless conditions improved, this was not going to be a profitable voyage.

An hour later Murrell's brooding was interrupted by his Third Officer, Mr. Lucas. Lucas had spotted a large steamer one point off the port bow, apparently in distress. Murrell altered his course to approach the stricken vessel.

It was the *Danmark* of Copenhagen, en route to New York with 665 passengers, most of them Norwegian emigrants with families, and a crew of some seventy men. The day before, a propeller shaft had broken loose, killing her chief engineer and tearing a huge hole in the ship's bottom before her engines could be stopped. As onrushing seawater threatened to overwhelm what pumps were still in operation, the *Danmark's* skipper, Captain Knudsen, asked Murrell if he could take off the passengers.

Murrell was flabbergasted. He had a crew of thirty-seven plus a few passengers, and might have been able to squeeze in another twenty or so, but the thought of taking on almost 700 was absurd. He offered instead to tow the *Danmark* to the nearest port, which was St. John's in Newfoundland. Knudsen accepted, and the crews of the two ships got busy with the complicated operation. Taking a ship in tow in mid-ocean is not

---

Captain Hamilton Murrell (the dark-coated figure in the upper right corner, stripes visible on his sleeve as he points downward) supervises the transfer of women and children from lifeboats to the Missouri *in this steel engraving presented to Murrell in honor of his deeds. The children are being lifted in coal baskets.*

like taking a car in tow on land. Imagine trying to attach a tow line to the other car's bumper during an earthquake when both vehicles are rolling back and forth, and rocking from side to side. Now imagine those vehicles thousands of times larger and heavier, and one begins to appreciate the difficulties involved.

Murrell steered the *Missouri* to windward of the crippled liner, and a boat from the *Danmark* brought over one end of a three-inch-thick manila rope. Once aboard the *Missouri*, it was used to haul over a monstrous ten-inch cable, which once transferred was secured to mooring posts, or "bitts" on the forecastle deck. The tow rope was 120 fathoms (720 feet) long, and on board the *Danmark* it was attached to another forty fathoms of anchor chain, so that the two ships, underway with the tow line taut, were about a thousand feet apart.

The operation was concluded by 4:30 that afternoon. Now the *Missouri*, steaming at its slowest speed so as to take up the enormous strain without any sudden jerks that could part the cable, turned the *Danmark* into the wind, and began heading into the waves on a course west-northwest, with St. John's some 650 miles away.

As night fell, lanterns were hung over the *Missouri's* stern to aid the steersmen aboard the *Danmark*. In the continued heavy seas, the strain on the tow line was frightful. A wire bridle was added to the line where it was tied to the *Missouri's* mooring bitts, but a gigantic wave smashed into the bow at about 11:30 that night, and carried the bridle away. The beams of the forecastle deck itself were pried up by the blow, and for a moment the *Missouri* shuddered and groaned like an animal in pain. But the tow line held, and in a few hours the wind had moderated enough to allow another wire bridle put on the cable. By dawn, wind and waves had diminished so much that the *Missouri* could increase its speed.

But the first light of April 6 revealed a new and deadly obstacle — ice. Captain Murrell realized that there was no way his laboring ship could force its way through the pack ice to be expected at that time of year in those latitudes. Reluctantly he ordered a change of course. The two ships reversed themselves and headed for the Azores, more than a thousand miles south and east.

As he gave the order, Captain Murrell must have wondered if his ship could endure the strain of dragging the much larger *Danmark* all the way to the Azores. But he needn't have worried. The *Danmark* was not going any farther. At 8:30 that morning, Captain Knudsen signaled: "AM LEAKING BADLY — FIVE FEET OF WATER IN AFTERHOLD." Half an hour later came a second message: "AM SINKING — TAKE OFF MY PEOPLE."

There was no longer any choice about it, and only one way it could be done. Captain Murrell ordered his men to throw the entire cargo — cement, linseed, bundles of rags, bales of wool, indigo, herring, and skins

— overboard. The tow line was cut, and the desperate people on board the *Danmark* were ordered to stand by to be taken off — women and children first. No baggage allowed. Murrell ordered two officers, Lucas and Forsyth, to take the *Missouri's* two lifeboats over to the *Danmark* and assist with the evacuation. He also ordered them to make sure that every boatload brought as much food as possible from the sinking ship. The *Missouri* had a fresh-water condenser capable of producing 8,000 gallons of drinking water a day, but there were provisions only for forty men for three weeks. Now began the most dangerous phase of the rescue. In all there were 735 persons on board the doomed *Danmark* — twenty-two of them babies less than a year old, sixty-five children under twelve, and 200 women. There were eight lifeboats, each capable of carrying twenty-three or twenty-four persons, and a smaller boat that was used exclusively for provisions.

At times, the waves were so high that the boats disappeared from view in the deep valleys between crests.

A quarter-mile of ocean separated the two ships, and a heavy swell from the southwest made transferring passengers from ship to boat and back to ship tricky. Mr. Forsyth was knocked down into his boat while trying to fend off from the side of the *Danmark*, and lost seven teeth. Had he fallen between the boat and the ship, he would have been crushed.

The *Danmark* had an accommodation ladder that could be used by older passengers, and the sailors on board the *Missouri* had rigged ropes and nets on her side, but getting the babies and small children from ship to boat and back again presented a problem. Captain Murrell came up with an ingenious solution. The children were placed in coal baskets and hauled up and down with ropes. By 10:15 A.M., the first boatload had arrived at the *Missouri* — two women and twenty-two infants, plus one large doll which a young owner had refused to leave behind. They were swung up on deck, where the sailors, unsure of how to handle them, put them all in the saloon cabin on the deck. When the other mothers arrived on the next boat, they found their babies rolling helplessly to and fro on the reeling floor of the cabin, squalling but safe.

By noon, all the women and children had been transferred, and the men began to come across. Murrell had the challenging task of continually keeping far enough away from the *Danmark* to avoid a collision. At times, the waves were so high that the boats disappeared from view in the deep valleys between crests.

The last boatload of passengers came aboard the *Missouri* at 4:30 that afternoon. The weather was worsening, and a light rain was turning to fog as Captain Knudsen, who had stayed on board the *Danmark* to direct the transfer operation, abandoned his ship. His last act was to shoot three valuable dogs that were being shipped to America. There was no telling whether there would be enough food for the people, so the dogs had to be sacrificed. At 5:30, the fog enveloped the *Danmark*, and the *Missouri* got underway. There being no room for them on board, the *Danmark's* six boats were scuttled, so that no other ship, coming across them in mid-ocean, would report the steamer lost with all hands. As it turned out, one of the *Missouri's* sister ships, the *Minnesota*, did spot some of the wreckage, and took the grim tidings to London.

Now it fell to the *Missouri's* chief officer, Mr. Gates, to find accommodations for the crowd. The officers and men of the *Missouri* gave up their berths to the frailest of the women and children. Captain Murrell's cabin was taken over by five women and a baby, while eleven young girls were squeezed into the 6'x12' wheelhouse. The empty cargo hold was crammed with refugees, and about two hundred were left to sleep on the deck, protected from the elements by sails, awnings, and tarpaulins. By midnight all were bedded down, in varying degrees of comfort, and the ship was running before a fresh gale towards her destination.

But the long day's labor and excitement were not over yet. At 1 A.M., a passenger gave birth to a baby girl in the chief officer's berth, assisted by the ship's doctor. (She was named Atlanta Missourie Linnie.)

It was a difficult night. The wind increased to a strong gale, and heavy seas washed over the unfortunate people on the deck. There was no hope of changing wet clothes, and no dry clothes to put on. Now that the exhilarating rescue was over, many of the emigrants had time to realize the enormity of their losses — all their possessions, and in many cases their life savings.

It was a cold and comfortless dawn as the passengers, jammed on the main deck, walked up and down disconsolately, trying to warm themselves and work out kinks in stiff muscles. Everyone was soaked to the bone, and mothers could only try to comfort their crying babies with murmurs and embraces.

But there was food enough for everyone — butter, cheese, biscuits, German sausage, and hot coffee. The people lined up for their provisions and shuffled through the galley for coffee, which was ladled out into buckets, meat tins, saucepan lids, and in some cases directly into open mouths. A tub of rice was boiled for the children, who sat around it with their mothers. Later that morning, Captain Murrell turned the ship into the freshening breeze so that clothing and sails could be dried, and for a while the *Missouri* looked like a floating clothesline.

As the day went on the weather improved, and with food and dried clothing, so did the spirits of those on board. It was a Sunday, and that evening several Lutheran preachers who were among the emigrants held a service of thanksgiving. One of the *Danmark's* cabin passengers, a Miss Lofgrin of the "Swedish Quartette," was a professional singer, and she sang for the gathering, among other songs, "Home Sweet Home."

The next day was also fine, and the seas were calm enough to allow the crew to improvise washtubs by cutting hogsheads in half. The passengers had a chance to wash themselves, everyone had three meals, and there was more worship and singing on the deck that night. The *Missouri* was making good time, and at 10 the next morning, April 9, land was sighted. It was Terceira, one of the Azores. Captain Murrell laid a course for Ponta Delgado, a harbor on the island of St. Michael's, and there was one more night of prayers, songs, and hardship before the anchor was let down on the morning of April 10.

Captain Murrell some time after the rescue, wearing his richly deserved medals.

Once on land, Captain Murrell met with the Danish consul, who told him that the mail steamer, the only form of communication with the mainland, had left the day before, and it would be two weeks before it would return. The consul and Captain Knudsen asked Murrell if he would allow some of the passengers to continue on to America on the *Missouri*. Murrell agreed, and it was decided that 365 — about half, all women, children, and married men — could stay on board, and head directly for Philadelphia, while the rest, all single men, were put ashore and quartered in an empty grain warehouse, where they would stay until the owners of the *Danmark* could provide alternate transport to New York.

Meanwhile, the *Missouri* was taking on fresh provisions, including two bullocks, a dozen sheep, a ton of fresh meat, twelve dozen chickens, a thousand eggs, biscuits, bread, fruit, vegetables, flour, rice, more blankets, and eating utensils. Captain Murrell promised his crew an extra month's pay in return for putting up with more crowding for the ten-day run. By sunset of the next day, April 11, the *Missouri* was underway again, leaving the harbor to the cheers of the islanders and the Norwegians on land and aboard ship.

The voyage to America was unremarkable. The crew made Easter eggs for the children on Good Friday, and the wrecks of two other ships were sighted on April 20. On Sunday, April 21, a last religious service was held, and at nine o'clock that night the pilot boat *Henry Cope* met the *Missouri* off Cape Henlopen. The long journey was over.

By now news of the rescue had been telegraphed and cabled around the world, and a huge crowd lined the banks of the Delaware River the next day as the *Missouri* made its way upriver to Philadelphia. Hundreds of steam whistles screeched in welcome, reporters flocked aboard the ship from small boats to get exclusives, and a crowd of five thousand strong waited on the wharf, cheering.

The passengers were eventually reunited with those who had been left in the Azores, who arrived in New York a month later. The Atlantic Transport Line approved Captain Murrell's actions, and gave the crew their bonus, as he had promised them. Murrell became the toast of the East Coast, and honors and decorations flooded in from around the world. The kings of Sweden and Rumania sent gold medals, Prince Bismarck of Germany sent a congratulatory letter, and the king of Denmark made Murrell a Knight of the Order of Dannebrog.

Murrell's rewards were not limited to the praise of princes. In the crowd that came to welcome the hero to Baltimore a few weeks later was a young woman who, shortly after meeting him, became his wife, and eventually bore him six children. The Murrells moved in 1901 to Massachusetts, where he worked for the Baltimore-Boston Barge Company.

Hamilton Murrell died of rheumatic fever in 1916, just four years after another passenger liner signaled desperately for rescue in the North Atlantic. But this time help came too late, and more than fifteen hundred passengers of the *Titanic* drowned, twenty-three years to the month after the rescue of the *Danmark*.

Author's Note: This article was adapted from material originally written by Catherine Murrell, the captain's mother, and privately printed in 1891. Catherine Murrell's account was supplied to *Yankee* courtesy of Esther Brittain Fry (Mrs. William J. Fry). She received it from Captain Murrell's son, Eric Hamilton Murrell, who is her uncle by marriage.

The Fisherman's Lot

One week after graduating from Wesleyan University, the author signed on as a deckhand aboard a fishing trawler out of Boston, bound for Georges Bank, to satisfy his lifelong dream of going to sea.

BY DAVID BOERI

ogbound, 150 miles off Chatham Light. Seven days without break, unrelenting drizzle, an occasional foghorn moaning out to warn approaching trawlers of our presence. Yesterday morning's rainbow circumscribed a throbbing red sun. "Rainbow in the morning, sailors take warning; rainbow at night, sailors' delight." True to prophecy, last night we had cold damp drizzle, today, agitated seas; cutting spray breaks over the rail, hammering our oilskins.

Eight days ago — or was it nine? — the 130-foot beam trawler *Sturgeon Bay* slipped down the Highlands past Cape Cod Light and out into the Gulf of Maine toward Georges Bank. Just out of college, I had signed on with a crew of fourteen Newfoundlanders for the nine- to thirteen-day cruise out of the port of Boston. At the time it seemed like the thing to do; I'm having second thoughts.

Prow dripping and soaring as it cuts through rolling gray-green hills, a four-story elevator shaft: up four floors, take a right at the end of the corridor, and go down five floors. Rocking forward and aft, starboard to port — these men must have gyroscopes in their stomachs! At the ship's wheel, the spokes run through my hand as I try to steer a straight course. With the crashing impact of boiling seas and the cracking sound of thunder, my head is a pinball machine screaming *Tiiilt!!!* as dull electricity flashes through torrential rain. Seasick, I wish I were dead, or, given a second choice, on shore. Another rebuke to the glamor and romance I had projected into the life of a fisherman.

* * * * *

"Thar she blows!" Two hundred yards to starboard two humpback whales blowing. They break water, flukes flying, godlike in size if not form. Humpbacks are zany creatures. Standing on their heads, they lash their flippers back and forth (lobtailing, it's called), and tiring of that, they leap from the water, if you can imagine a two-ton leap, crashing with abandon, their raggedy flippers flying every which way.

There's nothing amusing about sharks, though. Skulking figures with the lurid grace of Rasputin, they hover, circle, approach the boat with the menacing presence of Brando and his gang in *The Wild Ones*. Ten to twelve feet in length, they command the silent attention of even the old-timers (standard practice is to cut the eyes out of captured sharks before throwing them overboard). Nervous laughter, but not too loud.

Unable to penetrate the heavy fog, ship's spotlights glare through boiling vapors, barely illuminating the foredeck. Time to haul back, but the forward deckhands can't see their shipmates working aft. Waves gently lap the hull; it has become strangely tranquil. There is no wind, only the faint whirring of Mother Carey's Chickens — small black and white birds, better know to landlubbers as Wilson's Storm Petrels — as the winch begins to haul up its nets from the ocean's bottom a hundred fathoms below. A steady stream of droplets falls from the hanging rope, so called for its eerie resemblance, especially when highlighted by deck lights against a background of darkness and mist, to the hangman's noose. This is sea-serpent weather.

What will appear from out of this primordial ooze? Along with the usual catch of haddock, cod, halibut, flounder, and pollock, there is always some weird and fascinating creature in our nets: squid, long rubbery tentacles, and protruding black and white eyeballs; dogfish, sharp jaws, an unnerving stare, and glistening cartilage which squeals in the nets; goosefish, enormous jaws lined with dangerous teeth and a bloated belly to match the jaws' appetite; catfish, the body of an eel and the whiskered face of old Puss-in-Boots.

Ever so slowly the warp, or cable to which the net is attached, comes in and wraps around the winch drums, indicating a heavy load in the cod end — the end section of the trawl equipment which is connected to the net's belly. Once the cod end comes to the surface, it is pulled manually to the rail, and from there it is raised and brought forward by wire ropes attached to a system of pulleys where the load of fish is emptied into a forward deck compartment. When the catch is large enough, the expanding air in the fishes' bellies causes the bag of fish to shoot up through the surface and float there until pulled in. "Cod end up!" someone matter-of-factly states — there's not much that surprises a fisherman: all we can hear is the whoosh of water as the cod end breaks the surface. Going aft, I help haul in the net, hand over hand on the cold wire mesh. With the cod end later suspended over the forward checker, I untie the coiled knot and 2,000 pounds of cod drop out, along with a 400-

pound electric skate, body design out of Buck Rogers, a ray with a wing span of three feet. Enough for a fish story — but no sea serpent!

* * * * *

My work as a deckhand is physically demanding, alternately exciting and dull, challenging and tedious, always invigorating. At twenty-two I am the youngest of the crew. The next youngest is fifty!! and the average age falls between fifty-eight and sixty-five.

The men are old, but the fishing grounds are near dead, ravaged by an international fleet that, led by the Russians, invaded the Gulf of Maine in 1958. Every nation in Europe seems to have a fleet on those grounds: Italy, Spain, Portugal, Poland, Yugoslavia, East and West Germany. The Maple Leaf and Fleur-de-Lis are everywhere, but so are the Russians and Japanese. On some nights you can see a string of lights along the horizon, or a cluster of blips on the radar screen. At other times there is a much larger stern trawler, Canadian scalloper, or huge Russian "mother" (factory) ship looming above in the fog nearby. We have just heard that a New Bedford dragger was sliced in two by a Polish trawler (1971).

Like the great majority of Boston's fishermen, my shipmates are from Newfoundland (most of the others are from Nova Scotia). They came to the States in the twenties and thirties, becoming fishermen for lack of anything else. Along with the small farmer, they are among the most oppressed workers of the world.

* * * * *

They are gruff men, quick-tempered, hard-headed, stubborn, and unreasonable. Underneath all that, they are kind, gentle, self-effacing, decent. While they are as foul-mouthed as any men I have come across in twenty years, and highly inventive in the use of obscenities, they always direct their abuse outward to places or things, never at any specific crewmate or groups. A comedy of sorts is played out every time they are on deck together. Screaming violently at no one in particular as they work to get the nets back over the rail — you don't make any money when the nets are on the deck — they stalk back and forth spitting, more often frothing, chewing tobacco in emotional frenzy. Minutes later they sit and wait for the next haul back, and share loose-leaf tobacco, while cursing passively together. The strongest language I ever heard used on board to describe a shipmate was "nut."

* * * * *

They all speak in a thick and at times impenetrable Scotch-Irish dialect. Rather than tell them outright that they're unintelligible, a tactic as futile as it is presumptuous, I have carefully projected an image of stupidity, inducing them to repeat things several times, thus increasing my chances of deciphering their code.

They talk of freaks on dope, niggers on welfare, politicians on payola, the Red Sox, and the numbers game. Playing dogs, horses, and especially the numbers is one of their greatest pleasures. Along with drinking, it is their greatest vice.

We sit and wait under the whaleback (the forward section, under the bow, below which is the cramped fo'c'sle where we bunk). These men have little to say, few stories to tell, only inquiries about the health or whereabouts of other fishermen, factual questions and answers. Silence pervades their lives at sea; loneliness and isolation are the marks of their existence. For fishing is a way of life, not a trade. Most of my shipmates became fishermen by habit and the lack of other work. They find too late that they have no skills to sell ashore, no alternatives to the sea.

They have no friends ashore, just acquaintances. Having seen your wife and children no more than two or three days every two weeks for five, ten, twenty years, can you, do you, know them well enough to live with them for the rest of your life? Can you perform the ordinary without questioning the ordinary meaning of your actions? The sea effects a change in men far deeper than their haggard weatherbeaten faces. The mysterious attraction of the deep transformed into salt is absorbed into their blood streams. They curse the sea, the day they embarked upon it, the lives they have led. Futilely. They cannot escape. Perhaps this explains the large number of fishermen who have drowned in alcohol rather than salt water, why none of these men have sons who are fishermen. Certainly it explains why fishermen don't retire; they die as fishermen.

Their reaction to me is a curious blend of humor, respect, anger, and puzzlement. Unable to bear the intense, staring silence that haunts the whaleback, I spend most of my idle time on the bow reading, writing, and observing. My activities amuse them. They seldom use my name. "Professor" they call me because of the book under my arm. Or "Tonto" because I use a headband to keep the hair out of my eyes, or "Jane" for the same reason. But mostly it's "Young Fella."

They consider me, college graduate that I am, a disgrace to myself and my family in my present occupation. Uneducated men, they are angered by — resent — my position alongside them, as if I mock the dreams they have had for themselves and for their children. They also understand what I am beginning to grasp, that having gone to sea once, you lose some of your freedom, you begin to weave the web of a salty prison. In an admixture of wisdom, anger, and frustration, they tell me to "get the hell out." They cannot. Even now I sense this ambivalence in me; it is somewhat frightening to feel the magnetic force of green eternity.

Last Voyage of the *Hoogly*

R. G. F. Candage was born into a seafaring family in Blue Hill, Maine, in 1826. He shipped out first when he was sixteen, on coasting vessels. Eventually he captained clippers in the India and China trade, making many trips around the Horn and several times circumnavigating the globe — but of all the trips he wrote about in his autobiography, we believe this one to be the most exciting.

BY CAPTAIN R. G. F. CANDAGE
(Courtesy of his grandson, Richard C. Raymond)

Several weeks after my return from Valparaiso, I signed on as first mate of the ship *Hoogly* of Boston, a new half clipper of 1,300 tons, owned by D.G. and W.B. Bacon, built by Samuel Hall, Esq. at East Boston, and commanded by Captain John Chadwick. She had two decks, orlop beams, a long, full poop cabin extending nearly to the mainmast, and carried a crew of forty. There were thirty-nine passengers in the cabin, making seventy-nine persons all told.

We sailed on an extremely cold day in February, 1852. When we left Boston harbor the sky was clear, but less than a dozen miles outside the lighthouse, the wind came down from the Northeast thick with snow. We carried a press of sail to drive us clear of Cape Cod and out of the South Channel, and then reduced and reefed it to get clear of the coast. The next day the wind backened to the Northwest and blew a howling winter's gale. The ship rolled heavily in the rough sea and most of our passengers, not yet having acquired their sea legs, were miserably sick. We rode out the gale without difficulty, until we entered the Gulf Stream; but no sooner were we in it than, due to the change in temperature, the rigging became suddenly slack, and before anything could be done to tighten it, the three topgallant masts went over the side, taking with them the head of the main topmast and springing a fore topmast.

Our second night out was a dismal one, for the mass of spars, sails, and rigging hung in a tangled web over the lee side, thumping against the rigging that was undamaged and the planks of the ship. It was altogether too dark and rough to attempt any work that night. In the midst of this trouble an infant passenger died. By morning, however, the gale and sea had subsided enough to enable us to pass frapping lines around the wreckage to hold it still while we cleared it away. Meantime the infant's body had been prepared for burial, that is, wrapped up and weighted, and as soon as it had gone over the side, we squared away upon our voyage. During the next few days we replaced the rigging and sent up new masts. After a fair passage across the line we arrived at Rio de Janeiro, forty-two days from Boston. Rio was not one of our regular ports of call, but Captain Chadwick decided to put in there in order to procure extra spars, etc. We sailed again after a detention of two days.

Our run to the Straits Le Maire was an excellent one. We entered the Straits with a light fair wind, but this died away almost at once, leaving the *Hoogly* caught in the tide. As darkness came we were carried close to the Fuegan shore, where the natives had fires, as one of the sailors said, "in readiness to roast and eat us." It was an anxious time for all of us, expecting to strike any moment, for even if we escaped drowning we could hardly be sure of a hospitable reception. We barely managed to keep clear till morning, when a leading wind took us safely through. Outside we ran into a hard gale with squalls of snow and hail. We were forced to reduce sail to close reef as one blast after another hit us with such force that the ship shook from stem to stern. Captain Chadwick had gone below to catch up on sleep, leaving me in command. He came back on deck during a period of comparative calm and started to make some sharp remarks about the close sail. He was on the point of ordering the reefs to be let out when another and even worse squall struck us. He ordered the reefed mainsail taken in and furled, and said no more about close sail.

While furling the mainsail, Horace Smith, a Boston boy, fell from the main yardarm, struck the quarter boat davit, and then plunged into the sea where he sank and was lost. He was a fine lad.

For the next ten days it was make sail and take in sail, reef and turn out reefs, in the endeavor to round the Horn. When the struggle was over, the countenances of the crew and the passengers, like barometers, told of the pleasant change. The passengers came back on deck and played games and pranks, while the crew was kept busy refitting ship. Things worked smoothly as we glided through the trades, and then one day in May we passed through the Golden Gate and cast anchor in the harbor of San Francisco, one hundred and twenty-six days from the time we had left Boston. Here the passengers and all the crew left, except the Captain, a boy, and myself, expecting to make their fortunes overnight. And no wonder the crew left, for wages were five and six dollars per day, to say nothing of the loose gold that lay waiting (so they thought) in the hinterland. There were many forsaken ships in port which were being used for storage, houses, and piers for landings. Everybody here was busy and seemed happy, in spite of the rough and tumble life. The appearance of the town was decidedly ramshackle and its streets terrible. One of them was so bad that some jokester-teamster had selected it to tack up this sign: "Notice! All in favor of presenting the street commissioners with a leather medal, please deposit a tobacco cud!" The sign was plastered with them. Gambling houses were numerous and wide open. Everyone visited them, for they served as exchanges where one met one's friends. The Captain and I spent most of our time ashore at the Bella Union, for the captains and officers of other ships often gathered there, some to gamble, some to drink and spin yarns.

. . . nearer the Fuegan shore, where the natives had fires, . . . "in readiness to roast and eat us."

When the *Hoogly* had discharged and ballasted, we dropped down into the stream to get a crew on board. But because of the number of deserted ships and the bright prospects ashore, sailors were difficult to obtain. We eventually picked up twenty-four, to whom we had to pay $150 per man by the run to Shanghai — $100 down and the balance on arrival in China. The cook, steward, and officers were procured at proportionately higher wages. All told there were thirty-one of the ship's company, and one passenger, a certain Mr. Woodberry, who later brought disaster down upon us. Our crew turned out to be an excellent one.

Twelve days out we landed the mails and purchased some fresh fruit at Honolulu. The trades were fresh so we had an easy sail to the Island of Ascension, one of the Ladrones, and then shaped our course between Formosa and the Lew Chew Islands for the Yang-tse-Kiang. We sighted the Saddle Islands on the Chinese coast, passed Gutzlaff and headed for Wusung, the port of Shanghai. So far we had had fair weather, but now it became cloudy and rainy. The wind blew a fair gale and we were forced to run before it under double reefed topsails. We knew we were near the coast, but it was too low to be visible, and the water was very shallow. There were no lights or buoys, nor had we any pilot to guide us. Our only aid was the lead.

At this point Mr. Woodberry came forward to volunteer as pilot. He had been in Shanghai many times before and claimed he knew the coast well, for, he said, he had sailed up and down it on numerous occasions under all sorts of conditions. He seemed so sure of himself that the Captain turned the ship over to him. The Captain cannot be blamed, for he did not know the waters, and here was someone who did, or rather thought he did. Mr. Woodberry thought the ship was too near the coast, so he at once changed her course, and when the water shoaled, he changed it still more. In a few minutes we struck with a whack. The full force of the gale had driven us onto a reef. The *Hoogly* rolled over and thumped heavily in the high sea. We worked frantically to cut away the masts and to let the anchors go. She finally righted, but was already half full of water. We were then thirty-nine days from San Francisco.

The wind continued to blow a gale, and the rough sea pounded the wreck on the reef. We were afraid that the wreckage of spars would punch holes through the planks, but by working as hard as we could, we managed to clear them away from alongside before dark. At night the tide ebbed and the wreck lay more quiet. As there was nothing to be done till morning, the crew had a few hours of rest. Before turning in, we held a council. The general opinion was that we were on the mainland or on the south side of the channel, although no vessel or land had been seen since passing Gutzlaff. We decided to stay by our ship until she broke up, hoping either to be picked up or to be able to land when the weather cleared. No one was at all eager to embark in a small boat on such a sea.

In the morning, the gale and seas were still unabated. No vessel or land was in sight, and we were far from sure that any of us would reach shore alive. The tide made flood and came up to the main deck. The long boat and remaining quarter boat — one having been stove in by the falling spars — were shifted to the poop for safety, and then fitted with oars, spars, sails, provisions, and water, in readiness for leaving. We cut away the poop taffrail for their launching. At the next high tide the main deck was four feet under water, but when it ebbed the wreck again lay quiet and all hands spent the night upon the poop.

The morning of the third day brought no change in wind, rain, or sea. During this day it was low water, and the wreck comparatively quiet, but at flood it flowed over everything save the poop and forecastle, and even these were invaded at times. It was now evident we would soon have to leave. We hoped to stick until the following day, but that night the poop was pretty well under water and we could stay no longer. The Captain took the quarter boat and seven men; I the long boat with the remaining men of the ship's company, including our "pilot." We swung them round before the wind and sea and then shot out into the dark to go we knew not where. We had agreed to keep company, but soon became separated in the darkness. The sea was so rough that, to keep us from being swamped, the men sat on the gunnel of the boat to make a breakwater with their bodies, while one bailed with a bucket. Once we struck bottom in a hollow between two seas but kept moving. Otherwise the next wave would have filled the boat, and all would have been lost. As we advanced, the sea became smoother. Soon we grounded, and the men jumped overboard to track us along. After a quarter of an hour of this someone cried: "Land!" Sure enough. We headed for it and in a short while were on it. We had been tracking along parallel with the shore,

which proved to be an extensive salt marsh. It was after midnight when we landed. We hauled our boat out of the water, set a watch of two to the right and two to the left, made a tent of the sail, and in front of it suspended a lantern from an oar stuck in the marsh, as a guide for the other boat. Then we lay down for a bit of sleep, for we were exhausted.

These arrangements had scarcely been completed when the watch on the left ran up to the boat in great excitement yelling: "Get up and fight! Armed men are coming. Hear 'em shout!" Each man sprang up and prepared to defend himself with the various muskets and knives we had taken on leaving the wreck. The boat was to furnish a breastwork. Until daylight we awaited the attack, but none was made. Then we saw a herd of buffalo cattle feeding on the marsh and came to the conclusion that they were the "army" the watch had seen, their horns being their "arms," and their snorting at the approach of strangers, the "shouts."

Daylight showed neither man nor habitation. The water's edge was now two miles from us, our boat having come in over the marsh on the top of the high tide which was forced in by the gale. We ate our breakfast from the provisions in the boat and then set to work to get her afloat, by using the oars for skids. At noon we had her launched half the distance. After our noonday meal we resumed work. Up to this time we had seen no living creature except the cattle, but that afternoon two Chinese men came to the boat and talked, but no one understood them. After they had jabbered a while I pointed to the right and said, "Shanghai." They pointed in the opposite direction saying, "Shang hy yah!" And then to the ground and said something I could not understand. They left in a short time.

At dusk we got our boat to the water and after supper set sail up the coast. The boat jumped about in such a lively manner and so frightened some of the sailors that they begged to be landed. The sail was reefed, and we persuaded them to keep on. Soon, however, we began to ship water and the cry was given that we were sinking. We landed four or five miles from our starting point. Five of the sailors jumped out and started away, saying they would walk to Shanghai, that they had escaped with their lives and would not trust themselves in the boat again. I tried to reason with them, saying that they ought to stay by the boat as it might be the means of saving their lives, and that at least they should help haul her up out of the surf; but if they would not they should forfeit their right to her. They said they wanted nothing further of her and started off into the darkness. The rest agreed to stay. The boat was hauled up on the shore, a watch was set and the rest of us laid down in her to sleep until morning.

We ate our breakfast and were arranging plans for the day when a Chinese approached and said "chin chin" in a friendly manner. I said to him, "Shanghai?" and pointed to the right. He said, "Shang hy yah" and pointed to the left. Then he pointed downward and repeated slowly, "Tsung Ming! Tsung Ming!"

Now this was what the Chinese had said the day before. Then it dawned upon me that we were on the island of Tsung Ming and not on the mainland as had been supposed, and I decided to find out, if possible, just where we were before proceeding further. I knew that the word "taow-tai" meant governor.

I took from my pocket a Mexican dollar, held it up to the Chinese, pointed down, then landward, and said "taow-tai." The Chinaman caught the meaning, and by signs, agreed to guide me to the taow-tai for the dollar. I then arranged with the third mate, Mr. Harrington, to get the boat afloat and anchor her clear of the shore, free from intruders, and await my return from interviewing the governor. I also instructed him that no one but himself should handle a valise that contained five thousand dollars in gold. This belonged to the Captain, but in the hurry of leaving the wreck, had been passed into the longboat. Mr. Harrington and twelve sailors were left to care for the boat, and I, along with Mr. Woodberry, the cook, and the steward started with the guide for the interview with the taow-tai.

... no one but himself should handle a valise that contained five thousand dollars in gold.

The guide took us first to his house behind the dike and gave us melons from his garden. Then we started on a journey of five miles across the island. The paths were narrow, formed of the soil thrown out of the little canals or ditches for drainage purposes, with which the surface was intersected. The ground was closely cultivated and the island thickly populated. It had been formed from mud deposited by the Yang-tse in ages past and was not thirty miles long, five wide, and said to contain 200,000 to 300,000 people. By Chinese industry and skill, it had been reclaimed from the sea, protected by a dike from innundation, and made the abode of many souls. On our way across, we passed many villages whose thatched-roof dwellings were small but seemed to contain numerous persons. We passed a schoolhouse with doors and windows open, from which came the sound of boys' voices reciting their lessons in unison. They saw the passing strangers and came out to look. The guide spoke to them, and though they followed for a distance, they made no unfriendly demonstration. The men were quite as curious as the boys and asked questions of the guide, but offered no insults or indignities.

We reached the house of the taow-tai and were ushered into his audience room, where the guide made known the reason for our visit. The taow-tai waved us to seats at a table in the middle of the room, on which he placed a watermelon for us to eat. The room was large and was soon filled by a curious crowd. Others stood looking in through the doors and windows. The taow-tai was beyond middle life, of good presence and proportions, with gray hair, thin beard and moustache, and one seemingly fit to be in authority. At the table were Mr. Woodberry and myself on one side, and on the other the Negro cook and steward, and standing in the rear were the taow-tai and others. The women of the house, peering in through an open door, caught sight of the Negroes, and stepping up behind them, looked round into their dusky faces, felt their hair, and talked to each other excitedly, evidently never having seen a Negro before. The cook and the steward were frightened and when they felt their hair fingered, rolled up their eyes to me in a beseeching manner, and one most ludicrous to witness.

The melon had been eaten, but no definite plan had been arranged for the interview. In fact, none could have been as neither understood the language of the other, so matters were left to shape themselves according to circumstance. The melon had refreshed the party, and I was considering what I should do next when the taow-tai handed me a sentence written in Chinese characters. I took it, looked at it, shook my head, handed it back, and motioned to the taow-tai to pass me his pen and paper, which he did. I scrawled a sentence in English and passed it to him. He looked at it, shook his head, and passed it to others, who shook their heads, as much as to say, "We can't understand their language nor they ours, what can we do?"

All this time I had been thinking out of what I could make a boat and so convey to the governor what had happened to us. On the table lay the rind and seeds of the melon we had just eaten. I took a piece of the rind, and fashioning it into the form of a ship, stuck pieces of bamboo in it to represent masts, removed the rest of the rind to my left, and then moved my improvised ship across the table, ran it upon a pile of rind, and broke it to show that my ship had been wrecked. I then made two boats of the rind, in one placing twenty-four seeds and in the other eight to represent men; then pointed to the four present and counted on my fingers to make twenty-four, then downward and said, "Tsung Ming!" I placed eight seeds in the other rind boat, and moved it to the side of the table where it fell to the floor. I shook my head, meaning that they had drowned. Not a word had been said, but I watched the taow-tai and saw by the expression on his face that he understood. Next I took a silver dollar, held it up to the taow-tai, and pointing downard said, "Tsung Ming!" Then pointing westward said, "Shanghai!" meaning, "For how many dollars will you convey the party from Tsung Ming to Shanghai?" In answer the taow-tai raised both hands with fingers open, signifying that he would do it for ten dollars, to which I speedily nodded assent and the bargain was closed. In like manner arrangements were made to start for Shanghai. The next day we inspected the junk which was to take us and found her satisfactory. We agreed to return to the boat, get our effects and the other sailors, and, leaving the boat on the north side of the island, to come back that night. With these arrangements completed, we bade adieu to the kind taow-tai and set out to rejoin our companions.

We found the boat afloat and at anchor a hundred yards from the shore, and upon the marsh in front of her a villainous-looking body of two hundred Chinese armed with pikes and presenting an unfriendly aspect. It was then dusk, and the guide made signs that if the party attempted to recross the island that night, they might expect to be robbed and perhaps murdered, and he drew the edge of his hand across his throat in a manner not to be misunderstood. The wind had changed and was now fair to sail around the island. For an additional dollar, the guide agreed to pilot the boat around. We had kept quietly in the background and had not been seen by any of the cutthroats. Suddenly we came out before them, hailed the boat to take us aboard, and shoved off, leaving the pikemen standing on the marsh, before they could realize what had taken place.

We were surprised to find in the boat the five sailors who had deserted the night before to walk to Shanghai. I asked them, "What are you doing here? You were to walk to Shanghai and wanted nothing more of the boat. What do you mean by coming back to her?" They told a pitiful story of their wandering from the boat in the darkness, of being set upon and robbed of their money and clothing except drawers and undershirts, of being made prisoners under guard until morning, when they were released and found their way back to the boat, overjoyed to be received back by their crew. They each had lost a belt of gold worth several hundred dollars earned in California, which they had about their bodies.

I said to them, "You have forfeited your right to share in the boat by your conduct. You were told what the result would be when you went away, and you accepted it; but as you found the walking poor, you came back and wish to be reinstated as part of the boat's crew, but I am not willing to grant your request." They pleaded and promised good behavior and obedience to orders if allowed to remain. I answered, "You deserve to be made an example, and I for one, would not take you back, but will put it to a vote of your shipmates to decide." As I expected, the vote allowed them to remain, and the boat sailed away.

The result of the interview with the taow-tai was made known, which gave the crew great satisfaction. Mr. Harrington gave an account of his experience during the day: "We who were left to care for the boat, were surprised to see the five deserters return, nearly naked and half starved, and when they told their story we were frightened and set about launching the boat. We did not stop till she was afloat and at anchor. That had scarcely been done when the pikemen began gathering on the marsh, we thought to attack us, but we were beyond reach. Your return from the taow-tai and change of plan frustrated their intention and made us mighty glad."

We reached the harbor without any trouble, went alongside the junk, and made fast before midnight. The baggage was transferred, a watch was set, and preparation made for a nap. But the town was in an uproar. The people were hurrying about with lanterns, shouting and making a great noise. I sent the guide to find out what it meant. He returned, explaining by signs that the people, seeing a boatload of men come into the harbor at night, thought the town was going to be sacked, and they were preparing to meet the invaders. He explained the situation, the town quieted down, and there was no further disturbance.

In the morning we purchased food for the trip and paid the pilot. The taow-tai, captain, and the crew of the junk, consisting of ten men, made their appearance and all was ready to depart. The junk was gotten under way with the longboat in tow, the taow-tai waved his hand, and the shipwrecked crew of the *Hoogly* bade adieu to Tsung Ming and were off for Shanghai. We arrived at Wusung that afternoon. There, alongside of a receiving ship for opium, we saw the captain's quarter boat. We sent up three cheers. The junk was rounded to her anchor, let go, and all hands went aboard the opium vessel where the crews of the two boats had a joyful meeting a week after the wreck of their ship. Our effects were passed aboard the ship and as a sailor took up the valise containing the five thousand dollars in gold and felt its weight, he said: "Bill, there's money in that!" That was the only time a sailor had touched it since leaving the wreck. Two thousand dollars in silver were lost in the *Hoogly* for the Captain and I, who alone knew it was on board, agreed that its weight might imperil the boat's safety, or excite the cupidity of the sailors, so we left it behind.

Captain Chadwick was at Shanghai when the longboat arrived, but returned that evening and was overjoyed to find that the lost boat and the crew were safe. He gave me an account of his doings since our parting the night the wreck was abandoned. After passing the reef where the longboat was nearly swamped, he anchored his boat. At daylight he got under way and sailed to Wusung. As no tidings came of the longboat, he chartered a schooner, went to the wreck, found it submerged except the bowsprit and part of the forecastle deck, but gained no tidings of the missing boat. He returned and offered a reward of fifty dollars for any intelligence of the boat or of the crew, dead or alive, but no one came until the arrival of the boat herself.

The following day all hands went to Shanghai, the junk following with the longboat in tow. We appeared before the consul to settle the junk's hire. The circumstances relating to her hire were related and agreed to through an interpreter by the junkmen. The consul paid them the ten dollars for the hire, which was satisfactory, and then at my suggestion, gave each of the ten Chinamen a dollar as an incentive to treat kindly men who in the future should be cast upon their island. This was explained to them through the interpreter. They took the money and departed, highly pleased. There was no misunderstanding about the hire of the junk, and the terms were carried out faithfully and without a hitch, as well as though a charter party had been made, signed, and delivered.

The sailors were sent by the consul to a boarding house. The boats were sold and their proceeds divided among the crew. The officers were paid in full. The sailors got berths on other ships, the second and third mates came home the mates of the ships *Witchcraft* and *Snowsquall*, the Captain came home master of the ship *Oramingo*, whose former master had died at Shanghai, and I shipped first mate of the clipper ship *Eclipse* of New York, bound for London.

Four Days in the Rigging

By the third night, he was the only man still alive ...

BY BARBARA TALLMAN

My great-great-uncle was Charles Tallman of Osterville, Massachusetts, a mate on the two-masted schooner *Christina*. On January 7, during the storm which would become known as the Great Blizzard of '66, the *Christina*, laden with cement, was off Martha's Vineyard. She was captained by a Mr. Leach and carried Mate Tallman and a crew of four.

When they were off Cape Pogue on Chappaquiddick, which is on the east coast of Martha's Vineyard, a northeast gale arose with such rapidity and of so great an intensity that those aboard feared for their lives. Helplessly they watched as the *Christina* went aground on Hawes Shoal, a few miles easterly of the light.

Uncle Charley believed in preparing himself as well as he could, and while the other men hoped the storm would abate or chose to take their chances if it did not, he pulled on all the clothing his body would support, including extra sets of underwear and trousers, and covered all with a rubber coat — which act may have saved his life.

The sea was breaking mast-high in below-zero weather, and the men were being lashed with icy water, battered with cold wind.

Captain Leach, Charles, and the four other men climbed up into the rigging, above high water, and lashed themselves thereto: then began the slow tragedy. Uncle Charles was to watch as, one by one, his five shipmates froze to death, their bodies assuming strange postures silhouetted against the swaying masts.

Although the schooner could be spotted from the Vineyard, no boat could battle the angry sea to attempt a rescue. The hours became days, the days became years. To keep his arms from freezing and to encourage the circulation in his stiffening body, Uncle Charley had to thrash his hands and arms, although his fingers were now becoming frozen solid. So were his toes. On the third night, he was the only man still alive.

Charles Tallman, survivor.

The fourth day he was nearly without hope. If help did not arrive before sundown, he knew that he, too, would surely die. The only solace he found was to look through the "hole in the wall" and see, rising above the horizon, the steeple of the Osterville church. The coast, along Wianno, was heavy with pine groves, but opposite Eel River, for a hundred yards or less, there is an open space, and the church spire could be seen from the ocean through this so-called "hole in the wall."

What did Charles think about, swaying alone above an angry sea, his eyes on the church steeple? God? And the measure of his gratitude if he survived? God was ever-present to the men of Uncle Charley's generation — and to be depended upon.

On that fourth day, when the weather had cleared and the seas calmed somewhat, a longboat put out to rescue any survivors on the *Christina*, although it was believed there could be none. In the longboat were Captain Thomas Dunham, James Fisher, George Fisher, Charles Fisher, Edward Luce, and Eugene Wilber. My uncle, Joseph Tallman, Jr., of Osterville, has a picture, beautifully sketched by one B. Russell of New Bedford, showing the longboat alongside the schooner.

As Uncle Charles told it, his heart rose when he saw, at long last, help approaching, but to his great despair the boat circled the schooner twice, and the rescuers decided that all hands on board must have perished, that no one could have outlived such an ordeal. Those remaining in the rigging were dangling like wooden puppets with broken strings.

The rescuers had started to row back toward Chappaquiddick when they heard a feeble voice. It was ghostlike — supernatural — that sounds should be coming from the throats of dead men. Uncle Charles said that his words, no matter how they sounded on the winter air, were "Come back, you landlubbers, and cut us down!"

Of course they did, and Charles was taken to Edgartown, where the natives cared for him until he was removed to Holmes Hole (now Vineyard Haven). His feet had been so severely frozen that it was necessary to remove them to the ankles, and to remove his fingers. In February he was able to leave for home.

However, in *Martha's Vineyard, 1835-1935*, Henry Beetle Hough says, "The *Vineyard Gazette* referred to him as 'one of nature's noblemen' and, in the summer of 1874, the Oak Bluffs Land and Wharf Company, through the Honorable E.P. Carpenter, presented him with a small octagonal building not far from the Sea View Hotel."

Each summer thereafter, Charles Tallman occupied his small octagon, where he sold simple refreshments (including eighty-five bushels of peanuts in 1877), souvenirs, and pictures of himself with an account of his survival . . . survival made possible by a Cape Codder's determination and a rubber coat.

Offshore Hurricane

On the night of November 21, 1980, the offshore lobster boats Fair Wind *and* Sea Fever, *both out of Hyannis, Massachusetts, were heading for Georges Bank and, unwittingly, into an ocean hurricane of titanic proportions. ("Each wave came at us like a mountain.") One of the two survived.*

By Evan McLeod Wylie

Outward bound from Hyannis on Cape Cod in a light southeast breeze, the *Fair Wind*, a 55-foot offshore lobster boat, sped across Nantucket sound on Friday afternoon, November 21. In the pilot house of the trim green and white craft, the 30-year-old skipper Bill Garnos checked over his charts while at the wheel his mate, 33-year-old Ernie Hazard, held a course for the Great Round Shoal channel buoy east of Nantucket. Down in the galley, 22-year-old Rob Thayer whistled as he put together a supper of soup and sandwiches for all hands. On the open afterdeck David Berry, still a month away from his twenty-first birthday, mended a trapline and shouted an exuberant greeting to the crew of another outbound lobster boat, the *Sea Fever*.

Aboard the *Fair Wind* there was the relaxed atmosphere and easy camaraderie of a seasoned crew, but their mood this afternoon was exceptionally lighthearted because this voyage was to be one of the last of the year. Since early April, they had been working on a grueling schedule that kept them at sea much of the time. But high market prices for lobster and rich hauls had made many a trip a bonanza. The night before, they had celebrated their good fortune with steak dinners at the Back Side Saloon in Hyannis. Soon the *Fair Wind* would be dry-docked for winter overhaul while her crew scattered on winter vacations that ranged from the New England ski slopes to the Florida Keys.

Designed specifically for offshore lobstering, the *Fair Wind* was a rugged, all-steel vessel of twenty-seven gross tons propelled by a 265-hp diesel engine, strengthened with five watertight bulkheads, and outfitted with the latest in sophisticated electronic navigational gear, including loran, radar, sideband and VHF radios, power steering, and automatic pilot. In equipment and attention to safety, the boat was one of the most highly rated in the New England fishing fleet. In the six years since it had been launched from a Massachusetts shipyard, it had proved itself to be a highly seaworthy craft. It fulfilled the hopes of its young owner, Charles Raymond of Beverly, Massachusetts, that a truly modern fishing vessel with a top-notch crew could operate safely and turn a profit for all hands. So much attention was lavished on the boat by Raymond and his men that it had been nicknamed "the yacht."

Setting out to sea, the *Fair Wind* did not lack for company. Good weather and a favorable marine forecast for the weekend had brought forth scallopers, draggers, trawlers, and lobster boats from Maine to Rhode Island. Many were planning to work within ten to twenty miles of land. But the *Fair Wind* and *Sea Fever* were bound on a course that would take them into vastly different waters — destination: Georges Bank.

Lying far out in the Atlantic Ocean, 130 miles southeast of Cape Cod, Georges is one of the world's richest and most extraordinary fishing grounds. Its undersea terrain, spread over an area of 10,000 square miles, ranges from chasms and canyons thousands of feet deep to shoals so shallow that breaking seas often fling fountains of spray high in the air.

Here, near the edge of the continental shelf, the icy green waters of the Labrador current collide with the warm waters of the Gulf Stream as it sweeps up the east coast of the United States and swings northeasterly toward Europe. The mingling of these two mighty ocean currents creates an upwelling of ocean-bottom water mixed with the minerals and microscopic plankton on which fish thrive. Cod and halibut spawn in the canyons and rise to feed among the layers of plankton that drift toward the upper sunlit waters. Lobsters dwell in the depths and ascend the walls of the canyons and gorges.

Bathed in bright sunshine on a sparkling summer day, Georges can seem like a fishermen's paradise, but the immensity of its riches is matched by the perils of its dense fogs, treacherous tidal current, and shifting shoals. As autumn wanes, the low atmospheric pressures of the warm Gulf Stream pull toward it the cold air from the interior of the continent, to create savage winter gales.

By dusk, the *Fair Wind* had passed through Great Round Shoals channel and was breasting the long swells of the open Atlantic ocean. As the lights of Nantucket faded on the horizon, night watches were set, and all hands save the man at the wheel settled into their bunks. The overnight run would bring them to Georges Bank by 6 A.M. After that they would be hauling their traplines for forty-eight hours straight.

In the darkened pilot house, illuminated only by the faint glow from the loran and radar scopes, Ernie Hazard scanned the gauges of the droning diesel and held his course to the southeast. All seemed snug and serene. The 6 P.M. marine weather forecast on Friday, which the *Fair Wind* crew heard as they ate their soup and sandwiches, called for northwester-

ly winds fifteen to twenty-five knots, shifting to southwesterly on Saturday. This was definitely good fishing weather for a sturdy vessel the size of the *Fair Wind* and it was on the basis of this forecast that skipper Bill Garnos decided that they were definitely "go" for the weekend.

But in fact, they were heading into the path of a violent and unheralded ocean storm, heading northeast at fifty miles per hour. Clouds obscured it from conventional weather satellites. No ships or weather stations had noted the force and progress of this titanic ocean hurricane. It struck Georges Bank like an atomic explosion.

As the *Fair Wind* arrived on Georges on Saturday morning, Ernie Hazard awoke to find the boat plunging heavily through the screaming gale. Hurriedly he joined Bill Garnos and Dave Berry in the pilot house. They had already flooded the lobster tanks in an attempt to stabilize the boat. Hazard and Rob Thayer moved out on the deck to lash down all gear. The wind was now out of the northwest. It was too late to turn into the teeth of the gale and try to run back toward Hyannis. They were trapped on the Bank, with seas building behind them. Reducing speed, they ran with the seas, but the waves were enormous and were taking them on the stern. The *Fair Wind* was plunging deeper into the troughs.

Through heavy radio static they heard calls from another vessel. It sounded like the *Sea Fever*, but the words were garbled.

"Repeat your message," Bill Garnos responded. "We can't hear you. It's going crazy out here."

The *Sea Fever*, a 50-foot wooden-hulled offshore lobster boat from Hyannis, had also been taken by surprise by the lack of storm warnings. At 5 A.M., when the Boston weather forecasts still were predicting winds of twenty to thirty knots, it was already blowing fifty to sixty knots.

By 11 A.M., when Boston finally broadcast a storm warning for all of Georges Bank, the winds had reached eighty to a hundred miles per hour.

The fury of the winds combined with the shoals and turbulent currents of the Bank combined to produce towering, steep-walled, breaking seas such as most fishermen never see in a lifetime.

As the *Sea Fever's* skipper, Peter Brown, twenty-four, of Swampscott, Massachusetts, wrestled to hold his boat's bow into the seas, a monstrous wave rushed toward them. Looking up, Richard Rowland saw the wave cresting overhead. Then with a roar, it smashed down upon them, shattering the thick windows of the pilot house. A torrent of water surged into the boat, knocking out the navigational equipment and flooding the bilges.

Turning downwind to avoid taking any more seas through the windows, Peter Brown shouted, "We've got to close up the bridge! Gary, take the wheel and Dick, get me some boards."

As Peter Brown tied a rope around his waist so that he could climb out on deck to fix the broken windows, Rowland knelt down to saw up a slab of wood. He heard Gary Brown (no relation to Peter) cry out as a wall of white water picked up the *Sea Fever* and hurled it on its side. The deck lurched beneath Rowland, and he slid into a corner buried under water and wooden debris.

. . . the boat was wallowing on its beam ends with the pilot house half under water, and no engine power.

When he surfaced, he found that the boat was wallowing on its beam ends with the pilot house half under water, and no engine power. Gary Brown had disappeared. At first Rowland thought he might be still buried in the submerged debris, but Gary had been hurled through the wall of the pilot house and now Rowland caught sight of him drifting in the sea about fifteen yards off the stern.

While Peter Brown dove down a hatch to try to start the engine, Rowland scrambled back along the slanting deck and tossed Gary a lifeline, but Gary made no attempt to grab it. Peter had the engine going and he swung the listing boat around to bring the bow over to Gary. He was in plain view off the port side and they shouted and tossed him more lines, but he did not respond. His face was blank and glassy-eyed as if he was in shock. In another moment he had drifted out of sight.

On the radio, Peter Brown called, "MAYDAY, MAYDAY. We have a man overboard. We may be sinking."

On the 65-foot *Broadbill* about twelve miles east of the *Sea Fever*, skipper Grant Moore of Westport, Masssachusetts, heard the Mayday and turned his boat to respond. Taking seas that put his deck underwater from rail to rail, he fought his way through the storm, radioing reports on the *Sea Fever's* plight to Coast Guard stations on Cape Cod.

This great offshore storm had merely brushed the New England coast, so that most people were unaware that Saturday was any more than another blustery autumn day. The first persons on shore to discern the magnitude and intensity of the storm were the staff of the Operations Center of U.S. Coast Guard headquarters in Boston.

When Chief Fay arrived for a stretch of twenty-four-hour duty at 5:30 A.M. on Saturday, "The telephones were ringing off the walls." One hour earlier, Lieutenant Robert Eccles had received a Hot Line call from the Coast Guard Station at Point Judith, Rhode Island. Its radio room was picking up a Mayday from the 76-foot dragger *Determined*, which reported that it was sinking in heavy seas thirty miles east of Block Island.

On Eccles's list of available rescue craft the nearest large vessel was the Coast Guard cutter *Active*, en route to its home port in New Hampshire. At Eccles's request, *Active* swung around and sped toward *Determined*, which was wallowing close to the waterline in heavy seas, and they passed over a pump to try to stem the flooding.

At 6 A.M., as Lieutenant Eccles was briefing Chief Fay about this emergency, the Coast Guard station at Nantucket relayed a Hot Line report that the fishing vessel *Cape Star* was in serious trouble with a split bow off Chatham, Massachusetts. The Coast Guard station in Portland, Maine, came on the line with word that another fishing vessel, *Sea Rose*, was sinking fifteen miles east of the Isles of Shoals, and the Woods Hole Station on Cape Cod was relaying a message from *Nordic Pride* that the *Christina* was sinking on Georges Bank.

The Boston Operations Center began crackling out orders for patrol craft based in Portsmouth (New Hampshire), Boston, and Chatham to put to sea to aid the stricken vessels, and alerted helicopter crews at the Air Station on Cape Cod to stand by for a rescue launch.

Messages continued to come in from the *Active*. The *Determined* was going down. Seas were too rough for the cutter to come alongside. A team of swimmers donned wet suits and a cargo net was rigged. The crew of the *Determined*, clad in survival suits, leaped into the seas and were rescued by the *Active's* swimmers. At 8:15 A.M. all were safe, and the *Determined* disappeared beneath the waves.

*   *   *   *   *

Behind the *Fair Wind* on Georges Bank, the seas were building higher and steeper, causing the boat to plunge ever deeper into the troughs. Fearful that he might capsize, Bill Garnos maneuvered the boat around to face the towering waves. The wind, rising to a screaming pitch, was sucking the bait out of the barrels, and the surface of the ocean was lashed into such a boiling fury that the *Fair Wind* seemed to be buried in foam. The waves, Hazard guessed, were now sixty to seventy feet high. The *Fair Wind* rose to meet each one, battling toward the crest. Looking up, Hazard saw a huge wave looming up beyond the bow. It burst thunderously over the top of the pilot house and under the avalanche of water, the *Fair Wind* was almost driven beneath the sea.

The next wave was even more gigantic. As the *Fair Wind* fought its way up the slope, a rogue wave broke sideways and spun the boat completely around. Caught on the face of the wave, the *Fair Wind* hurtled headlong down into the trough. As her bow buried itself in the sea, the stern shot skyward. In a matter of seconds the *Fair Wind* had "pitch-poled," turning completely upside down.

Ernie Hazard found himself underwater in icy darkness. Groping and struggling, he collided with hard metal and realized that he must still be inside the pilot house. His head broke out into a pocket of air and he gulped it down into his lungs. He knew he had to get out, but it was impossible to get oriented. He saw a block of dim light and swam and groped toward it, desperate for more air. He bumped hard on a metal doorway, swam through it, and then suddenly emerged, gasping and choking in the sea beside the overturned boat. The exposed propeller was screaming as the engine raced out of control. Waves surged over the hull. He had surfaced on the windward side and the overturned boat was blowing away from him. Alone in the sea, he thought, "I've got to make it back to the boat. Maybe the hull will float." Spying a floating bucket, Hazard overturned it to trap its air and clinging to it as if it were a barrel, kicked and bodysurfed down the next wave to try to reach the boat. As he reached the hull, he was astonished to see that an orange-colored canopy raft was bobbing in the water on the far side of the boat.

It was a Givens Buoy Life Raft, invented and built by Jim Givens of Tiverton, Rhode Island. An all-weather, self-righting raft, the Givens consisted of two rings of heavy-duty neoprene, five feet in diameter, surmounted by a protective nylon rip-stop canopy supported by three inflated arch tubes. Attached to the bottom of the raft was a submerged ballast chamber with a capacity of 2,900 pounds of water designed to keep the raft stable in high winds or heavy seas. Within the circular shelter of the canopy was space for six men.

Hazard battled his way around the drifting hull until he reached the raft. There was a small door in the side of the canopy and he pulled himself inside, hoping he would find himself reunited with his crewmates, but the raft was empty. Hazard recognized it as the raft that had been stored in a canister on the roof of the pilot house. When the *Fair Wind* overturned, it had been torn loose and some miracle had yanked the lanyard, which caused it to inflate automatically. Now it bobbed and tugged at the end of the lanyard, which was still attached to the boat.

Crouched inside the raft, Hazard caught his breath and waited, praying that he would see one or more of his shipmates rise to the surface. They might still be alive in air pockets inside the pilot house and might escape at any moment. He was shaking from shock and immersion in the icy cold water. In his fight to stay afloat he had kicked off his shoes and cast aside a wool jacket, and now he was wearing only soaking wet jeans, socks, and sweatshirt.

Despite the huge seas that surged over the partially submerged *Fair Wind*, the Givens raft was riding well at the end of its tether. An orange canvas bag containing a kit of survival items was washing about in the water inside the raft, and Hazard grabbed it and managed to tie it securely to rings in the canopy's wall. The large ballast bag beneath the raft had filled with water and was providing great stability, but the constant yank-

Ernie Hazard kicks his way free of the ballast bag.

ing and tugging on the line that secured the raft to the boat was placing a great strain on the undersea bag, and it was being ripped open.

About one hour passed and still there was no sign of life from within the *Fair Wind*. The submerged hull was sinking beneath the waves. Fearful that he and the raft would be pulled under, Ernie Hazard loosened the line and the raft drifted swiftly away, still engulfed in winds and seas of hurricane force. Only one other life raft is known to have survived passing through the center of a hurricane at sea and that, too, was a Givens. But the damage that Ernie's raft had suffered while he was tethered to the submerged hull had made it less stable, and as giant seas hurled it from the crests to the troughs, it tipped and pitched so wildly that Hazard considered lashing himself to rings in the canopy's wall. He decided against it, fearing that if the raft overturned he might not be able to escape, but a moment later he regretted his decision as a wave burst in through the door and swept him out of the raft. As the raft drifted away, Hazard swam frantically to overtake it and climbed back inside.

Within a short time, another mammoth sea picked up the raft and turned it completely upside down. As the submerged canopy filled with water, Hazard groped his way to the door and swam to the surface, but now he was without shelter from the driving spray and screeching gale. He glimpsed a hole that had been ripped in the bottom of the ballast bag and thrust himself down inside it. He was in water up to his neck, but at least he was protected from the terrible wind.

Then another wave rose beneath the raft and heaved it on its side. The wind caught the canopy and flipped it right side up. Hazard was again in underwater darkness inside the ballast bag, and when he tried to swim free, he found that his sweatshirt was snagged. Battling with his last breath as the bag filled with water, Ernie tore off his sweatshirt and left it behind. Kicking and swimming, he wriggled out of the hole in the ballast bag, swam back to the surface, and crawled back inside the canopy. He found himself seated in two feet of water, naked to the waist.

Grimly he told himself, "So long as this thing floats, I'll hang on!"

Locking his hands in the straps in the canopy's wall, he braced himself within the raft with his back against the rear wall and his feet toward the front door. Once again he felt another mountainous sea carrying the raft toward its crest. Up it went and then again turned upside down. Briefly Hazard hung upside down, spread-eagled within the canopy, and then the breaking crest of the wave surged past and the raft righted itself.

Hazard was like a man in a barrel going over Niagara Falls. Relentlessly the seas tumbled the raft, spun it, buried it, and sent it careening from crest to trough. Tons of water smashed over the canopy's arched roof and surged in and out of the door hatch, but the raft continued to float. Hazard hung on.

*   *   *   *   *

Night had fallen over the Atlantic Ocean when Helicopter 76, piloted by Lieutenants Buck Baley and Joseph Touzin, was airborne from the Coast Guard Air Station on Cape Cod with pumps for the *Sea Fever*. As they flew out over Nantucket the moon was shining, but soon they encountered the solid cloud mass of the storm and were forced to drop down to within a few hundred feet of the ocean. The wind, still strong out of the northwest behind them, propelled the big twin-engine helicopter at a fast clip, but its crew was keenly aware that on the return flight they would be bucking that wind as their fuel tanks emptied. If the helicopter went down in the violent seas beneath them, it would probably capsize and there would be no one who could rescue them.

Flying on instruments, they arrived on Georges Bank and began calling the *Sea Fever* and the *Broadbill*, homing in on their radio signals. Two other fishing vessels had joined the *Broadbill's* vigil over the *Sea Fever*. They were the *Reliance*, commanded by Allan Eagles of Newport,

Rhode Island, and the *Stephanie Vaughan*, a longliner. Finally the helicopter sighted the cluster of white deck lights in the black sea.

Hovering fifty feet above the water, Lieutenants Baley and Touzin inched their helicopter closer until they were directly over the *Sea Fever*. In the glare of the chopper's floodlights they could see that part of the pilot house of the boat was missing and waves were breaking over the stern.

"Do you wish to remain with your vessel or do you wish to be lifted off by hoists?" they radioed. It wouldn't be easy: winds were still over forty knots and seas were running twenty feet.

"We will stay with the boat," Skipper Peter Brown answered.

"Stand by for the pump," replied the chopper.

Down went a drop line and Petty Officers Davern and Smith wrestled the pump into the open doorway of the helicopter. Below, on the heaving deck of the *Sea Fever*, Richard Rowland and Peter Brown were grabbing for the line. There was little time for mistakes. Fuel limits would soon reach the point of no return. Now Brown and Rowland had the drop line aboard and Davern and Smith winched down the pump.

As soon as the pump was safely aboard the *Sea Fever*, Helo 76 veered off and switched on its "Night Sun." In its three-million-candle-power beam, they searched the sea for any sign of Gary Brown, who had been washed overboard that morning. Then, with fuel gauges dropping, the helicopter swung around and started the flight back toward Cape Cod.

*　*　*　*　*

In the Coast Guard's Boston Operation Center, Lieutenant Robert Eccles reviewed the situation at 11 P.M. Saturday. From Georges Bank came reports that the pump that had been delivered to the *Sea Fever* was stemming the flooding. The cutter *Active* was due on the scene at daybreak. The sunken *Christina's* men were safely aboard the *Nordic Pride*. Motor lifeboats from Chatham and Provincetown were towing in the *Cape Star*. A helicopter from the Cape Cod Air Station had guided the *Christina Marie*, another disabled fishing boat, through the treacherous shoals north of Nantucket, and the cutter *Cape Horn* was escorting the vessel toward Hyannis. The dragger *Barbara and Christene* had sunk, but her four crewmen had been rescued. No other ships were reported missing. Eccles concluded that one of the most hectic days in the history of the Center was ending, and after being on duty for more than thirty-eight hours, he bade Fay, Krizanovic, and Decker goodnight and went home.

*　*　*　*　*

Out on Georges Bank, Ernie Hazard was still alive in the Givens raft. Before darkness fell, he had discovered that the raft contained two paddles. Using the blade of a paddle as a shovel, he scooped and bailed water out the door until he was exhausted. Outside the storm still raged and gusts of wind-driven spray hammered on the canopy like machine-gun bullets. Alternately bailing and dozing off, Hazard fought to hold on until morning.

Hazard awoke at dawn. It was Sunday, November 23. The wind had dropped but there was still a heavy sea running with tremendous swells. The raft wallowed in them and when Hazard craned his neck out the door, he could see nothing.

Taking stock of his situation, Ernie found that he was bruised and sore from being flung about within the raft, but no bones appeared to be broken. Sorting out the contents of the survival bag, he found that it contained six 10-ounce cans of fresh water, a can of high-protein cookies, a can opener, a small bellows pump for the raft's air chambers, two packages of hand-held signal flares, and a small canister of Smith and Wesson flare cartridges. Secured to the canopy outside the door of the raft was a coil of heaving line and a small, blunt-nosed knife.

The cans of fresh water were badly dented from the pounding of the seas, but still intact. He opened one and drank it slowly and allowed himself one protein cookie. The sea seemed warmer. Hazard estimated it at about fifty to fifty-five degrees and guessed that wind and current were carrying the raft southeast, toward the edge of the Gulf Stream. This also meant that he must be nearing the edge of the continental shelf, and the chance of being sighted by a fishing vessel was slim.

He massaged his legs and feet, which were numb and blue from the cold water in which he had been kneeling and sitting, finished the cookie, and decided to rest until dark. The chance of such a small raft being sighted by day was slight. He would stay awake during the night and if he heard an aircraft or a boat's engine, he could risk firing a flare into the sky.

An ominous hissing aroused him from his doze. A damaged valve in the neoprene ring that formed the base of the raft was leaking air and above his head, the inflated arches that supported the canopy were sagging. The roof was literally falling in on him as the canopy enveloped him in its folds. He seized the small hand pump and began pumping air back into the valve. It reinflated the arches, but now there was another hissing sound behind him. Another valve in an opposite corner of the raft was leaking. With his knife he cut patches from the survival bag and tried to tie off the leaks, but could not stop them completely. It became clear there would be no time for sleeping. He would have to keep pumping one valve, tying it off, and then turning to pump the other. His legs were numb from kneeling and there was no longer any feeling in his swollen feet. He was afraid that they were already frostbitten and that, without dry clothing, hypothermia would soon overwhelm him.

"You don't want to admit you're going to get beat," he told himself. "It's better to keep working."

It also helped to keep his mind off the *Fair Wind*. "Better not to think when you're alone," he said. "Keep going. Keep busy." And so, during the blackness of Sunday night, he pumped air, rested, dozed, and then awaked to pump again.

*   *   *   *   *

Arriving on Georges Bank at dawn on Sunday, the Coast Guard cutter *Active* found the *Sea Fever* still afloat. The three fishing vessels were standing by and the *Broadbill* had passed over hot coffee and nails and plywood to patch up the smashed pilot house.

As the *Active* undertook to escort the crippled *Sea Fever* back to Cape Cod, there was talk between the ships about other boats on Georges that might be in trouble. No one, it was learned, had heard from the *Fair Wind* and at 7:30 A.M., Grant Moore, skipper of the *Broadbill*, recalled that he had last had radio contact with the boat at 10 A.M. on Saturday.

In his home in Beverly, Massachusetts, the *Fair Wind's* owner, Charlie Raymond, was aroused by a ringing phone. "This is the radio marine operator," a voice said. "I have a call for you from the fishing vessel *Broadbill*."

"Charlie," said Grant Moore, "I am out on Georges. We have been in a bad blow. Have you heard from your boat?"

It was the first inkling Raymond had that the *Fair Wind* might be in trouble. So strong was his faith in the boat and her crew that he assumed their radio antenna had been damaged in the storm.

Quickly he notified the Coast Guard. In the Boston Operations Center, Chief Fay and Lieutenant Decker, who had been looking forward to going home after a hectic twenty-four hours, found themselves swept up in a new search-and-rescue effort. The cutter *Active* was directed to turn over the *Sea Fever* to another fishing vessel and return at once to Georges Bank to resume the search.

Once more helicopters were launched from Cape Cod. A large HU-16-E aircraft out on patrol from Otis Air Force Base was summoned to fly a search pattern that scanned 5,000 square miles. Coast Guard shore stations from New Hampshire to Rhode Island began calling the *Fair Wind* on their radios and a bulletin about the missing vessel was broadcast.

But the *Fair Wind* and its crew had vanished. By late Sunday, Boston Operations was convinced that the boat had sunk. Next was the question of survivors.

Lieutenant Joseph Duncan, Search Planner, backed by a computer, began calculating the area to search, based on winds and currents. The major offshore search would continue through Sunday night with a C-130 from Elizabeth City, North Carolina, scanning another 10,000 square miles. On Monday there would be the *Active* and three large patrol planes. The search area was now beyond the range of helicopters.

Seeking further assistance, Lieutenant Duncan picked up a Hot Line and called the U.S. Naval Air Station in Brunswick, Maine. Based there was a squadron of long-range P-3 patrol planes whose anti-submarine and reconnaissance flights carried them far out into the Atlantic Ocean between Nova Scotia and Bermuda. Carrying a crew of eleven airmen and sophisticated electronic scanning equipment, each huge P-3 could stay aloft a full day or night and search an immense range of ocean. At dawn on Monday, a P-3 from Squadron VP-10, headed by Commander William Lash and Lieut. Commander Alfred Linberger, was airborne to search an area 350 miles east of New York.

He was finding it difficult to move his legs. He was now too weak to pump air much longer.

*   *   *   *   *

Peering out of the door of his raft on Monday morning, Ernie Hazard noted the skies were clearing. His raft seemed to be drifting toward the rising sun, farther and farther away from land. A few birds flashed by, flying close to the water, and he recognized them as stormy petrels and shearwaters, which dwell hundreds of miles at sea.

The sun would slowly warm the raft's interior, but Hazard doubted that it would do him much good. Exhaustion and hypothermia were overwhelming him. He was finding it difficult to move his legs. He was now too weak to pump air much longer.

Dimly he became aware of the drone of a large jet aircraft and, craning his neck out the door of the canopy, saw a plane passing on a course to the west. Lunging for his survival bag, he seized the Smith and Wesson signal flare kit and pressed the trigger, praying it would fire. There was a sharp pop and a red flare, trailing smoke and sparks, shot skyward, arching high into the sky before it dropped back into the sea.

Had they seen it? He could not tell, and not daring to wait, Hazard fired again. Another flare rocketed skyward and this time Hazard saw the wing of the plane dip.

Aboard the P-3, radioman Craig Martin had just reported to the pilots that he thought he spotted something, possibly a life raft. Commander Lash swung the aircraft around for a closer look and then saw the flares and a man in the raft waving an orange cloth.

It was 8:35 A.M. when their radio message was flashed to the *Active* and relayed back to Boston Operations.

The P-3 came thundering low over the waves to drop a smoke buoy as Ernie Hazard hung out the raft door feebly waving his orange survival bag.

Soon there were other planes in the sky. A Coast Guard C-130 dropped a portable radio but it fell some distance from the raft and before Hazard could retrieve it, another Coast Guard plane dropped a string of orange marker buoys in a scatter pattern. As Hazard's raft drifted close to one, he picked it up. Within it was a message: "If other crewmen aboard raft, wave."

For the first time, Ernie felt deep anguish overwhelm him. It confirmed what he had been putting out of his mind for two days: he probably was the only survivor.

On the horizon he glimpsed a hull, the bow of a white cutter emblazoned with bright red-orange stripes — the cutter *Active* steaming in for a pickup.

Aboard the *Active*, Hazard was buried in blankets and revived with mugs of coffee and clam chowder. He was suffering from multiple abrasions, frostbite, and hypothermia, and needed hospitalization as soon as possible, but they were 180 miles at sea. A helicopter was dispatched from Nantucket.

Ernie Hazard, reviving after treatment on the cutter, protested when he was carried out on the afterdeck in a stretcher and saw the hoist line dangling from the chopper. The prospect of being plunged once again into the icy ocean terrified him, but in a few moments he had been winched aboard the helicopter and was en route to a hospital in Beverly. Prompt medical treatment enabled him to make a complete recovery.

Throughout Monday and Tuesday, the *Active*, assisted by Navy and Coast Guard patrol planes, continued to search the ocean, but no more survivors or wreckage were found. The weather had cleared and in the serenity of the long ocean swells, all traces of one of the most violent storms in the history of Georges Bank had disappeared.

The *Fair Wind* is believed to lie in water nearly two miles deep. Its three crewmen and Gary Brown of *Sea Fever* join the legions of fishermen whose lives have been lost at sea.

Saga of the *Widge*

The story of a love affair . . .

By Hobart Bauhan

On a warm spring day in 1926, two men drove across the Delaware River from New Hope, Pennsylvania, to the New Jersey side north of Lambertville. One of the men was William L. Lathrop, a nationally known landscape artist, the other his son-in-law, Rolf Bauhan, an architect from Princeton, New Jersey.

Lathrop, who had sailed for years on other people's boats, had decided to build one of his own. He was not deterred by the fact that he had never undertaken such a project, nor by the fact that he was sixty-seven years old. For a long time he had been making plans and models of the ideal craft, and it was time to make that ambition into reality.

Lathrop did not drive, so he enlisted Bauhan, and together they began their search for materials for the boat in a grove of white oak. They were beautiful specimens, averaging at least two feet in diameter, their tall shafts straight and true. But Lathrop wasn't impressed. "If they're like this in here," he said, "there's probably one in a hedgerow that would be better. It will have stronger fiber for having fought the winds."

Sure enough, when they reached an open field, there, standing in a hedgerow, was a grand big oak almost four feet at the base and sixty feet high. The two men went to the farmer who owned the land, and he took fifteen dollars for the tree — provided the branches were cleaned up.

During the next week, a local sawmill cut the tree into planks and timbers, then delivered it to the Lathrop place, where it was allowed to season for a year. Out of this giant oak came all of the structural members of the boat, which Lathrop called *Widge* — short for the sea duck widgeon.

The keel of the *Widge* was over twenty feet long, six inches thick, and sixteen inches deep; it had 700 pounds of iron bolted into it. The big oak also supplied a husky stem post, stern post, sampson post, and enough knees to make two boats. Besides this, there were ten-foot timbers that were sawed into 2x2s for the ribs. During the fall, Lathrop found a lot of yellow pine logs more than a foot thick and fifty feet long. He selected several and had them sawed into one-inch planks for the outside of the hull.

The project got underway in the spring of 1927. Stakes were set and the keel was laid down. On the weekend of the Fourth of July, the ribs

were set into the keel. Section forms were built for the shape of the hull, the curvature taken from Lathrop's favorite model, and batten strips fastened from stem to stern at twelve-inch intervals against which the ribs were to be fastened. Bauhan brought a thirty-gallon hot water tank from Princeton with several lengths of pipe.

A steam box of 2x10 spruce boards about twelve feet long was fashioned and plugged at both ends with burlap bags. The hot water tank was placed at one end, horizontally, with a pipe leading into one end of the steam box. Coal was used to fire the boiler.

On this hot weekend of the Fourth, the 2x2 oak pieces were inserted into the steam box and the fire lit. A dozen or more were spoiled before the two men got onto the trick of just how much steam to administer. Bauhan would open the far end of the steam box, pull out a ten-foot rib, and run with it over to the cradle of the boat where Lathrop was waiting with the clamps. The rib would be heeled into the keel and then bent against the battens and clamped fast. Hot, exhausting work. Ribs were placed on twelve-inch intervals. As the oak was bent to the curve of the hull, many ribs broke because they were too dry, but finally the two got the hang of it and after three days they had her ribbed.

By the end of the year, the framing, with knees set, deck planking, and mast bracing, was completed. She was nine feet across the beam, twenty-six feet at the waterline, and had a draft of four feet six inches. *Widge* was a "pinkie" type, modeled on a North Sea fishing boat with a double end so that following seas would not be annoying. She was to be gaff-rigged with a reefing bowsprit. The mast was thirty-five feet high, made of spruce.

Planking was begun in the spring of 1928. This was a tricky job, for every plank had to be sawed to fit the curve of the hull. Each plank was beveled toward the outside to allow for caulking. The placing of the planks, which averaged five inches at the widest part, was accomplished with four operations on each rib. A hole was drilled through the plank into the rib for the screw. Then a wider hole was drilled so that a wooden plug could be let in to cover the screw; the screws were then set, two per plank, per rib, and after they were tightened, the plugs were dipped in white lead and set and smoothed off with a chisel.

The next two years work progressed slowly, primarily done by Lathrop alone — roofing the cabin and putting down the canvas over the deck. Rigging was next.

Although he was 67 when the project started, William Lathrop built most of the Widge *by himself. A single giant oak tree provided most of its framework. This photo originally appeared in a 1927 article in* American *magazine.*

In the meantime Lathrop's boat-building project had excited a good deal of curiosity and attention, not only in the community but among the national press. It was noted in *The New York Times,* and in 1927 *American* magazine sent a reporter to the scene; the result was a feature article on the white-bearded but still vigorous painter, with a photograph of him at work on the hull of the *Widge.*

By Labor Day, 1930, *Widge* was ready to launch. Neighbors, Lathrop's fellow artists and their families, visitors from as far away as New York, gathered to help and to celebrate. Their task was to haul the boat from behind the shop about two hundred feet across the lawn and garden to the canal — the old Delaware and Lehigh Canal that bordered the Lathrop property. *Widge* was laid over on her side on power pole rollers cut six feet long. All hands tugged on the ropes and inched the heavy boat toward the canal. Mrs. Lathrop prepared a generous picnic lunch for the noon break. By one o'clock they were underway again with boys and girls pulling on the cables with blocks and falls rigged and anchored to various trees along the way. At four o'clock the *Widge* was ready at the edge of the canal. Mrs. Lathrop broke a bottle of champagne on her bow, and amid much cheering, Lathrop jumped up on her deck and she plunged into the water. The *Widge* floated! Above the waterline to be sure, but level and balanced — it was a great triumph for William Lathrop, who that year had celebrated his seventy-first birthday.

During the next month, she was outfitted with sails. Bauhan brought two tons of old lead pipes for the ballasting. The mast was stepped and everything tried and tested. Then in the last week in September they stacked the shrouds and took down the mast so that she could pass under the canal bridges between Lathrop's and Bristol, where she would pass out into the Delaware River on her way to the sea. Besides Lathrop, her crew on this "maiden voyage" down the canal included Rolf Bauhan and Lathrop's closest friend, the marir ᛦ artist Henry B. Snell.

Lathrop, although he had lived inland at New Hope for some thirty years, was no novice to boat handling. He had grown up on the shores of Lake Erie, where as a youth he had built his own sailing canoe, and later had put in a good deal of time sailing larger craft with friends on Lake Erie and along the Atlantic coast.

October 13, 1930, saw the *Widge* under sail for the first time gliding by the city of Philadelphia on her way around Cape May to New Gretna, New Jersey, where she would be winterized. The following is an excerpt from *Widge's* log.

Saturday, November 1, 1930. Got underway this morning and sailed joyously out of Mahon's Ditch before a fresh northwest breeze. Headed for Cape May forty miles E.S.E.

Had a glorious sail, strong wind. Dead aft. under main and staysail. *Widge* behaved like a perfect lady. We were soon out of sight of this low coast and for two hours we might have been in the open sea, except for the oyster bed stakes which are everywhere except in the steamer channels. Wind and sea increasing, finally had to lie to and reel my mainsail. Then finding myself in the midst of the oyster fleet, I followed them into Maurice River Harbor instead of Cape May.

The next day turned bitter cold with the wind out of the north. Lathrop awoke to the sights of the extraordinary little town of Maurice River, New Jersey.

Hundreds and hundreds of snow-white schooners moored for miles along the shore! Huddled about the warehouses until their masts look like forests and shooting out into and from the open water at high speed from their powerful engines. They are very gallant and handsome craft — the slowly developed perfection of a type. Almost all of them carry great weatherbeaten gray tri sails at their work in the Bay.

That morning, Lathrop got underway for Cape May, foreseeing a quick and easy passage before a strong north wind. If he had only known! What it turned out to be was a strenuous twenty-two hours.

The strong north wind reversed itself and became a light south wind — a head wind. An hour later the tide did the same thing, so I spent the entire afternoon beating back and forth across the Bay and about 9 P.M. found myself abreast of Brandywine Shoal in a dead calm but with the tide again in my favor. So through the night partly drifting, sometimes sailing gently. About 2 A.M. I was out in the open Atlantic on a dark night trying to unravel the mysteries of Prissy Wicks Shoal. Unforgettable name! I was anxious, but from a study of the chart and such beacons and buoys as I had been able to identify I believed myself safely outside of the dangerous places. There was little wind, so little that the boat was hardly manageable, but there were the usual big Atlantic rollers. Suddenly in the quiet darkness off my port bow, not a hundred yards away, one of them burst with a thunderous roar into a breaker. I did some quick work with the helm and sheets and slid away from there like a scared hen. I worked myself a good mile further off shore before I dared again turn eastward.

Widge *was a "pinkie" type, with a double end.*

Sometime before sunrise the breeze freshened, and Lathrop worked eastward and toward the shore, finding himself abreast of Cape May City at dawn with the harbor two miles farther up the coast.

It looked easy, but the breeze which had freshened with the dawn suddenly took on a vicious strength N.E. *Widge* was carrying whole sail and I had a strenuous time making that last two miles, luffing where I had to and sailing when I could. I was very thankful when I finally rounded the end of the south breakwater and let her go with lifted sheets straight up the harbor and drop anchor handsomely before the Coast Guard station. Then into my blankets and sleep before I thought of breakfast, though I had had nothing but bread and cheese since breakfast the day before. So ended the *Widge's* first encounter with the Atlantic Ocean! Humiliating as to Prissy Wicks, but that was not her fault.

The *Widge* sailed the bays, rivers, and the ocean from Cape May to Cape Cod for eight years, skippered by Lathrop and crewed by friends, many of whom were famous in their own right, such as Albert Einstein. Lathrop made the most of these years, sailing and living aboard *Widge* from spring of the year until the late fall, when the cold north winds sent him back to New Hope and his anxious family for the winter. Many of his paintings — seascapes and sketches of the coast — were done from the cockpit, and his impressions and experiences were recorded in the log.

The balance between sails and hull of *Widge* must have been exceptional, as hinted by the log entry made by Lathrop while sailing alone at night off Port Jefferson, Long Island, July, 1931.

> ... squared away on a course for Plum Island and Coacles Harbor. Being very tired and sleepy, I was delighted and surprised to find that *Widge* would steer herself with the wind almost directly aft, slightly on the starboard quarter. I carefully adjusted sheets, lashed the tiller and after a trial of half an hour, finding her still accurately on her course, I went to sleep for over two hours and woke to find dawn approaching and Horton's Point abeam!

Sailing *Widge* with no engine of any kind, especially in and around New York Harbor, the Hellgate, and the Kill von Kull River in Jersey, must have been hair-raising at times, as we may picture from this log entry of the summer of 1936 after leaving Keyport, New Jersey.

> Had a wonderful sail up here yesterday, north across the Bay, through all the windings and heavy traffic of the Kill von Kull to an anchorage here almost under the famous Goethals Bridge. A strange, appalling place. Miles of huge, sooty buildings, smoking chimneys, manufacturing mysterious and mostly ponderous things which are loaded into freighters and lighters and barges to go to the ends of the earth. A four-masted schooner, a rare sight in these days, is just passing me. Sailed up the Kills to Shooter's Island. Fascinating navigation to one unfamiliar, especially under sail, to crowded traffic, ponderous, huge 500-foot, four-story freighters from all parts of the world. I dodging about with my little sails was persona non grata to everyone but the Scandinavian sailors to whom the North Sea rig of my little ship seemed to bring a thrill of homesickness. They always cheered and swung their hats.

Late October of 1937 saw *Widge* and her skipper leaving Montauk, Long Island, for New Haven in a gale. *Widge*, with her double-ended sheer lines and deep keel, sailed her best under these conditions.

> Got underway four in morning, bright moonlight and wonderful morning star. Wind hauling S.E. getting strong, half a gale. Heading for Plum Gut. I think you could call it a

whole gale. With my roof it is all she can carry. Seas washing the foredeck. Glad the fore hatch is fastened.

The next year the famous hurricane of 1938 struck the New England coast with its center passing across Long Island at Montauk on September 21. William Lathrop, at the age of seventy-nine, was aboard his beloved *Widge*. One gets an eerie feeling from reading the last entries of *Widge's* log, later found aboard her. At the time, *Widge* was moored along with several trawlers in the harbor at Montauk Point.

> September 20, 1938. It has been a day of beautiful but disquieting skies. At the edge of dark tonight Anderson got a radio report of a hurricane coming up the coast and already north of Hatteras with easterly gales! It was decided the best place for me was in the lee of Indian Hill on the east side of the Pond, and that I must get there at once before night set in. I cut my mooring line with the hatchet, got up sail, and away in the teeth of a dangerous-looking squall coming from the S.E. which broke and drenched me just as I was trying to anchor and get down sail. So here I am and feeling decidedly uneasy. It will be an anxious night.
>
> September 21, 1938. Bar. 29.65. The night was windy and rough. Indian Hill directly behind. I can see cows grazing. Evidently they are unaware of radio alarms. Perhaps they are right and there is nothing to be alarmed about. I am already beginning to feel a bit irritable about cutting ten feet of my best hawser.
>
> 10:15 A.M. Bar. 29.50. Blowing hard from S.S.E. but sun is shining brightly and I have just-washed dungarees drying in rigging. I have the big anchor down with a long scope and it seems to hold.
>
> 1 P.M. Bar. 29.36, Anchor still holds, the wind is ferocious. The two big trawlers have just come in to hug the eastern hills for shelter, others are here or coming.
>
> 2:30 P.M. Bar. 29.00!

That was the final entry. During the storm, a fisherman drifted past the *Widge* in his boat, and saw Lathrop slumped in the cockpit, still as a statue. Authorities concluded from that that he had suffered a heart attack. Lathrop's body was found several weeks later washed up by the tide, near the point where *Widge* had been anchored.

As for *Widge* herself, a fishing trawler apparently cut across her anchor line. She was found afterwards clear across the bay, empty, banging against a yacht club dock. On board, on the bunk in his cabin, were Lathrop's violin and an unfinished painting dated September 21, 1938.

Trapped in a Dead Submarine

"Submarine sunk here. Telephone inside."

By David L. Sudhalter

I t was May 23rd, 1939. The local newspapers were carrying news of ominous events in Europe, while just outside Portsmouth Harbor, the submarine U.S.S. *Squalus* was getting under way for the last of her sea trials. The *Squalus* and her sister ship, the U.S.S. *Sculpin*, each cost around five million dollars and represented the latest in a growing arsenal of new weapons that the Navy knew would soon be needed.

Lieutenant Oliver F. Naquin, skipper of the new submarine, had a crew of fifty-nine experienced men with him as the *Squalus* weighed anchor and sailed out the mouth of the Piscataqua River. Most of the crew were on deck, smoking last cigarettes and getting a last sight of the open water when the order came, "Station the special sea details." Like clockwork, the crew set about the tasks that they had learned so well. Also aboard for this special sea trial was Harold C. Preble, the naval architect who knew more about the *Squalus* than anyone else, and two other civilian technicians. Their mission on this starchy May morning was to take the *Squalus* into a succession of rapid dives about twelve miles off Rye Beach. The *Squalus* had performed magnificently on her shakedown cruises. At 8:30 A.M., Lieutenant Naquin ordered full speed on the four diesels as the *Squalus* worked up to her limit of sixteen knots. This dive was to simulate a "crash" dive as though the *Squalus* was under attack. The vents and gear were checked. Dials and gauges were being carefully monitored. The radioman sent out the last position signal to Portsmouth.

"Stand by to dive!" came the skipper's order as the klaxons cranked out their harsh, raspy warnings. The skipper descended from the conning tower and spun the wheel that dogged the hatch. The indicator lights were green, showing everything in working order and ready for the dive. The diesel inductions were closed as the submarine shifted over from the noise of the diesels to the quiet hum of the powerful batteries. The *Squalus* was now sealed tight. It was 8:40 A.M. Lieutenant Naquin and Harold Preble were watching the depth gauges and recording the diving time with great satisfaction. They had already reached sixty-three feet — a record dive for the *Squalus*.

The quiet atmosphere of the control room was broken suddenly by a frantic message from the engine room. The main induction valve was stuck open, and sea water was pouring in! The skipper reacted immediately. "Blow the ballast! Rise, rise! Close all watertight doors!" But the weight and rush of tons of sea water was too much for the *Squalus* to cope with, and she began to sink, as her stern fell. Men and gear crashed into each other as the sub tilted to a 45-degree angle, and in those few seconds, the lives of the crew hung in a precarious balance. At that moment Electrician's Mate Lloyd Maness was stationed by a bulkhead door to the rear compartment. As the rear compartment began to flood, Maness grabbed for the watertight door that would seal off the control room of the sub from the flooded rear compartments. The sub was already at an angle, and the 200-pound steel door had to be pulled upwards in order to close it. Maness had almost brought the door up when five shipmates appeared and shouted, "For God's sake, leave the door open!" Maness complied, and five more men were able to escape the flooding compartment. The task of closing and dogging the watertight door was one of those superhuman feats that seem possible only in emergencies. Among the twenty-six men left behind in the flooded compartment and doomed to certain death was Maness's best friend, for whose wedding he was to have been the best man the next Sunday.

At the same moment, Chief Electrician's Mate Gainor realized what was happening, and headed for the battery compartment. The rushing seawater would make contact with the batteries and cause fire and explosions unless they could be disconnected. Gainor entered the battery compartment and crawled over to the two big switches that would disconnect the batteries. The powerful batteries emitted a bright blue arc as Gainor finally reached the switches. These two acts — closing the rear compartment door and pulling the battery switches — saved the men from immediate destruction. Now as the *Squalus* settled on the muddy bottom, twelve miles from the New Hampshire coast in 240 feet of water, the problem was survival.

It was 8:45 A.M. Just fifteen minutes had elapsed since Lieutenant Naquin first gave the order to prepare for the dive. As he looked around in the half-lighted gloom of the control room, Naquin began a head count. Twenty-three men were alive and well in the control room; ten more were in the forward torpedo room. In the flooded after section were twenty-six men for whom there could be no hope. A signal flare sent from the *Squalus* surfaced and arced over the desolate emptiness of the sea. Lieutenant Naquin then ordered the release of the telephone buoy, which floated to the surface. It bore a sign that read, "Submarine sunk here. Telephone inside." The men settled down to wait for a rescue that might never come, for they knew that at great depths, submarine rescues were still pretty

Jimmy Jones of the Boston Post *photographed the* Squalus *breeching like a steel whale from the depths, only to sink again within seconds.*

shaky propositions. To preserve what oxygen there was, the men were ordered to lie still, not to talk, and not to exert themselves. Most of them huddled silently in blankets trying to keep out the gnawing cold that added to the fear and isolation of being trapped in a dead submarine. The most immediate dangers to their safety were the increasing concentration of carbon dioxide and the possibility of chlorine gas seeping from the storage batteries. If rescue came, the *Squalus* had aboard a new lifesaving device, the Momsen Lung, which could enable the crew to escape from the sunken sub and slowly float to the surface. But it would take at least two hours to negotiate the 240 feet, and it was doubtful that anyone would be able to survive the icy water.

Finally, at 12:55 P.M., the anxious crew heard the beat of propellers. Their sister ship, the *Sculpin*, had located the *Squalus's* position. Just as the *Sculpin's* skipper, Commander Wilkins, reached Lieutenant Naquin on the buoy telephone, the line snapped. There was no other means of direct communication.

In the meantime, all of the rescue facilities of the Navy began to swing into action. Amphibious aircraft, ships, and Navy divers all began

Each Navy diver working to rescue the trapped sailors required a surface support team of six men to maintain airlines, lifelines, and ropes.

to stream northward. The Cape Cod Canal was cleared as were the streets of Boston, while police escorts with wailing sirens guided the Navy divers and their equipment towards Portsmouth. For the next three days, all of New England's attention would be riveted on the tiny band of men trapped in the *Squalus*, and the gathering army of rescue personnel racing against time to save them.

Aboard the *Squalus*, some of the men began to vomit and complain of lightheadedness, a sure sign of the increasing concentration of carbon dioxide. Since the telephone line was broken, the rescue vessels knew only the approximate position of the *Squalus*. They had to use grappling hooks to locate her. At 7:30 P.M., almost twelve hours since the *Squalus* began her fateful dive, contact was made by the tug *Penacook*. Rescue operations could not begin at night, and the long wait for daybreak began. The *Falcon* arrived with a McCann rescue bell, a recently developed device that had never been tested in an actual emergency. By 10:00 A.M., the first Navy diver was able to reach the *Squalus*, now spending her second morning on the bottom. The crew could hear his leadweighted shoes clomping on the deck as he tried to attach a cable to the *Squalus* that would anchor the McCann bell to the sub's hull.

The temperature inside the sub was now forty-five degrees, the pressure was building, and humidity was almost 100 percent. Lieutenant Naquin picked the weakest men to leave the sub first. It was almost 1:00 P.M. when the rescue bell was connected to the *Squalus* and the men waiting in the forward torpedo room were able to break the hatch open and slip into the waiting rescue bell. Fresh air lines were inserted into the open hatch of the dead sub and new, clean air from the surface began to revive the crew. The diving bell began its ascent to the surface with the first of the survivors. At 3:00 P.M., the McCann rescue chamber returned and took nine more men. Finally, at 8:00 P.M., Lieutenant Naquin and seven other survivors were the last to leave the watery grave of the *Squalus* and her dead crew of twenty-six. Halfway up, the rescue chamber stopped suddenly. Navy divers found that the cable had been frayed, and a diver went down to cut it. The lives of the men in the chamber could not be risked by a sudden rush to the surface, so the rescue bell was lowered to the bottom once again until a new cable could be attached to the *Squalus*. Finally, after an agonizing four hours, the tiny rescue chamber began its slow ascent. At 12:30 P.M., it broke through the surface into the glare of floodlights from the rescue vessels. Cheers greeted the haggard crew and passengers. Lieutenant Naquin and all of the thirty-three men who survived the sinking of the *Squalus* had been saved. Despite the loss of twenty-six men, it was a day of great rejoicing for Navy veterans who had witnessed many such tragedies before when rescue equipment was not available. Ironically, a few days after the *Squalus* went down, a British sub, the H.M.S. *Thetis*, was lost off the English coast. The *Thetis*, too, was a brand-new submarine, but her crew was not so lucky — all hands were lost.

The work of salvaging the *Squalus* began. Never before had the Navy tried to salvage a submarine from such deep water. Several methods of salvage were discussed, including trying to drag the sunken sub along the bottom until shallow water was reached.

Finally, the idea of attaching pontoons and then blowing out the tons of water from the *Squalus* was agreed on. The salvage operation was to take 113 days, and would see the *Squalus* rise to the surface twice in a rush of compressed air, only to sink back to the bottom just as quickly, until delicate balancing adjustments were made that allowed the sub to be towed back up the Piscataqua River to the base in Portsmouth. It was now September 13th. The dead were removed from their watery grave. A malfunctioning valve was found to have caused the disaster.

Two years later, the *Squalus* was recommissioned and given the new name of U.S.S. *Sailfish*. She proved worthy of her resurrection from the deep. During World War II she torpedoed and sank six Japanese merchantmen, and won a Presidential citation for sinking a Japanese aircraft carrier during a typhoon in the Pacific. On V-J Day, October 1945, the *Sailfish* was decommissioned at her old home base, Portsmouth. The career of the gallant *Sailfish* came to an end when she was sold at auction on May 3, 1948, for $43,167 to a Philadelphia scrap-metal firm. The ship is long since torn apart and melted down, but she'll never be forgotten.

Adrift in the Blizzard

I never met my grandfather, but he had great influence on my life — mostly because we shared the same experience. Seventy-odd years apart, we shared the miracle of survival in a blizzard, all night, at sea.

By Charles Wesley Greenleaf
(as told to Patricia Kettner Greenleaf)

At noon on Monday, February 6, 1978, I packed up my gear, knowing there'd be no more work that day. The island marina was closing early because a blizzard was due by nightfall. No need to take chances. By leaving now, we'd all get home well ahead of the storm.

Though home lay across seven miles of Sound, I was well used to making the crossing in all kinds of weather. Commuting to my island job in a 17-foot Boston Whaler had long been routine. My co-worker, Lance, was bundling up to go with me; he, too, wanted to play it safe and get across early.

The crossing would be a bit exposed but short — fifteen minutes at most. Fishers Island, part of Suffolk County, New York, but located just off the southeastern Connecticut shore, creates its own Sound out of the larger Long Island Sound. This small and fairly protected body of water was the one we proposed to cross.

We listened to the marine weather station report. A storm warning was in effect, with high winds and heavy seas due in our area at about 3 P.M. We computed course corrections for existing wind and tide. Usually I'd just take a compass reading and head out, but when I had a passenger I was more cautious.

The wind had reached about twenty knots. We were accustomed to anything up to thirty knots. Many times we had had to turn around because of gusting or high seas, and today we would use that option if necessary. When we got to the head of West Harbor on the Island, we'd have a good look at things.

"Now, if we don't get a phone call from you guys by 12:55, we'll pick you up in the *Sea Stretcher*." Peter Sanger, marina owner and lifelong Island resident, aware of the risk that accompanies any winter crossing, helped us make emergency plans. He and a crew of volunteers would come after us with the Island's hospital emergency boat if necessary.

As we rounded the head of Pirate's Cove and entered West Harbor, we set the compass for thirty degrees northeast. That would put us in at Noank and Singer's Boatyard on the mainland. The edge of a cold, northeast wind had stung our eyes. It would be a push to get across into the wind, but she seemed a steady wind in direction and speed; we'd just have to adjust our time a bit.

We pounded some. The icy spray showered over the port and glazed our foul-weather gear, but home and warmth were closer with each lurch and that gave us reason enough to endure. I ran my 65-hp Johnson at a safe two-thirds throttle. Snow had been falling for a few hours, but visibility was still fair, about one and one half miles — enough to see the coastal markers that would direct us to the channel buoy and safe harbor.

As the channel marker slipped astern, I checked our time. Just past 12:30, and right into the harbor! I had just glimpsed the familiar Mystic Spindle when the engine quit.

Darn! Of all the rotten luck! I had my tools as always, but it was a darned cold spot to fool with the engine.

We had a full tank of gas and six gallons in reserve, so the problem was in the engine. Most likely an electrical failure, we agreed. I put my gloves down on the deck and checked the ignition system, where I found the beginning of the problem. I disconnected a ground wire to the power pack, and the engine turned over. We regained some of the distance we had lost, but then the engine quit again. I dreaded the thought of more engine work. My hands were already red and numb, and the storm wasn't getting any nicer.

In fact, something was very wrong here. This storm was very quickly getting really nasty — much nastier than predicted. Growing gusts of wind churned the water, making our little boat pitch so wildly that I could barely steady myself, let alone examine the silent engine. Waves smacking us hard in succession showered us with ice water. I was making no time, and time was the key to regaining our rapidly diminishing headway. By now we had drifted yards from the channel marker.

My several attempts to restart the engine caused it only to sputter, then quickly die. (Days later we discovered that a tiny spring in the ignition had fallen out of place and shorted everything. Our breakdown had not been caused by the weather or by routine engine failure. A rare, unforeseeable accident was our undoing.)

Finally, a fuse blew. As I had no fuses on board that day, I put a penny in the bypass, but it didn't do the trick. The engine, open all the time I was working, was soaked. We were drifting with our stern facing into the still-rising waves, by now large enough to break against or slightly over the low transom. There was no juice left. The battery was dead, and we had to begin bailing.

I had repaired outboards for years, and Lance had put in as many years on the water. Without words, we both knew the graveness of our predicament. We were both suddenly, unexpectedly, sick.

"We're overdue by nearly an hour now. Peter and the *Sea Stretcher* crew must be out here, too." Straining to separate the sound of boat engines from the din of howling wind and crashing waves, we discussed dropping anchor because we were probably in the path of any rescue attempt. We decided to drift to maintain better control over the boat. By drifting, the drag of the engine would keep the bow from pointing into the driving wind, which was easily strong enough to scoop the boat up and flip it. We'd lose control over our direction by drifting, but our first objective had to be to keep the boat afloat.

"I can't believe we haven't crossed paths with the *Sea Stretcher* by now. This wind should be shoving us right back to the Island."

"Hope we land close enough to hike to a warm house for a late lunch. Hay Harbor, Silver Eel Pond, or Race Point are my guess."

But with no fix on a land mass for a compass reading, we could only guess at our heading. Dead reckoning works only as long as the wind and the current don't shift. The swirling snow and water that enveloped everything was moving so crazily that we could only pray that land would soon appear. Any land with a place for shelter would do. The area was full of coastal inlets on both shores and numerous little islands between, so we felt we'd be on land in no more than two hours.

Hope of sighting or being sighted by Peter's vessel diminished steadily as the minutes passed. As we bailed, we listened. Working against the rising water was the only way to save our hands from frostbite, our minds from panic.

Then in the midst of the deafening racket of wind came the piercing blare of a horn. Another blast, and our hearts froze as we recognized the sound of the New London Light that marks the mouth of the Thames River. The wind must have veered to the east, taking us far from our hoped-for course toward land or rescue.

We tried dropping the anchor, but the Whaler took on too much water. We would surely be spending the night in the boat now, and any water in our clothes or shoes would increase the danger of hypothermia.

So again we were drifting slightly southwest, straight toward the treacherous waters of the Race and beyond. These waters would take us forty or more miles to Long Island at best, or to infinite miles of open ocean at worst. In either case, we would be exposed to the potentially fatal chill of wind and water.

The Coast Guard was certainly out there by now, risking their own lives in the hope of saving ours. Our senses strained for any sign of rescue. We knew that our chances were lessening with each minute away from the sound of the New London Light.

... our hearts froze as we recognized the sound of the New London Light that marks the mouth of the Thames River.

We bailed together, and I silently prayed, tensing every muscle against the cruel exposure. Our legs and arms, already stiff from the cold, cramped quarters, had to be kept in constant motion. Lance used the battery cover as a makeshift bailer while I used the hand pump. But pretty soon I had to stop. Without gloves, I couldn't bear the pain of prying my frozen fingers from the pump every few minutes. My worst fear now was the dread of frostbite. I exercised constantly — deep knee bends and arm flexes to keep active and stay awake.

Lance bailed continuously. I cursed the clothing I hadn't worn, the gloves that lay soaked beneath the ice-encrusted deck.

Through layers of sleet we glimpsed our last readings of time and direction before being swallowed up by total darkness. Though only a few feet apart, neither of us would see the other for the rest of the long night. We were completely cut off in this madness. The dead battery left us with no hope of any light until dawn. There would be no way of knowing for hours how much time we had spent or what direction we had taken. The only contact we could make would be to shout periodically to each other to startle and reassure — to make sure the other was still on board.

No one could have found us in that raging darkness. The odds against our survival were frighteningly high. The relentless waves driven by 70-mph gusts were pouring over us in rapid succession, a big one followed by several smaller. Three successive big ones would have capsized us. Each time, the boat rose to frightening heights, then pitched wildly into the trough between the two mountains of water. Would the next trough be filled with rocks that would dash our small Whaler to pieces? Would we be effortlessly flipped by one of the endless cresting breakers that we could hear on every side? The water was heaving over the gunwales so rapidly that Lance had just enough time between hits to bail the icy water to a safe level.

To keep my mind and body under control, I had to keep exercising. My gloveless hands wanted to stop moving. I sat with my back to the wind, my arms wrapped around the railing to keep from pitching out. I knew the seat of my pants had long since frozen to the gas can. As I tensed

> *... my grandfather and his crew survived on their wrecked schooner by lashing themselves to the rigging overnight through a raging blizzard.*

and relaxed my muscles, I felt the pull of the ice and the creeping numbness. I responded to Lance's shouts, but the urge was growing to give in to the fatigue, to just lie down, forget the endless nightmare, sleep. I knew there was no hope of rescue. We had reached the limit of our endurance; we would die in this hurricane.

I couldn't grasp anything real. I just fell in and out of a deep, sleepless trance. Sometimes I saw strange things like lights. Sometimes I would forget where I was for a moment.

I shook myself, and the sharp sound of ice cracking off my shoulders roused me.

I shouted to Lance. I wanted to tell him that I had been dreaming of one of my favorite family stories, which related how my grandfather and his crew survived on their wrecked schooner by lashing themselves to the rigging overnight through a raging blizzard. By some miracle they had survived, and although there might not be a miracle out here for us, one *had* happened for them, and the thought strengthened me somewhat. I had prayed so much that night, and this time I gave thanks — thanks for the glimmer of hope to hold on to. I was not afraid to die, though. That surprised me. The sorrow was in the fear of leaving my family without enough. My little girl was only two and had so many years, so many needs; I hated to think I wouldn't be around.

As I thought of her, I noticed several clear, bright lights in the swirling darkness. Stars. A break in the storm. Soon the entire night sky was visible. Brilliant, naked stars shone all around. The first light in hours — it was so welcome. But the clearing brought with it an almost immediate temperature drop. I could feel it through water-soaked layers of rain gear, snorkel coat, woolen sweater, flannel shirt, and underwear. Water had been running down my neck all night, and now I began to shiver uncontrollably. I think Lance thought I was freezing to death. He huddled beside me under the protection of a frozen tarp to create what little warmth he could. We drained the accumulating water from our boots as we had been doing all night, with grim thoughts of hypothermia. I warmed my hands as best I could by tucking them inside my coat against my skin or under my arms. When my exposed skin became too chilled, I would warm one finger at a time in my mouth.

The Whaler had turned into a misshapen iceberg. Ice humps had formed on the console and motor. When I tried to kick a wind-formed icicle off the side of the motor, my leg felt like a lifeless stump. The extra weight of all that ice wasn't going to help us any, but there was nothing we could do about it.

Though the skies had cleared, the seas were unrelenting. Wave after wave crested around and over us in an endless barrage. The unabating wind chilled our bodies. There could be nothing worse for me. Even as the eye of the storm passed and the heavy clouds and darkness returned, a determination came with it. Dawn was approaching. The longest night I had ever known was coming to an end. Lance was the first to spot land.

"Mattituck!" He recognized the snow-covered bluffs of Long Island's North Fork and Mattituck Inlet. We had drifted nearly fifty miles from our intended port. We put the helm hard to port and began to drift slowly toward shore.

As we drifted, we listened for the approach of rescue copters, not realizing that the blizzard had grounded all helicopters. An hour passed, then two. We could see the dangerous, breaking surf between us and the shore. We shivered and steered as best we could toward the nearest sandy section. It was 5 A.M. As we closed in on the surf, a wave caught us, and Lance was swept out of the boat. I held on a little distance, stuffing an emergency blowtorch and flint igniter into my coat, before I followed him into the foaming waves. I hit bottom, then surfaced. The terrible shock we'd expected from the mid-winter water hadn't come. The ocean felt warm as waves lifted us toward shore.

Tossed onto the snow-drifted beach close to each other, we tried to stand and we both fell. We didn't have so much as an hour left. We had to *move*, get our blood circulating.

"We've gotta run," I said, breaking into what I thought was a strong sprint. But as I looked at Lance walking slowly beside me, I realized that we could barely move. We had to find shelter quickly.

We settled into a stiff shuffle in ankle-deep, icy water, covering about a half mile in this fashion. The entire beach was covered with deep drifted snow. All we could see were snow-covered beaches and the sheer bluffs of Jamesport. We made our way eastward to avoid the rocks blocking the way to the west. But which way meant shelter? People?

Then about thirty yards away we spotted a set of old summer sea stairs leading up the bluffs. We could only pray that up there we would find signs of civilization. As we carefully crawled up the snow-drifted, ice-slick steps, several rotten steps gave way. As we gained the top, we spotted some deserted-looking beach cottages, welcome shelter even without people. Four hundred yards of high-drifted snow lay between us and the first cottage. Lance and I took turns falling into the drifts. The first got the foothold and made the trough. The other followed. We knew we'd make it now. Nothing could stop us. The crisis had passed. On the beach we could have wandered too long and frozen to death. But here by the cottages we could laugh.

When we got through to the nearest cottage I was all for breaking down the door and burning the whole place for warmth, but there was a half-buried car parked next to the porch, so we pounded on the wooden door instead, not really expecting to find anyone at home. The door gave way to our pounding fists, and we fell in just as a couple who turned out to be John and Mary Taber rounded the corner of their living room to see what the commotion was about. They saw us shivering on the floor and thought we were stranded motorists. We said we were shipwrecked.

They warmed and fed us, and we called our families, the Coast Guard, and local authorities. Friends were already on their way in snowmobiles to transfer us to the Central Suffolk Hospital. They had been searching for us on land and on the water all night. My best friend, Alan Chaplaski, a commercial fisherman out of Stonington, Connecticut, had come after us in his 52-foot commercial fishing vessel, *The Black Whale*. He had followed us into the heart of the storm, then had cut his engines off Noank, and let his boat drift for a half hour. Then, with power on, he had followed our course as far toward Long Island as possible. He had missed us by moments, risking his own life. When warned to return to port at 10 P.M., he had shut down the radio and gone on until he was satisfied that he had covered all the possibilities.

We were unspeakably grateful to everyone, and I could only marvel at the miracle of it all.

"Come In, *Can Do!*"

"We've lost it! It's all gone ... we've had it!"

By Evan McLeod Wylie

I t was early evening on a cold and cloudy night in January, 1978 when the *Can Do,* a sleek 45-foot craft with the word PILOT emblazoned on both sides emerged from Gloucester (Massachusetts) Harbor, rounded the long breakwater, and sped out into the Atlantic Ocean. Soon she was on station, pitching and rolling in sea swells near the shadowy shape of a flashing whistle buoy off Cape Ann's Eastern Point.

On the horizon appeared the red and green running lights of a large vessel. The Greek tanker *Global Hope,* bound into Salem with a cargo of 180,000 barrels of heating oil from Venezuela, slowed to ten knots. Floodlights switched on, illuminating a rope and wooden ladder dangling over the ship's side. Revving up her engines, the *Can Do* swung around and maneuvered amidst the choppy seas surging around the tanker until she was close alongside and her passenger could reach out to seize the dangling ladder and clamber up it. When a blast from the ship's whistle signaled that the pilot was safely aboard and on the bridge, the *Can Do* veered off and set a course for a run back to her berth in Gloucester.

Captain Frank Quirk, Jr., skipper of the *Can Do,* had completed another routine assignment in his daily job of transporting pilots to and from large vessels moving in and out of Salem and Gloucester.

Pilots are compulsory for all large foreign and U.S. vessels entering or departing from Salem or Gloucester. Meticulous navigation is necessary to avoid the hazards that lie close to the deep-water channels. Salem Sound is studded with islands, jagged rocks, and sunken reefs. The approaches to Gloucester abound with massive ledges, treacherously submerged or menacingly awash with breaking surf. After twenty years cruising these waters at all hours of the day and night, in all kinds of weather, and constantly in the company of seasoned harbor pilots, Frank Quirk was as at ease among these perils as a man in his own backyard.

Stocky, cheerful, and energetic, Quirk, forty-nine, was a master plumber by trade and a mariner by choice. He had served as a U.S. Navy "Seabee" in the Korean War and had taken the motto of the Navy's famed construction battalions as the name for his boat. It suited him and his swift steel-hulled craft perfectly. Quirk and the *Can Do* met every piloting assignment and were involved in countless rescues and boating mishaps.

"No matter when it was, where it was or who . . . if someone was in trouble, Frank Quirk would be there," said Gloucester Deputy Harbormaster Charlie Lindbergh.

Storms and high winds did not faze him. Quirk was fond of comparing his boat to "a little submarine. You just batten down the hatches and she'll go through anything." In heavy weather, seas broke over the wheelhouse, but Quirk had installed extra thick glass in the windshield, and felt that it could take the worst that the ocean could offer.

Normally the *Can Do's* next meeting with the *Global Hope* would have taken place within about three days, after the tanker had discharged her cargo and was dropping off the pilot as she put out to sea. Instead Quirk was directed to meet the ship in the middle of Salem Sound. Additional time was needed to separate water from some of the oil cargo she was carrying, and the pier space she was occupying at the Salem Power Company was needed for another vessel.

Under the supervision of Harbor Pilot Captain George Landrigan, the *Global Hope* steamed slowly north to Salem Sound. There, at 8:30 P.M. on February 4th, she was anchored in forty feet of water on a muddy bottom with five shots of chain to one starboard anchor. After supervising the anchoring, Captain Landrigan took radar bearings to points on shore so that the ship's position could be precisely noted on her bridge charts, and he pointed out the local lighted navigational aids to the Captain of the tanker. Prior to departing, Landrigan also cautioned the Captain concerning changing weather conditions and recommended that if the weather worsened, he should (1) ballast his vessel to lower the bow, (2) put out extra chain on the starboard anchor, and (3) put out a second anchor.

This accomplished, Landrigan stood by to wait for the pilot boat. Soon the *Can Do* was alongside, and Frank Quirk took Landrigan aboard, put him ashore in Salem, and then headed back to Gloucester. Plans had been made to move the *Global Hope* back to the Salem pier the next day, but delays ensued, and she still lay at anchor on the morning of February 6th, a memorable date. During the night it had become apparent that a heavy winter storm was about to strike the coast. Gale warnings were broadcast to mariners and coastal communities. At 10 A.M., the National Weather Service in Boston changed the gale warnings to a full storm warning. However, no effort was made to move the *Global Hope* from its exposed position in Salem Sound. At noon, the Captain of the tanker instructed the chief engineer to keep the engine-room crew on a standby alert and his engines on standby.

At noon, the storm, sweeping up the coast, was enveloping Cape Cod with snow and gusting winds. Coast Guard stations had been placed on alert and the 210-foot cutter *Decisive*, on patrol in the Atlantic southeast of the Cape, had been ordered to proceed to a sheltered anchorage in Provincetown. All over southern New England, communities were responding to the threat of what was now predicted to be a great blizzard.

On the *Global Hope*, the total response to the approaching emergency was made at 3:10 P.M., when the main engine was ordered to dead slow ahead to take the strain off the anchor chain, but this effort was continued for only two minutes. And although the tanker's bow, riding high out of the water, caught gusts of wind like a sail, no attempt was made to lower it by re-ballasting.

By 4:30 P.M., the U.S. Weather Service marine forecast was urgent and ominous: "East to northeast winds forty to sixty knots with gusts of hurricane force. Visibility to be near zero in snow. Seas eight to ten feet and building to ten to twenty feet. Tides above normal."

At 5 P.M., thick, swirling snow driven by rising winds struck Cape Ann, and shoreline residents of Beverly now began to telephone the Coast Guard Station in Gloucester, warning that the *Global Hope* was in trouble.

At 5:15 P.M., the tanker was contacted by radio, but the captain of the *Global Hope* said that there was no problem. Apparently the anchor was holding.

Captain Frank Quirk's "little submarine" — the 45-foot pilot boat Can Do.

The weather on the scene was steadily worsening. Winds out of the northeast were reaching sixty knots. Heavy, driving snow was cutting visibility to zero. Sea conditions were rough.

At 5:30 P.M., the *Global Hope's* engine was again ordered dead slow ahead, but at 5:58 P.M., a jarring shudder was felt throughout the ship. A few minutes later the tanker's captain was on the radio in great excitement and apprehension.

> *Global Hope* **to Coast Guard:** WE ARE IN A DANGEROUS POSITION! WE ARE IN A DANGEROUS POSITION! AND WATER — SHE IS COMING INTO THE ENGINE ROOM!
> **Coast Guard:** DID YOU SAY YOU ARE TAKING ON WATER?
> *Global Hope:* ENGINE ROOM! ENGINE ROOM! YES. THE HULL IS BROKEN, AND WATER IS COMING INSIDE INTO THE ENGINE ROOM!
> **Coast Guard:** CAPTAIN, SLOW DOWN, WHAT IS BROKEN?
> *Global Hope:* HULL IS BREAKING DOWN; IT'S BREAKING DOWN, AND WATER IS UP IN THE ENGINE ROOM.
> **Coast Guard:** YOU SAY THE HULL IS BROKEN, AND YOU ARE TAKING ON WATER IN THE ENGINE ROOM?
> *Global Hope:* THAT IS CORRECT.
> **Coast Guard:** ROGER. WE WILL DISPATCH A BOAT WITH A PUMP AT THIS TIME.

Shortly after this, radio contact with the tanker was lost.

In the rapidly building storm the Coast Guard now found itself in a quandary. At its Gloucester station, the only two boats available were a 41-foot patrol boat and a 44-footer, neither meant for the tremendous seas and winds making up at Cape Ann and in Salem Sound. The nearest larger vessels were a 95-foot cutter, the *Cape George,* dispatched immediately from Boston, and the 210-foot cutter *Decisive,* instructed at once to get underway from Provincetown, Cape Cod, fifty miles away.

A radio call to Warren Andrews, director of Salem Control, which supervises all shipping in the area, asked if there were some other vessel in the area that might be able to help the stricken tanker. There wasn't.

Frank Quirk, on the alert aboard the *Can Do* at her dock in Gloucester Harbor, broke into the exchange to say that he and his boat would be standing by in case they could be of help.

On the other side of Gloucester Harbor, the Coast Guard station dispatched the two small boats out into the howling wind, driving snow, and darkness. The 41-footer, *41353,* built for high-speed patrol and pursuit duties, was immediately in serious trouble. As she skirted Round Rock Shoal just outside the harbor, giant waves sent her reeling as tons of water crashed aboard. She had to turn back.

The *44317*, a 44-footer designed and built for rescue work in rough seas, was still underway. She weighed twenty tons, having a heavy steel hull, eight watertight compartments, and big twin-diesel engines. Heavily reinforced with welded steel, she was one of the strongest rescue boats in the world. But only a canopied bridge, protected by a canvas curtain, protected her crew of four young enlisted men from the weather.

Now with coxswain Bob McIlvride gripping the wheel, seamen Roger Mathurin and Robert Krom taking turns on the radarscope, and fireman Tom Desrosiers monitoring the engine gauges, the *44317* battled toward Salem Sound. A terrific gust of wind carried away the canvas curtain. Seas burst aboard, pouring into the open pilot house, burying the men waist-high in icy water. Snow and ice blanketed the windshield, forcing them to peer through tiny slits at the blinding snow and monstrous seas. An enormous, barnacle-encrusted shape reared suddenly out of the sea — a huge channel buoy that had been tossed skyward by the raging seas. For one terrifying moment, it loomed above the boat, about to topple straight down on her. Then another giant wave picked the *44317* up and hurled her sideways, sweeping her from beneath the falling buoy.

As she entered Salem Sound, driving snow and sheets of spray began to short-circuit her instruments. The depth recorder was becoming erratic. The radar was blurring.

Coast Guard: *44317*, WHAT'S YOUR POSITION?
44317: (Shouting into mike to be heard above howling winds and tumult of the storm): ABOUT ONE-THIRD OF THE WAY TO THE MAYDAY (tanker) BUT IT'S PRETTY HARD TO SPOT WITH ALL THESE SEAS. WE THINK WE HEARD A WHISTLE.
Salem Control: I BELIEVE THAT BOB IS CORRECT ON THAT. WE HEARD A WHISTLE AS WELL. (At this time, it appeared that the *Global Hope* was sounding blasts on her whistle as a distress call, but there was no way of telling whether the big tanker was breaking up.)

In Gloucester Harbor, Frank Quirk, standing by aboard the *Can Do*, was becoming increasingly restive about the tanker, and particularly concerned about the young Coast Guardsmen on the *44317*.

Quirk: WHAT'S THE STATUS OF THE 44? HOW ARE THEY MAKING OUT?
Coast Guard: SHE'S ABOUT ONE-THIRD OF THE WAY DOWN THERE. WE HAD TO TURN THE 41 BACK.
Quirk: LET'S WAIT A FEW MORE MINUTES. IN ABOUT ANOTHER FIFTEEN MINUTES I MAY GIVE IT A SHOT. WE'LL GIVE IT A TRY TO GET OVER THERE.

But the prospects for the 44-footer operating without compass or radar in the blinding snowstorm and raging seas were not good.

With Quirk aboard the *Can Do* were four friends, Kenneth Fuller, Jr., thirty-four, of Magnolia, and Donald Wilkinson, thirty-five, of Rockport, enthusiastic yachtsmen active in offshore powerboat racing, Dave Curley, thirty-five, an electrician, and Charles Bucko, twenty-nine. Until recently Bucko had served in the Coast Guard. A seasoned and able coxswain, he had been at the wheel of one of the Coast Guard boats that had taken part in the rescue of the men from the tanker *Chester A. Poling*, and had received the Mariner's Medal for his heroism. Charlie Bucko was the sort of young man who couldn't help getting involved when there was trouble. "He was a born rescuer," his father said. "He was the kind of guy who would rush into a burning building when you and I wouldn't. There's a type of person, and there's very few around, who when everyone else is backing away, will go forward. Charlie was like that and so was Frank Quirk. With them it was almost a compulsion."

All four of these men had stopped by the *Can Do* at her berth in a dock slip in the South Channel off Parker Street to discuss the storm. Preparing to get underway, Quirk told the others to leave, but all four volunteered to assist in the attempt to aid the Coast Guard boat and disabled tanker, both in increasing danger.

Coast Guard: *44317.* WHAT'S YOUR APPROXIMATE POSITION? (Time: 7 P.M.)

44317: OFF THE LIGHTED BUOY OFF BAKER'S ISLAND. (But the *44317's* fathometer had quit, the compass was going, and the radar, their only eye in the blinding storm, was fading. And no other rescue vessel was anywhere near them.)

Coast Guard: *44317.* THE MOMENT THAT YOU CAN IDENTIFY A FLOATING AID, ANY KNOWN AID, AND YOU CAN WORK YOUR WAY INTO BEVERLY, DO SO IMMEDIATELY.

44317: ROGER. THAT SURE IS WHAT WE'RE GOING TO DO. WITH THESE SEAS WE'RE TRYING TO STAY AS CLOSE TO RANGE AS POSSIBLE.

Coast Guard: YOU CAN FORGET ABOUT THE VESSEL (tanker) AT THIS TIME. PROCEED TO BEVERLY.

44317: PROCEEDING TO BEVERLY.

But the prospects for the 44-footer operating without compass or radar in the blinding snowstorm and raging seas were not good.

At this point Frank Quirk announced his decision to go to the aid of the *44317* and the *Global Hope*.

Coast Guard to *Can Do:* IF I CAN GET THAT BOAT (*44317*) BACK TO SAFE WATER, THAT'S WHAT I'M GOING TO DO. DO YOU FIGURE ON GOING UP THERE?

Quirk: WELL, WE'LL TAKE A SHOT AT IT. I DON'T KNOW. IT LOOKS AS IF IT'S GOING TO BE ONE HELL OF A MESS FROM HERE.

Coast Guard: ROGER. AT THIS TIME, WE DON'T KNOW FOR SURE WHETHER ANYBODY IS IN FACT IN JEOPARDY (on the tanker). WE KNOW THERE IS A PROBABILITY THE SHIP IS DRAGGING HER ANCHOR. WE HAVE OTHER COAST GUARD FACILITIES COMING ON THE SCENE, A 210 (cutter) AND A 95. I DON'T SEE ANY REASON FOR JEOPARDIZING A SMALL BOAT CREW THAT DOESN'T HAVE THE FACILITIES AT THEIR DISPOSAL.

Quirk: ROGER ON THAT. WELL, WITH YOUR OKAY, I'D LIKE TO TAKE A LOOK OUTSIDE THE HARBOR AND SEE ABOUT HEADING UP THAT WAY OR WHETHER I STAY HERE.

Coast Guard: ROGER. PROCEED OUTSIDE, FRANK, AND GIVE IT A LOOK. I APPRECIATE IT.

Quirk: OKAY, WE'LL GIVE IT A LOOK. THE WAY IT LOOKS, WE MIGHT BE RIGHT BACK.

Along the shore of Salem Sound, in the communities of Beverly and Salem, volunteers were setting out to try to help save the *44317*.

Salem Control: *44317.* WE HAVE ALERTED SEVERAL SURF PATROL PEOPLE AND HARBOR MASTERS TO TAKE UP POSITIONS AT HOSPITAL POINT, SALEM WILLOWS, AND DANE STREET BEACH. THEY WILL ATTEMPT TO SPOT YOU AND HELP YOU INTO BEVERLY HARBOR.

44317: WE'RE SURE GOING TO GIVE IT A TRY. OVER.

Quirk: WE'RE UNDER WAY, WARREN. JUST GOING UP BY THE COAST GUARD STATION HERE. WILL SEE WHAT IT LOOKS LIKE OUTSIDE. (Whether the *Can Do* could reach the *Global Hope* was questionable, but if Quirk could at least pick up the *44317* on his radar, he might escort or guide the Coast Guardsmen to safety.)

Strong enough to bulldoze her way through the thick ice or even tow a 378-foot cutter, the *44317* was absorbing tremendous punishment. Cresting seas driven by the northeast gale picked up the craft like a chip. At times, the 44-footer was "surfing" bow down, stern out of the water, propelled at high speed into whatever lay in her path, as coxswain Bob tried to head towards Beverly Harbor.

At 8:30 P.M., there was a jarring thud as the *44317* struck an underwater object, stalling out both engines. Fireman Desrosiers flung open the hatch, and dropped down below. Crawling into the engine room, he tried to get the engines going.

> **Coast Guard:** DROP YOUR HOOK.
> *44317:* ROGER.
> **Coast Guard:** HAVE YOU RESTARTED YOUR ENGINES?
> *44317:* WE'RE WORKING ON IT.
> **Coast Guard:** LET ME KNOW IMMEDIATELY.

There was an agonized wait for radio listeners, then —

> *44317:* ENGINE RESTARTED THIS TIME. WE'RE GOING TO TRY TO CIRCLE INTO THE WIND AND WAVES.
> **Coast Guard:** IF YOU SEE ANY AID (to navigation) AT ALL, MAKE A REAL ATTEMPT TO TIE UP TO IT OR STAY AS NEAR TO IT AS POSSIBLE. COMMENCING NOW, I WANT YOU MEN TO GIVE ME A RADIO CHECK EVERY TEN MINUTES. OVER.
> *44317:* ROGER. OVER.
> **Coast Guard to** *Can Do:* FRANK, WHATEVER HE HIT, HE'S CLEAR OF IT. HE'S MANEUVERING. A LITTLE DISORIENTED AT THIS TIME. HE DOESN'T HAVE COMPASS OR RADAR. IF IT'S AT ALL POSSIBLE, COULD YOU HEAD OVER THAT WAY?
> **Quirk:** OKAY, WE'LL GIVE IT THE BEST SHOT WE'VE GOT, MIKE, AND BELIEVE ME, YOU NEED A COMPASS AND RADAR OUT HERE TONIGHT. YOU WOULDN'T BELIEVE IT. ONCE WE GET A POINT OF KICKOFF, WE'RE GOING TO STAND OFF FOR SALEM AND KEEP YOU POSTED.

Surf Unit 172 had identified the *44317* off Hospital Point and was talking to him directly to steer him away from the beach. He was within twenty yards of shore.

While the *Can Do* was making its way toward the area, the *44317* again lost an engine; once again Desrosiers restarted it. But the battering, pounding, and numbing cold were overwhelming the crew.

> **Coast Guard:** IS YOUR FATHOMETER WORKING?
> *44317:* IT'S WORKING BUT NOT ACCURATELY.
> **Coast Guard:** I SUGGEST YOU TAKE YOUR LEAD LINE OUT AND SOUND. IF YOU HAVE SHALLOW ENOUGH WATER OR WATER THAT WILL HOLD YOUR ANCHOR, I SUGGEST YOU THROW IT OVER. LET ME KNOW BEFORE YOU DO.
> *44317:* ROGER.

If worse came to worst, they could anchor down and lock themselves below. Unless she split a seam on rocks, the 44-footer should last until daylight. Or until the *Can Do* arrived. But then another message, in a relieved voice.

> *44317:* WE HAVE OUR RADAR BACK AT THIS TIME. WE ARE ATTEMPTING TO NAVIGATE INTO BEVERLY HARBOR.
> **Coast Guard:** AM I TO ASSUME YOU ARE A LITTLE OUT OF JEOPARDY? SEEING YOUR WAY CLEAR?
> *44317:* THAT'S A ROGER. FOR THE TIME BEING. AS LONG AS WE HAVE RADAR, I'M GOING TO TRY TO WORK MY WAY INTO THE HARBOR.

With the Gloucester Station in close contact, the *44317* cautiously maneuvered toward the invisible shore.

A disturbing message from Frank Quirk.

> **Quirk:** I HAVE TO TURN AROUND. MY RADAR WENT OUT FOR SOME REASON, PLUS THE FM ANTENNA. THAT WENT OVERBOARD WITH A BIG CRASH. SO IF I CAN GET TURNED AROUND, I'LL BE A WHILE GETTING BACK. I'VE GOT NO RADAR TO WORK WITH SO I'LL JUST BE TAKING IT SLOW.
> **Coast Guard:** ROGER, FRANK. PROBABLY A GOOD IDEA TO CALL US IN FIFTEEN MINUTES.
> **Quirk:** IF I DON'T GET BACK TO YOU, GIVE ME A CALL. WE'RE GOING TO BE BUSY HERE FOR A WHILE.

While the *Can Do* groped blindly in the howling blizzard, there was good news from the *44317*.

> *44317:* RED FLASHER BUOY NO. 16 DIRECTLY BEHIND US. WE BELIEVE WE ARE HEADING INTO BEVERLY HARBOR NICE AND SLOW.
> **Salem Control:** BE ADVISED THAT THE LIGHT YOU SEE AHEAD IS THE JUBILEE YACHT CLUB SPOTLIGHT. WE HAD THEM TURN IT ON FOR YOU ABOUT AN HOUR AGO.

On the *Can Do*, Frank Quirk was now in an extremely perilous position. Trapped between Baker's Island and the approaches to Gloucester Harbor, without radar he dared not try to run before the storm into the treacherous waters of Salem Sound. Yet to make it back into Gloucester, he would have to point the bow of the pilot boat into the towering seas and shrieking winds of the northeaster.

The storm was still increasing in fury, with winds now up to hurricane force, gusting from eighty to ninety knots. In fact, the storm had become that most rare and dangerous form of weather, "a hurricane-blizzard." In communities along the shore, huge waves were battering down concrete seawalls. Granite breakwaters which had stood for more than a century were crumbling. Surging high tides swept coastal homes into the sea and flooded through entire towns. Inland and up and down the coast, all traffic had come to a standstill. Highways were blocked by deepening drifts, and thousands of motorists had abandoned their cars.

As the *Can Do* fought for her life, radio messages continued to be her only contact and lifeline with those on shore.

Coast Guard: *CAN DO*, HOW FAR OUT WERE YOU WHEN YOU TURNED AROUND?
Quirk: I'M NOT QUITE SURE. WHEN THE RADAR WENT OUT, I WAS TAKING A READING ON BAKER'S ISLAND. WE'RE TRYING TO NURSE ALONG HERE, BEST WE CAN, SO CAN'T TELL YOU JUST WHERE WE ARE RIGHT NOW. TRYING TO MAKE THE MOUTH OF THE HARBOR.
Salem Control: PILOT BOAT *CAN DO*. GO AHEAD, FRANK. HOW'S IT GOING?
Quirk: WE'VE GOT PROBLEMS HERE WITHOUT THE RADAR AND EVERYTHING ELSE. BOY, I'LL TELL YOU IT'S SOME WILD NIGHT OUT HERE. SO WE'RE JUST POKING ALONG. I'VE GOT PLENTY OF WATER UNDER ME. I'M JUST TRYING TO PICK UP SOMETHING TO GO BY.
Coast Guard: IF YOU WOULD LIKE AN ESCORT, WE'RE STAND-ING BY.
Quirk: OKAY. IF YOUR RADAR IS ON, YOU MIGHT TRY TO PICK US UP OUTSIDE THE HARBOR. WE HAVE NOTHING TO WORK WITH, AND WE ARE JUST TRYING TO FISH AROUND AT THE PRESENT TIME.

At that moment, while the *Can Do* and the men on the Coast Guard vessels who had gone to the rescue of the *Global Hope* were in peril of their lives, the tanker was in far less difficulty. Hard aground on a rocky ledge on Coney Island, the tanker was pounding and shuddering under the impact of heavy seas, but her hull was not breaking up, and there was no immediate danger.

Then an urgent radio message in a voice that was not Quirk's.

Can Do: THIS IS PILOT BOAT *CAN DO* . . . A MAYDAY! A MAYDAY!
Coast Guard: KEEP SENDING YOUR TRAFFIC.
Can Do: WE'RE NOT SURE WHAT HAS HAPPENED AT THIS TIME. WE FEEL WE MAY HAVE HIT THE BREAKWATER (outside the harbor).

Frank Quirk, who had twice earned Gloucester's Mariner's Medal for heroism, receiving a special commendation from the Coast Guard for his part in the 1977 rescue of the Chester D. Poling.

Coast Guard: KEEP ON TALKING TO US HERE. DO YOU KNOW YOUR LOCATION?
Can Do: WE ARE IN SHOAL WATER. OUR WINDSHIELD IS OUT. LOST OUR RADAR AND POSITION UNKNOWN. ACTION EXTREMELY VIOLENT.

The storm had struck the *Can Do* another catastrophic blow. A huge sea had smashed through the windshield of the pilot house, leaving Frank Quirk knocked unconscious and bleeding badly from cuts inflicted by the shattered glass. The water soaked the boat's radio electronic equipment and threatened the power for the main engine and generator.

The Gloucester Coast Guard's 41-footer immediately got underway to try to contact the *Can Do*. But as soon as the little boat drew near the mouth of the harbor, heavy seas threatened to swamp her as before, and again the crew had to turn back.

The only other Coast Guard vessel nearby was the 95-foot cutter *Cape George*. Although this vessel had finally reached Cape Ann, Lieutenant Snyder and his crew were battered to the point of complete exhaustion. Helmsman Bob Donovan's forearms were bruised black and blue from fighting the wheel. Sheets of icy spray had short-circuited the loran so that they could not get a navigational fix on shore stations. The radar was faint and fading. Visibility in the black night and heavy snow was near zero. Even though all hatches and steel doors were tightly sealed and dogged down, the shrieking winds forced jets of seawater through, filling the bridge with an icy mist, and soaking their navigational charts. Water was in the ventilation system and had flooded the mess deck. Between the ship and the safety of Gloucester Harbor lay the huge rocks of Eastern Point and its mile-long breakwater. A collision with the breakwater would mean the end of the *Cape George* and her crew.

As the *Cape George* groped her way towards Gloucester Harbor, she was asked to sweep the area where Frank Quirk and the *Can Do* were presumed to be. With Chief Quartermaster Myron Verville navigating by the fading radar, the ice-laden cutter wallowed through the storm, venturing closer to shore. Suddenly the breakwater loomed ahead, buried in high tides and waves, and visible only as a mass of seething foam. Uncertain as to where its submerged tip lay, the *Cape George* veered off. A huge sea picked up the cutter and hurled her sideways. By a miracle they were safe inside the harbor, but Lt. Snyder had difficulty letting the Gloucester Coast Guard Station know, because by this time his ship also had lost the radio antennas. Her remaining electrical equipment shorting out, the *Cape George* moved slowly up the North Channel and tied up.

Despite the Coast Guard's continuing attempts to reach the *Can Do*, there was no response until forty-five minutes later when Frank Quirk came back on the radio.

> *Can Do:* THEY HAVE PATCHED ME UP AND WE ARE HOLDING OUR OWN FOR NOW.

Quirk thought he might be nearing the mouth of the harbor and holding a position in deep water, but the *Can Do* apparently was being swept southwestward into Gooseberry Shoals, south of Baker Island. Suddenly the pilot boat reported shallow water and then struck bottom.

> *Can Do* (voice not Quirk's): WE'VE LOST IT! IT'S ALL GONE! WE'VE HAD IT!

At this point, further communication between the Coast Guard and the *Can Do* faded out. Repeated calls brought no response.

In his home atop Indian Hill in Pride's Crossing, near Beverly, amateur radio operator Melrose Cole had been listening to the tense radio communications all evening. An electrical engineer and designer of highly sophisticated electronic equipment, Cole had an unusually wide range of radio transmitting and receiving equipment in his basement, and had even installed a tall antenna tower outside which could be rotated to serve as a direction finder. The antenna was not as high as the huge pines and hemlocks which surrounded his house, but tonight, in the midst of the blizzard, this was an advantage, since the big trees shielded the antenna from the tremendous winds and driving snow.

Monitoring the *Can Do's* calls on his marine radio, Cole realized that he alone had the capability of making contact with the pilot boat. Swiftly he "jury-rigged" a marine transmitter to his directional antenna to focus on the waters south of Gloucester. With a call to the Coast Guard headquarters in Boston, he obtained permission to contact the *Can Do* and relay any message he might receive or that the Coast Guard wanted sent.

> *Can Do* (10:47 P.M.): WE HAVE BEEN AGROUND, BUT WE'RE OFF NOW. STILL UNDER OUR OWN POWER.

Then a little later:

> *Can Do:* HARD AGROUND. NO POWER. TAKING ON WATER.

Cole worked feverishly to get a radio beam fix that would place the *Can Do's* position. Another amateur radio operator, Robert Wood of Topsfield, rigged a portable direction finder in his van, and drove out into the blizzard. Heading for a beach in Manchester, Wood was trying for a cross-bearing that, together with Cole's beam, would tell them where Quirk and his companions were putting up their desperate battle for survival.

> *Can Do* **to Cole** (at midnight via walkie-talkie): WE'VE GOT AN ANCHOR SET AND ARE HOLDING OUR OWN. TAKING A BEATING BUT NO FURTHER INJURIES. TRYING TO BUILD UP SOME POWER AND GET THINGS STARTED AGAIN. OUR POSITION UNKNOWN.

Wood's van was now at Singing Beach, Manchester, but unfortunately the walkie-talkie's transmissions were too weak for him to pick them up. After talking with Cole, Wood started off for a beach in Beverly Farms for another try.

> *Can Do* (Quirk): NO LUCK ON THE POWER. THIRTY-TWO VOLT BATTERIES ALL SHORTED OUT. CAN'T GET THE ENGINE STARTED. I HAVE A MATTRESS STUFFED IN THE WINDOW TO KEEP THE SEAS OUT. WATER NOT BUILDING UP IN THE BOAT AT THIS TIME.
> **Cole:** OKAY, FRANK, I COPY. STAND BY. ON YOUR LAST TRANSMISSION SO MUCH SNOW STATIC THAT WE COULD NOT GET A CROSS-BEARING ON YOU. SORRY WE CAN'T PIN YOU CLOSER.

Can Do: THESE BATTERIES WON'T HOLD FOR MUCH LONGER. I'LL CONTACT YOU IN THIRTY MINUTES.

Cole (2:15 A.M.): ROGER, FRANK, WILL BE HERE WHEN YOU WANT US.

Cole (2:25 A.M.): *CAN DO . . . CAN DO . . .* I HAVE BEEN ADVISED THAT A TRUCK WITH AN EXTREMELY POWERFUL SEARCHLIGHT IS HEADED FOR MAGNOLIA BEACH. KEEP YOUR EYES OPEN FOR IT. WARREN SUGGESTS YOU CONSIDER HOOKING YOUR RADIO LEADS TO A TWELVE-VOLT BATTERY FOR MORE POWER.

Can Do: WE'D NEVER GET TO THE BATTERY. ACTION OUT HERE TOO MUCH.

Cole: WOOD IS NOW ON HIS WAY TO SINGING BEACH WITH A PORTABLE RIG. CALL ME IN THIRTY MINUTES AND WE'LL TRY FOR A FIX. SAVE YOUR BATTERIES UNTIL THEN.

Can Do: OKAY, MEL. GETTING PRETTY COLD AND WEAK HERE — GUESS THE LOSS OF BLOOD CAUSED IT. GETTING WET, TOO.

Cole: FRANK, WHY DON'T YOU GET OUT OF THE WHEELHOUSE AND GO BELOW? I KNOW WATER IS COMING IN THAT WINDOW. GO BELOW WITH THE OTHERS AND TRY TO WARM UP. YOU CAN'T DO ANY GOOD UP THERE IN THE WHEELHOUSE, AND IF SHE DOES BEACH, YOU'RE BETTER OFF DOWN BELOW WITH THE OTHERS. TUCK YOUR WALKIE-TALKIE RADIO BESIDE YOU WHEN YOU LIE DOWN AS YOUR BATTERIES ARE GETTING LOW. THE WARMTH WILL REVIVE THEM.

Apparently Frank Quirk agreed to go below, because his next transmission was fainter. He asked Cole — Can you copy me from here?

Cole: ROGER, FRANK. DO YOU WANT TO TRY YOUR CB?

Can Do: DON'T THINK WE'LL TRY TO MOVE. WE'RE PRETTY WELL WEDGED IN BESIDE THE TABLE. IT'S REALLY RIPPING OUT HERE.

Then, at 3:30 A.M., heavy seas pounded their way through a forward hatch on the pilot boat.

Can Do: WE'RE GETTING PRETTY WET UP HERE. HATCH IS LOOSE. WE ARE GOING TO TRY TO MOVE AFT.

Cole: OKAY, FRANK, TRY TO LOCATE SOME FOOD. YOU COULD USE THE ENERGY. KEEP CLOSE TOGETHER FOR WARMTH. KEEP THE RADIO PROTECTED BETWEEN YOU TO WARM UP THE BATTERIES. FRANK, IT'S ONLY ABOUT TWO HOURS UNTIL DAWN AND LATEST WEATHER PROMISES ABATING SEAS. GLOUCESTER COAST GUARD WILL GET A 44-FOOTER UNDER WAY TO YOUR POSITION THEN.

Can Do: OKAY, MEL. WILL HOLD ON. SURE WISH WE COULD

RAISE SOME POWER. IT'S REALLY HOPPING OUT HERE BUT WE'RE
MAKING IT.
Cole: OKAY, FRANK. GET SOME REST AND I'LL BE HERE WHEN
YOU CALL BACK.

The crucial question now was: would the *Can Do's* anchor hold? If
the pilot boat could maintain her position, the five men inside the steel
hull might survive. If the anchor line, constantly wrenched and chafed by
savage seas, were worn through, the *Can Do* would be carried before the
storm until it foundered.

At 4 A.M., Cole renewed his radio calls to the *Can Do* but there was
no reply. At 4:30, he tried again, without success.

At dawn, Cole, supplied by the local fire department with a list of
names and phone numbers of homes along the water, set up a coast watch
for the pilot boat. But the blinding blizzard raged through most of Tuesday, and no sightings were reported. The *Decisive* escorted a fishing vessel
with damaged radar to the entrance to Gloucester Harbor and then proceeded to Salem Sound. The *Global Hope* was still hard aground on the
ledge, but the snow and high seas made it impossible for Coast Guard
helicopters or boats to reach the tanker. The *Decisive* spent the rest of the
day and night searching for the *Can Do*.

On Wednesday, the *Decisive's* small boats removed the twenty-
eight man crew from the *Global Hope*, and members of the Coast Guard's
Atlantic Strike Team were set aboard the tanker to combat its oil spill into
Salem Sound.

The same day, the bodies of Frank Quirk, Donald Wilkinson, Dave
Curley, and Kenneth Fuller were recovered from beaches at Nahant and
Marblehead. One week later, a private plane sighted the submerged
wreckage of a boat near Marblehead Neck. Divers were transported to the
scene, and the wreck of the *Can Do* was found lying in approximately
twenty feet of water. A body found by the divers in the engine room was
identified as Charles Bucko.

Attempts to refloat the *Global Hope* were unsuccessful, and it was
not until a month later that the tanker was finally towed to Boston for
further disposal.

After intensive investigation, a Coast Guard Board of Inquiry concluded that the captain of the *Global Hope* was personally negligent and
responsible for the grounding and loss of the tanker because he had failed
to make adequate preparations to ensure that his vessel would not drop
anchor and could safely ride out the forecast storm.

But it was the *Can Do* and her valiant crew that paid the price.

Above and Beyond the Call of Duty

"Engines! For God's sake give us steam ...!"

By DON AND HELEN ROSS

A lthough the Medal of Honor is usually associated with heroism in time of war, 177 Medals (all but six to U.S. Navy personnel) have been awarded for bravery during peacetime.* One such was awarded sixteen years after the action to Charles Willey of Penacook, New Hampshire, in 1932.

Born March 31, 1889, in East Boston, Massachusetts, Charlie apprenticed as a machinist after graduation from high school. At nineteen, he was rejected by the Navy because he was underweight for his 5' 2" stature. Undaunted, he ate a dozen bananas and drank a half gallon of water to up the scales at the Boston Naval Recruiting Station to the required weight.

The wiry New Englander, physically barely acceptable, was overtrained for entrance as an ordinary recruit, but a long-established rule barred men under twenty-one years of age from entering the ranks of Petty Officers, where Willey belonged. However, the Navy Department broke that rule, and Willey enlisted in the regular Navy as a Second Class Petty Officer in the Machinist specialty. He progressed through the ranks at a speed unheard of for peacetime. In eight years he was a Warrant Machinist aboard the U.S.S. *Memphis*.

The armored cruiser *Memphis*, originally named *Tennessee*, was often assigned special duty. At the outbreak of World War I, she returned United States citizens who had been traveling abroad; transported $10 million in gold bullion to Europe during the war; served twice in the Mediterranean transporting refugees; carried Marines to Haiti and Santo Domingo; and took President Wilson's daughter to Buenos Aires, Argentina, to a Commission which convened on May 25, 1916, the same day that the ship's name was changed from *Tennessee* to *Memphis*.

* As of April, 1975, the date this story appeared in *Yankee* magazine.

On the return trip, the ship anchored on August 29 in the harbor of Santo Domingo, British West Indies. She had borne her new name for over three months. Superstitious sailors said that changing a ship's name was bad luck. Others added to the dark talk with "Just as bad as having a woman aboard."

Sunday afternnoon, August 29, 1916, was balmy. Warrant Officer Willey was playing cards with mess-mates in his stateroom aboard the *Memphis*. The ship swung peacefully on the starboard hook in the harbor. At about 3:15 P.M., Captain Edward Beach noticed that though the sea was calm, a long, slow swell was causing the ship to roll. "The most amazing thing of all, most impressive, was the high breakers plainly receding rapidly from the beach," he wrote in his August 30, 1916, report to the Secretary of the Navy.

Another Navy ship, U.S.S. *Castine*, anchored closer to shore than *Memphis*, was suddenly engulfed in breakers. "Huge seas buried *Castine* out of sight," Beach wrote. "But she hove up her anchor, and, despite a disabled steering wheel, she pulled out and sailed clear of disaster. *Memphis* rolled in mounting waves, and water came over the deck."

Captain Beach sent a message to Warrant Officer Willey directing him to go at once with his emergency watch of men to raise steam, as the sea was getting rough. Hastily slipping dungarees over his uniform, Wil-

On May 25, 1916, the Navy changed the name of this armored cruiser from U.S.S. Tennessee *to U.S.S.* Memphis. *Bad luck, some sailors said.*

ley grabbed flashlight and leather gloves and hurried below. On his way, he noticed that the ship was rolling at an alarming degree.

Down below, the crew hastened to light off four boilers that were all primed and ready for any eventuality. Two live boilers with 250 pounds of steam pressure were already being used for auxiliary machinery. From these, fire was carried by shovels to light off the additional boilers.

In the meantime, Willey's men closed watertight doors and hatches. Vertical sliding doors in the boiler room were closed with slow-turning handwheels. Doors in the uptake passage swung shut and were clamped tight by ten dogs, or clamps, against a rubber gasket around the frame.

"In a few minutes, the draft blowers hurled air under pressure from the ventilators into the firerooms. Men worked like Trojans," Willey wrote in his personal account. "They brought coal from the bunkers to the floor plates and worked the various eighty-two doors of those great water tube boilers, perhaps sensing that their lives depended on their actions."

By 4:00 P.M., Captain Beach realized that conditions were serious. Everything loose was secured, closed, or battened down to keep the ship from filling completely with water.

The ship began to heave violently, throwing men about. The captain gave orders to the engine room to have engines turning within a few minutes. He said the ship was in the grip of a tidal wave and in danger of swamping.

This is how Captain Beach described the unusual actions of the water in his report: "Breakers reached *Memphis* about 4:20 P.M. The ship sank in a hollow trough. The sea came and without breaking flowed across the decks. These seas, getting higher and higher, simply pushed across the decks. I saw none curl over and break. First they flowed across the forecastle and quarterdeck. Then they pushed across the boat decks, the lower and upper bridges, and tops of the ventilators. One simply saw a great smooth mountain of water along the starboard side, then this mountain toppled on board. Finally the water was as high as the smokestacks and in toppling buried the stacks. There was no spray, no violent gust of wind, no sheets of water being blown about. Simply immeasurable quantities of water toppling on board in great volumes. Sometimes this water was cold, sometimes, towards the end, noticeably warm."

Below decks, the men in the engine room had no time to take note of the unusual condition of the sea. "In the matter of a few minutes we realized we were fighting a grim battle of death and destruction," Warrant Officer Willey wrote in his personal account. "As watch officer of those men I went from boiler to boiler, directing and encouraging them. Stripped to their waists, they gave their all . . . . The giant waves pounded the ship, pouring sea water down ventilators. Water washed over coal on the floor plates. Slice bars flew about. Coal buckets jerked from coal-passers' hands. The men tried to work those fires on wet, slippery plates, trying to hold their feet on the pitching, pounding ship."

A cry came over the speaker tube: "Engines! For God's sake! Give us steam . . . !" Thirty-five minutes had passed from the time the crew had arrived in the firerooms. In that unprecedented time, boilers were cut into main steamlines, and engines started to turn.

In hopes of clearing Torrecella Point in a crablike maneuver, Captain Beach ordered, "Full right rudder. Full speed astern starboard. Full speed ahead port." The starboard engine responded immediately, followed a few seconds later by the port engine. But just then a heavy sea carried the bow of the ship to port, pushing her well inside the Point.

"Water — tons of it — poured aboard, coming down the stacks, putting out some fires. Out went the lights. All hell broke loose."

From now on *Memphis* repeatedly struck the bottom. There was no hope of clearing the Point. The only possibility of getting out was by going out sternwards, slipping the starboard chain. The Captain reversed the port engine telegraph to full speed astern, while holding full right rudder.

Willey's account describes what happened then in the boiler room: "Water — tons of it — poured aboard, coming down the stacks, putting out some fires. Out went lights. All hell broke loose. The main steamline of the port engine room burst as cold water hit hot boilers."

In less than a minute, word reached the bridge that the main steampipe had burst. Then — "Dynamos have stopped." All engines ceased completely. The ship dragged rapidly towards shore, striking bottom heavily with monstrous seas continuing to sweep over her.

Captain Beach directed the port anchor be let go, and, in spite of powerful waves sweeping the decks, men struggled to obey this last command for their ship. Now, at 4:50 P.M., *Memphis* was on the rocks. Down in the boiler room, men rushed to stop-over valves over boilers in the darkness of an inferno. Tubes leaked from strain at headers. The only light was fire flame and Willey's flashlight. "There in pitch blackness," Willey wrote, "those men showed their mettle. They stuck to their posts and to me until beaten by the elements. Only when we struck the reef and the boilers let go did they flee for their lives."

Up the hot ladders they fled, to the air locks of the uptakes, hoping to release the ten dogs. All were too weak to undog the door, and they were trapped. Steam cooked their bodies. "I can hear their screams today," Willey said years later.

Word came down the speaking tube, "Abandon ship!" Willey could have escaped through the coal bunkers, but instead he chose to help his men. He rolled in the water, then, removing his jumper, wound it around his head and struggled up the ladder through scalding billows of steam.

"It was a desperate battle to undog the door leading to the open passageway. Yet God gave me the strength to do it. The moment when the last dog yielded and the door opened was the most thrilling of my life."

Willey pushed and dragged the six nearly unconscious men into the passageway. Only when rescuers came, did he lose consciousness.

Of the 844 Navy personnel aboard that morning, 98 were lost. This disaster was the worst the Navy had sustained in peacetime. Among those rescued was the unconscious Willey — and reportedly he remained in that state for three months. He was hospitalized for a total of eighteen months. It was a long, painful recovery since much of his body had been badly burned, and he had lost one lung. He retired from the Navy when he left the hospital.

Charlie Willey settled on a small farm in Penacook and began writing technical articles. To gain background for a specific set of articles, he wandered into Hoyt Electric Company. He so impressed a foreman that he was hired full time. (Forty-two years later, he retired from Hoyt, but continued as a consultant for many years.)

One day in 1932, when Charlie opened the shop door at work, he was greeted with, "Here comes the conquering hero!" Before official word had reached Charlie, the morning newspaper carried a story that Charles Willey was to receive the Medal of Honor.

Sixteen years after the action, Willey's heroic deed was disclosed only by chance. In reviewing the career of a fellow officer for advancement, the Navy Board read the details of the *Memphis* disaster and Willey's part in it. Better late than never, his resourcefulness and compassion for his fellow men were rewarded.

The Medal was presented by Admiral C. S. Kempff in ceremonies at Portsmouth Navy Yard, home port of *Memphis*.

> **Citation:** For extraordinary heroism in the line of his profession while serving on board the U.S.S. *Memphis*, at a time when that vessel suffered total destruction from a hurricane while anchored off Santo Domingo City, 29 August 1916. Machinist Willey took his station in the engineer's department and remained at his post of duty amidst scalding steam and rush of thousands of tons of water into his department as long as engines would turn, leaving only when ordered to leave. When boilers exploded, he assisted in getting the men out of the fireroom, carrying them to the engine-room where there was air instead of steam. Machinist Willey's conduct on this occasion was above and beyond the call of duty.

A Historic Tête-à-Tête

Americans, upwards of three quarters of a million of them a year, still turn off the fast lane for a moment to be piped aboard their heritage, to tread the decks of the oldest commissioned vessel in the United States Navy, to see and feel for themselves what happened. To feel the oak and the iron and the hemp of the U.S.S. Constitution is to plumb our national depth, our American gut. Only a fraction of her frame is original, and yet, like all creatures that continually replace their tissue, she lives on. The moment in history that justifies a hundredfold the preservation of a wooden ship whose expectancy expired a century and a half ago took but four days in the early weeks of the War of 1812 with England.

By Joseph E. Garland

Since the end of the Revolution, the young nation had been caught in the backlash of the grim stuggle between the mother country and France — its ports under unpredictable blockade, its merchant vessels searched and seized, its commerce in chronic jeopardy. President Jefferson's Embargo of 1807 turned out to be a feeble threat. On the 18th of June, 1812, President Madison had had enough and declared that we would fight again for our rights.

Within two months the frigate *Constitution* in two consecutive actions had ended Britannia's absolute rule of the waves forever, and established the infant American navy as something more than a dog barking in the night.

Constitution carried thirty long 24-pounders on the gun deck, twenty-two short 32-pound carronades on the top or spar deck above it, and two 24-pounders and an 18 on the forecastle as bow chasers — fifty-five guns in all, most of them cast in England. Her complement at this time was 456; the men slept in hammocks, slung like hams in a smokehouse, or on the berthing deck below the gun deck. She was 204 feet long over all, and her mainmast reached up for the breeze 220 feet from keel to truck.

The War of 1812 was four days old when two squadrons under Commodore John Rodgers sailed out of New York to avoid being blockaded by the enemy fleet and to intercept, if they could, a convoy of

English merchantmen reportedly en route home from Jamaica. The next day, June 23, a long British frigate of thirty-six guns, *Belvidera*, was sighted, and Rodgers made chase. Though his flagship, *President*, was the bigger, *Belvidera* was bound for Halifax and could afford to jettison boats, spare spars, anchors, and fourteen tons of fresh water. The American commodore personally fired the first round of the war, and Captain Byron returned the compliment. Both suffered hits, but *Belvidera* escaped and arrived at Halifax with substantive evidence that hostilities were under way.

When confirmation reached the British naval base soon after, Captain Sir Philip Bowes Vere Broke was ordered to sea on July 5 with a squadron made up of four frigates. Four days out they were joined off Nantucket Island by another frigate, *Guerrière*.

All the while, Captain Isaac Hull, the short, stoutish, amiable, but superlatively able bachelor who had taken over the command of *Constitution* from Rodgers in 1810, was chafing up in the Potomac, under orders to complete his refit, put to sea, and join the American fleet on the double. Rodgers had complained that his former command was a slow sailer, and small wonder. Hull's divers reported the equivalent of ten wagonloads of mussels, oysters, barnacles, and seaweed clinging to the worn-out copper sheathing. Hull had her hove down, cleaned, and recoppered while signing on a new crew, most of them with no man-o'-war experience, to replace those whose hitches were up.

On July 5 *Constitution* proceeded slowly out of Chesapeake Bay, taking on more stores, guns, ammunition, and recruits as her draft allowed in the deeper water, with Hull and his officers drilling their green men day and night in seamanship and gunnery. On July 12 they cleared the Virginia capes and stood to the northward in search of Commodore Rodgers. The American squadron, as a matter of fact, was by then on the other side of the Atlantic, just as fruitlessly looking for that fat convoy from the Caribbean.

Constitution was about fifteen miles off Egg Harbor, New Jersey, when at 2 P.M. on July 16, the cry came from the masthead: "Four sail to the nor'ard and inshore, look like men-o'-war!" The enemy or Rodgers? Captain Hull ordered all canvas on in chase, for the wind was very light. Then a shape appeared on the northeast horizon. They crawled toward each other over an almost windless sea. That evening Hull tried the American private night signal on the mystery ship, but drew no response. The lot must be British, he decided, and hauled away from them to the southeast; Hull had no thirst for baptizing his greenhorns in the dark.

Dawn of July 17 disclosed that the near-encounter had been with *Guerrière*, now five or six miles astern. Other frigates, *Belvidera* and *Aeolus*, drifted along some miles off *Constitution's* lee, the rest of Broke's

The Constitution *being towed by rowboats and alternate kedges in her attempt to escape the British "hounds" in an almost flat calm.*

squadron bringing up the rear, all flying English colors and pointing for the American prey like lazy hounds on a sleepy hare.

The rising sun dispelled the night breeze so thoroughly that the torpidly fleeing Americans lost all steerageway. Two cutters were swung over the side, hawsers were run out, and the rowers commenced the old torture at the sweeps — but now with patriotic zeal — of swinging 2,200 dead tons of frigate back to the southward, towing her out of the reach of the British Empire. Two heavy cannon were rolled aft on the spar deck and aimed astern. On the gun deck below, a couple of 24-pounders were rumbled back to the captain's cabin and their snouts stuck out his windows.

The July sea undulated and glistened under the morning sun, and now the English had their boats over too and were pulling with might and main. It was almost comic, were anyone in a laughing mood, to see these giant ships of war, their lofty sails limp, in antlike chase across the vastness of the Atlantic. The effort to move the frigate hit the height of desperation when Hull and Lieutenant Charles Morris, second in command, decided to kedge. Every inch of rope heavy enough for the job was rounded up and spliced into nearly a mile of cable. The first cutter and the launch were assigned alternately to row the lightest anchor on board, the kedge, ahead to the length of its cable and drop it while the bully boys at the capstan walked it in, foot by foot, warping their frigate on its own hook, so to speak, as the second kedge was being rowed forward. An old trick for coming to an anchorage in a calm. But here, in the middle of the Atlantic Ocean, in a life-or-death chase?

Naturally British spyglasses had been active, and soon Captain Byron, who was closest astern, had *Belvidera's* kedges out and was warping in pursuit — and rather more effectively. The gap was narrowing.

Thus the chase literally dragged on all the rest of that day, into the evening, and through the night, towing and kedging, kedging and towing, shift after shift, with only brief respites for the weary men of both sides from infrequent and slight breezes. *Guerrière* — whose commander, Captain James R. Dacres, is said to have bet Hull his hat, during a friendly meeting before the war, that he could beat him in single-ship combat — was some distance off *Constitution's* lee beam at the break of the second day, July 18, when occurred one of those unaccountable close encounters that might have altered the entire outcome.

Another light breeze had materialized, carrying *Belvidera* ahead of *Guerrière* to a position off the American's bow, where she tacked; to maintain his weather gage (his superior position upwind), Hull had to tack also, which brought *Constitution* unavoidably within range of *Aeolus* on her lee quarter. For some reason the commander of the smaller frigate refrained from firing his broadside, and instead tacked in *Constitution's* wake. It was claimed later that he was afraid the recoil of his guns would stop him dead in the water; as it was, he appears to have muffed Britain's best chance to end the chase then and there.

And at last, a real breeze freshening! Eagerly, they scrambled aloft at their captain's order and set the skysails flying to catch every breath of it. By noon the American frigate was laying into it, all her boats safely up in their davits, the wind on her beam, knocking off ten knots. Twelve and a half by two o'clock in the afternoon. At four the closest of the pursuers, who in desperation to catch up with the quarry had cut their cutters adrift, was six miles astern.

No sooner was his ship lost from the enemy's sight than Isaac Hull roared out to sheet 'em home. Eight more days and the U.S.S. *Constitution*, having twisted the lion's tail, sailed happily into Boston. "Nothing," wrote

Captain Byron of *Belvidera*, "Can exceed my mortification from the extraordinary escape of the American frigate."

Captain Hull put a disclaimer in the press, commending the bravery of his men who, though "deprived of sleep, and allowed but little refreshment during the time, not a murmur was heard to escape them."

It took but a few days to reprovision. By the end of July Hull had still received no new orders. Not wishing to take a chance on being bottled up in Boston for the duration by the enormously superior enemy fleet and thirsting for action, he simply risked his career by sailing on August 2 without orders.

Captain James R. Dacres is said to have bet Hull his hat, during a friendly meeting before the war, that he could beat him in a single-ship combat ...

Heading east in hopes of intercepting British shipping in and out of Halifax, *Constitution* captured and burned two merchantmen, then on August 15 scared off a marauding enemy sloop of war that escaped after burning a captive brig, and took over two already-taken prizes, one American and one British. Prisoners reported that Broke's squadron was cruising the Grand Bank not far to the northward to defend against just such depredations as *Constitution* had been committing. Hull had no hankering for a rowing and kedging rematch and headed south.

The following day Captain Dacres, once again on his way to Halifax, left an invitation to any one of the Yankee 44-gunners to meet his *Guerrière* at sea "for the purpose of having a few minutes' tête-à-tête."

Three more days and *Constitution* was bowling along under a good northwest breeze about 650 miles east of Boston. Cloudy but clear. At 2 P.M. the masthead reported a sail to the east-southeast. Hull bore off to investigate. It was clearly a ship of war. At 4:45, up fluttered British ensigns to all three mastheads. She was *Guerrière*. Dacres was about to have his tête-à-tête.

Again, as luck would have it, *Constitution* held the weather gage. Captain Hull with due caution ordered *Constitution* brought up to the wind while he took in light sails and cleared for action.

Constitution was about two miles off when *Guerrière*'s broadside all at once exploded in a row of ominous puffs, the cannonballs plummeting into the ocean in geysers of spray well up ahead of them. Already the enemy frigate wheeled in a sharp U-turn and in a matter of minutes brought her opposite guns to bear.

The object of the confident Captain Dacres in these maneuvers was to place each shot where it would wreak the greatest mayhem. And the object of the cagey Captain Hull, as he had his helmsmen twirling their great double wheel back and forth between port and starboard, was to make the target the harder to hit. In this he succeeded, firing off his bow guns in the bargain when *Guerrière* chanced to come in their sights as she, too, wore downwind on one tack and then the other, firing off one broadside as the gunners across the deck feverishly sponged, doused, and served their smoking, steaming barrels.

Like an enraged but calculating bull, *Constitution* charged on into broadside after broadside. The tête-á-tête was at hand. Dacres put *Guerrière* nearly before the wind, his sternguns blazing an invitation to close. At 6 P.M., *Constitution's* bow was abreast of *Guerrière's* port quarter, distance about 200 yards and narrowing. The American gunners and their crew stood half-naked beside their "iron dogs," waiting tensely for the word.

"No firing at random!" cautioned their commander calmly. "Let every man look well to his aim."

The black frigate drew up on her enemy, which was firing sporadically. Twice Lieutenant Morris came up from the gun deck to report casualties and request permission to fire. Twice Captain Hull restrained his first officer. A third time Morris appeared with his urgent plea.

The enemies were beam and beam. "Now, boys, pour it into them!" bellowed their Captain, leaping up in his excitement and splitting his britches from fore to aft.

The frigates were within half a pistol shot now, pouring out broadside after thundering broadside staccatoed by the crackle of musketry from the marines halfway up the masts in the fighting tops. In ten minutes *Guerrière's* entire mizzen mast, with yards, sails, and rigging, toppled over the starboard rail with a stupendous crack, followed immediately by the main yard. Someone shouted as the cheer went up, "We've made a brig of her! Next time we'll make her a sloop!"

The enemy broadsides slammed an occasional round against *Constitution's* oaken hull, twenty-one inches thick in places, which bounced into the sea, inspiring the immortal Yankee yell: "Huzzah! Her sides are made of iron!"

The loss of *Guerrière's* aftermost mast and her main yard took the wind out of perhaps a quarter of her canvas, while the drag of the spar in the water veered her hard to starboard. Instantly Captain Hull ordered his helm over; swinging around her crippled enemy's port bow, "Ironsides" delivered two raking, devastating broadsides.

But her braces and jib halyards had been shot away, and *Constitution* couldn't hold her windward advantage. *Guerrière* was now half-sailing, half-drifting into a position that might give Dacres just time to rake the Yankee's stern. Hull countered by falling off the wind, across *Guerrière's* course. The collision was inevitable. The British frigate drove her long, angling bowsprit up over *Constitution's* larboard quarter, where

it tangled in the mizzen rigging, stuck fast, lunging up and smashing down on the rail and quarterdeck with every sea.

Another fifteen minutes of close in-fighting ended at 6:30 P.M., when the heavy seas and the wind parted the embattled frigates. Hardly were they clear when the whipping of *Guerrière's* bowsprit, transmitted through the stays of the foremast and back to the mainmast, snapped both almost at the deck, and down they crashed — yards, sails, rigging, and all in a hopeless mess.

Constitution stood to the eastward a short distance for repairs. *Guerrière* wallowed in the trough of the sea, a scene of despair. The frigate with the sides of iron returned at 7:00 P.M. to resume battle if challenged, but Dacres could do no more. Having not a mast left from which to strike his colors, he fired one gun to leeward in surrender.

Lieutenant Read brought the British commander back aboard *Constitution* for the formal surrender. "Dacres, give me your hand," offered Hull, as his wounded enemy labored up the rope ladder. "I know you are hurt." The victor refused the proffered sword, but thought, remembering their bet, that he would trouble him for his hat.

Constitution's boats took off the 267 British prisoners, 63 of them wounded. Fifteen had been killed in contrast to seven American dead, only seven more wounded, out of 456.

Ghastly was the scene in *Constitution's* cockpit that night, deep in her after hold where side by side the American and British surgeons amputated mangled limbs. There bled to death an English tar whose lower jaw had been shot off. How many of his miserably maimed mates coughed and screamed and mercifully expired? Dick Dunn, a Yank, suffered what was left of his leg to be sawed off without flinching, growling through grinding teeth, "You are a hard set of butchers."

Nothing, however, could save the stricken *Guerrière*. The upstart ex-colonials had done their job well. No hope of towing the prize back to Boston. She was filling, and her pumps couldn't keep up. At three the next afternoon Captain Hull ordered her set on fire.

The U.S.S. *Constitution* sailed back into Boston Harbor on August 30, 1812. Her stunning victory brought exultation to the land, extravagant honors to her officers and crew, and the deepest chagrin to Britain. For the wiser heads on both sides of the Atlantic saw that the frigate's victory had secured the future of the young nation — if not forever, then for as far as anyone dared peer into it.

Collision — CQD!

"Do your utmost to reach her . . ."

BY WILLIAM P. NOBLE

T he cold New York wind whipped around the sleek hull of *Republic* as she backed from her west-side pier into the icy waters of the Hudson River. She shuddered a moment as the pilot ordered the engines stopped, and then very gradually *Republic* pointed her stem down river, moving slowly forward. It was January 22, 1909, and for 461 eager passengers it was to be a mid-winter excursion to the warm waters of the Mediterranean. No more snow, no more cold, no more freeze — at least for a while.

Republic was perfect for the job. Fast, comfortable, and luxurious, she was the pride of the White Star Lines, only five years old, and big — 570 feet from stem to stern. Ocean crossings were her specialty, and she once held the record for the Boston-Queenstown (Ireland) run. Only the most experienced White Star Line sailors were assigned to her.

Republic nosed her way into lower New York harbor through a darkening night while the passengers barely noticed. In the dining saloon with its ornamental wood carvings, waiters bowed over the loaded platters of whole salmon and roasts of meat; some of the passengers were already walking off the evening meal; others let their dinner settle in the library or smoked in the privacy of the smoking room.

Up on the bridge, Captain William Sealby and his watch detail prepared to enter the heavily traveled sea lanes outside New York harbor. For Sealby it was nothing new; he had made the North Atlantic crossing a number of times. He was comforted, too, by the presence of Jack Binns in the wireless shack far aft. Only in the past few years had ocean-going liners added wireless. In fact, the first wireless distress call at sea had been flashed just ten years before.

Old-timers, though, weren't sure wireless was worth getting excited about. Because the equipment was expensive, there were few trained operators, and weather conditions could make everything unreliable, many shipowners didn't bother to install wireless equipment, waiting until it proved itself of value.

Republic moved ahead through the dark night, leaving the glare of New York behind. As she cut through Ambrose Channel, passengers unpacked and got ready for bed.

The weather had begun to grow murky. The cold slap-slap of the sea against *Republic's* slicing hull threw a biting spray into the January night. Captain Sealby could sense a change in the air, which seemed heavier and wetter than usual. As the ship plowed through Ambrose Channel towards Ambrose Lightship and the transatlantic sea lanes, visibility began to diminish. The lightship's blinking light could still be seen in the distance, though its glow was anything but clear.

Soon, *Republic* cleared the lightship and turned north, heading for the Nantucket sea buoy where she would turn east and begin her great-circle course across the North Atlantic. Though a number of miles at sea, she was still in well-traveled waters with dangerous shallow areas nearby. It was important to keep a close eye on position at all times. A course error of just a few degrees could put *Republic* on Nantucket shoals, and a sleepy watch detail could jeopardize other shipping as well.

Then, almost without warning, no one could see anything! *Republic* had slipped into a thick, dense fog. Visibility was gone.

"Lookouts!" came the sharp order from the bridge, and sailors ran to positions on bow and stern where they might give a few seconds advance warning of impending danger. Below decks passengers pulled their cozy blankets up and settled into reading the latest novels.

On the bridge, however, Captain Sealby had no such comfort. He knew that the fog off Nantucket could be treacherous and extensive, that it could wrap itself around a ship tighter than a cocoon, making it impossible for someone standing on the bow to see the bridge. Worse — it was the middle of the night, and the darkness coupled with the fog gave the sensation of being totally alone in a black hole.

"All ahead one-half!" Captain Sealby ordered, and the high hum of *Republic's* engines slowed.

"Commence sounding whistle!" and preparations were made to blow the ship's foghorn, in accordance with recognized rules of international seamanship. Ooooooooooooogah! came the ear splitting blast, six seconds long, once every minute . . . Ooooooooogah! . . .

"Lookouts look alive!" came the reminder as *Republic* sliced through the quiet sea, a ghostly apparition in the dark and the fog. In spite of the adverse weather Captain Sealby and his crew knew their ship was among the safest afloat. *Republic* had twelve watertight compartments and a double-thick hull; she was a modern ocean-going liner in every sense of the word.

Even the U.S. Navy thought so. Down in *Republic's* cargo hold were huge supplies of fresh and smoked meats, turkeys, potatoes, sugar, butter, and eggs, all to be delivered to the Navy in Gibraltar. It was for President Theodore Roosevelt's Great White Fleet, preparing for the final leg of its triumphant around-the-world cruise under the command of

White Star Line's S.S. Republic *after the collision, the great hole in her side covered with canvas in an effort to check the inrush of water.*

Admiral Sperry. Without these supplies the fleet would have to limp home, abandoning the President's purpose.

As *Republic* continued to move cautiously northeast, the fog never let up. The tense early morning hours ticked by; only the deep hum of the engines and the occasional slap of a wayward swell against the hull broke the quiet on the bridge. *Republic's* course became a steady 084 degrees, almost directly east, as she settled into the great-circle track. On the navigator's chart, the last few hours showed a series of estimated positions along a dead-reckoning course, the best that could be hoped for in the dense fog. It was impossible to get a land fix, and just as difficult to take a star sight. But the navigator could estimate *Republic's* speed from the number of engine revolutions, and positions could then be estimated at hourly intervals. By 5:30 A.M., Captain Sealby was confident *Republic* was more than thirty miles southwest of Nantucket and moving easily through the winter sea.

Most of the passengers were fast asleep in their staterooms, the January darkness and the fog a pall on early waking. For many, the loud blaring of the foghorn had made sleep difficult until the early morning, and they were now in the deepest part of their rest.

Ooooooooogah! . . . blew *Republic's* monotonous foghorn. . . . "What was that?" someone on the bridge said. It was now 5:45 A.M., and the fog was thicker than ever. "Someone's out there!" the whisper flew around the bridge.

"All engines stop!" came the order, and the steady engine hum died away immediately. A few rushed to the port side, straining to peer through the gauze-like air. That signal sounded close. Through the darkness it seemed as if something loomed out there, a shape, a shadow. . . .

"Full speed astern!" a shouted order. "Left full rudder!" Ooooooooogah! sounded *Republic's* whistle . . . oooooogah! . . . oooooo-gah! . . . three whistles, signalling a sudden change of course and a reversal of engines.

As the water boiled beneath *Republic's* stern, there was time only to watch transfixed a cluster of bright lights that suddenly broke through the fog directly off *Republic's* port side — lights that could only come from another ship, lights that seemed to be moving closer to *Republic*, bearing down on her, white lights straddled by red and green running lights. That meant only one thing — a ship was headed straight for *Republic*; it could slice her in half. . . .

"All ahead flank!" *Republic's* engines screamed in agony at the violent change from full speed astern to full speed ahead.

Still the lights came on . . . closer . . . closer . . . No doubt now — it was a big ship . . . oooooogah! it whistled, oooooogah! But there was nothing to be done. In the thick, wet fog about thirty miles southwest of Nantucket at 5:50 A.M. on January 23, 1909, while most of her passengers slept, *Republic* received a jagged, vertical gash in her middle, penetrating far below the waterline and opening her up like a clam shell, right into the engine room. The large ship which rammed her rebounded, blew her whistle furiously, reversed engines, and staggered off into the fog.

"All engines stop!" came the immediate order from *Republic's* bridge. The shock of the collision left everyone momentarily stunned. One of the finest, most seaworthy ocean liners in the world lay wallowing in the cold North Atlantic with a large hole in her side, unable to move, unable to see, unable even to identify the ship that had wounded her — a pitiful, helpless sea creature.

Captain Sealby recovered quickly. "Find out the extent of the damage," he ordered. "Get Jack Binns to the radio shack, we've got to notify people. Rouse the passengers, get them on deck immediately. Never mind waiting for them to get into their clothes. Have the stewards prepare coffee and solid food."

The shocked ship's company jumped to their duties. A few thousand yards away, swallowed by the fog, lay Lloyd Italiano Line's S.S. *Florida*, her bow crushed in, her passengers and crew equally shocked. How could this have happened? What went wrong?

On *Florida's* bridge, 29-year-old Captain Ruspini reviewed the past few minutes, sensing that the damage his ship had inflicted on *Republic* could be catastrophic. It was a good thing he had been on the bridge at the time of the collision, that *Florida* had been giving regular whistle signals. He remembered hearing a strange whistle off the starboard side; he had answered it while reducing speed . . . and then suddenly, right across his path, there had been a mountainous shape, a dark blob in the fog-shrouded early morning, moving from right to left. He had shouted for right full rudder and tried to reverse the engines, but there just hadn't been time. Reports began to flood in . . . three crew members killed instantly in their berths in the fo'c'sle, the passengers — mostly Italian immigrants bound from Naples to New York — milling about the decks on the verge of panic, an entire bow section mashed in, with only a watertight bulkhead holding back the sea. There was no way he could inform the outside world of this tragedy in the fog. *Florida*, even though she was almost four hundred feet long and built less than five years before, carried no wireless.

Water in the engine room had shorted out the ship's power. But he had to transmit now!

On *Republic* damage reports were coming in also, and Captain Sealby did not like what he was hearing. The collision had sheared a hole right into the engine room, the largest compartment on the ship. Water was pouring in; there was no way to stop it. The engine crew had fled topside, closing all watertight doors to the engine room.

"Tell Jack Binns to get on the wireless!" Sealby ordered. "We need immediate assistance!"

But Binns was already in the radio shack, one side of which had been ripped open by the ramming. Binns hunched his shoulders against the penetrating cold and fog and surveyed his equipment. It was up to him, he knew; he had to get help.

Gingerly, he tried his equipment — the power seemed to be on — and readied himself to transmit. Then, ploof! off went the power. The light in his radio shack was out, the hum of the ship's engines ceased, and emergency lights lit up around the ship. Binns knew immediately what had happened. Water in the engine room had shorted out the ship's power. But he had to transmit now!

He switched his equipment to a storage battery, knowing that the transmission range would be cut tremendously — to fifty or sixty miles at best — but at least the storage battery wasn't dependent on the ship's power. He just had to hope there was someone out there, somewhere.

"C-Q-D," he tapped out. "C-Q-D." (This was then the only recognized international distress signal, predating SOS by several years. It meant "Come Quick Danger.") As fog and cold swirled about him, Binns continued to send, waiting briefly for a response, then sending again. At 6:15 A.M., with the winter dawn seeping through the fog, there was a response. The lifesaving station on Nantucket's coast as Siasconset acknowledged Binn's CQD, "WHAT IS THE NATURE OF YOUR EMERGENCY?"

"WE HAVE BEEN RAMMED BY AN UNKNOWN SHIP," Binns began. "WHAT IS YOUR POSITION?"

Jack Binns had no idea. Nor did he know the extent of *Republic's* damage. He asked the lifesaving station to clear the air, and he would get the information. As Binns made his way along *Republic's* wreckage-strewn deck to the bridge and Captain Sealby, he couldn't help noticing passengers dressed in whatever they could find to hand. There was an elderly gentleman with a lady's petticoat around his shoulders; a woman in baggy men's trousers; others wore overcoats over their nightclothes or had blankets draped over their heads. They milled about the deck near the bridge, the stewards serving them hot coffee and sandwiches, smiling, trying to appear unworried, politely answering questions. Then Captain Sealby appeared, a megaphone to his mouth.

"May I have your attention, please," and he told them about the collision, mentioning that *Republic* had been damaged but was in no immediate danger of sinking. He urged them to keep calm, that help was being summoned, and that his first concern as captain of *Republic* was the safety of his passengers. To Jack Binns, he said, "Try and get in touch with other shipping. Hurry!" Binns answered that he had been in contact with Siasconset lifesaving station. They needed *Republic's* position and the extent of the damage.

"Right," Sealby said, sending Binns back to the radio shack.

Within moments Siasconset radioed that the air was now clear for traffic from *Republic*. There was no let-up in the fog, and Binns knew that the small storage battery connected to his wireless was the only thread that tied them to outside help. He had better take care of that battery. A message from Captain Sealby was handed him. It was to be the first official notification that *Republic* was in trouble.

Binns contacted Siasconset, waited for acknowledgment, and slowly tapped out, "REPUBLIC RAMMED BY UNKNOWN STEAMSHIP, TWENTY-SIX MILES SOUTHWEST NANTUCKET, BADLY IN NEED OF ASSISTANCE."

A few thousand yards away in the thick gloom, *Florida* lay, unmoving, her whistle sounding its regular deep belch every minute . . . ooo00-gah . . . ooogah! The situation with *Republic* seemed ominous to Captain Ruspini. For a few moments after the collision, he could hear *Republic's* fog whistle blowing regularly, but then it just stopped. An ominous sign. Could the two ships have drifted out of range? It was possible, but more likely *Republic's* damage made it difficult to generate enough steam to continue sounding the whistle. If so, *Republic* was in deep trouble. Ruspini knew there was nothing so vulnerable as a large ship drifting aimlessly near Nantucket Island. The chart showed the dangerous shoals nearby, and in the winter there were those sudden terrible storms with icy, bitter winds and huge seas that could last for days.

Ruspini wasn't sanguine about his own situation, either. More than thirty feet of bow had been crushed in, weakening the whole structure of the ship. *Florida* could still maneuver, however, as her engines had not been damaged, but she simply was not as stable as before. Then there were the passengers; Ruspini had a feeling that few could be relied upon to remain calm. He had more than eight hundred immigrants aboard, most of whom were survivors of the Messina earthquake just weeks before, in which more than 83,000 people had died. Memories of that horror were still so vivid, he feared to expose his passengers to new terrors. Still, he must do everything possible to help *Republic*; that was his mariner's code. What would he expect if the tables had been reversed?

Jack Binns, *wireless operator of* Republic.

By this time Siasconset had *Republic's* first message, and the lone radio operator, Jack Irwin, was frantically sending it on with his much stronger equipment. Irwin had just replenished the coal fire in the little lifesaving shack, when he got the first CQD from Jack Binns; the heat would keep his finger limber for the extraordinary signalling he was to do in the next few hours. "REPUBLIC RAMMED BY UNKNOWN STEAMSHIP," he tapped out, repeating what he had received from Jack Binns. And he added, "DO UTMOST TO REACH HER."

Well over a hundred miles away, out in the North Atlantic, the steamship *Baltic*, bound for New York from Liverpool, was moving cautiously through the same thick fog that blanketed *Republic* and *Florida*. Breakfast was being served, and the passengers wondered if the fog would mean delay in their arrival in New York. On the bridge, Captain J. B. Ranson was checking course and positions as *Baltic* moved into the coastal sea lanes.

"A message, sir!" said a sailor, materializing suddenly. He held out a hastily scribbled note from the radio shack.

It was the CQD from *Republic*, as relayed by Siasconset. Ranson looked at his watch: 7:15 A.M., an hour and a half after the collision. He made his way to the chart table, motioning for the navigator to join him. Carefully plotting *Republic's* estimated position, they compared it with their own. Down below, *Baltic's* passengers prepared for their last day at sea, packing up, exchanging addresses, and writing letters, sure they would be safely in port and docked by nightfall.

This was not to be. The chart on the bridge showed *Baltic* and *Republic* only sixty-four miles apart — little more than three hours sailing at *Baltic's* top speed.

Ranson knew it wasn't going to be easy to find *Republic* in the fog, but he had to try. "Send the following," he told his radioman. " 'RECEIVED MESSAGE FROM *REPUBLIC* OF RAMMING, WILL PROCEED TO HER ASSISTANCE. REACH HER AT 11:00. NOW 115 MILES EAST OF AMBROSE CHANNEL.' "

By 8:15 A.M., Siasconset, the White Star Lines offices in New York, and Jack Binns on *Republic* had all learned that *Baltic* was on the way. For Captain Sealby, however, the real question was whether *Republic* would still be floating. With thirty-five to forty feet of sea in the engine room, the ship was a lot lower in the water. He had no steam and no way to maneuver his ship in case of sudden storm. *Republic* was virtually a floating derelict, with 461 agitated passengers.

As he stared out at the swirling fog, he perceived a dense shadow, then a sudden whistle blast. Shouts erupted from the scores of passengers lining *Republic's* railing. The shadow was coming closer — a ship — the same ship that had rammed them. It was scarcely more than a few hundred feet away. The bow looked as though a giant fist had smashed it flat. More whistle signals, then the engines stopped, reversed, and gradually, ever so slowly, through the haze and mist, the strange ship began to turn off, bringing itself alongside *Republic*.

Words floated across the water. "S.S. *Florida*, out of Napoli, bound for New York. What assistance?"

Sealby reached for his megaphone. *Florida*, was it? No trouble remembering that. No wireless either, he'd bet, or Jack Binns would have raised them by this time. "We are *Republic* out of New York," Sealby shouted. "We have no steam, a flooded engine room, large hole port side amidships. We are taking on water."

Once again the voice floated across the water. "I am Captain Ruspini. We have steam. Our collision bulkhead is holding."

Sealby surveyed his passengers milling about the boat deck, ill-dressed and uncertain of their fate. Two of the passengers, Mrs. Lynch from Boston and Mr. Mooney from New York, had been killed instantly when *Republic* had been rammed. *Florida's* bow had knifed into their staterooms and crushed them to death. The bodies were below decks, laid out in coffins. At least two other passengers had been severely injured.

Sealby feared that the rumors were building, rumors that could lead to panic unless he took decisive action.

He took up the megaphone once more. "My passengers must be transferred," he shouted, "for their safety without delay." He made a formal request that *Florida* take aboard all *Republic's* passengers and a portion of her crew.

The response from Captain Ruspini was quick. "As you wish!" Both captains alerted their boat crews and boat-handling parties. Sealby now had to deal with his passengers. If they got the idea the ship was sinking beneath their feet . . .

Aiming his megaphone at the boat deck, he barked, "Your attention please . . . !" Anxious-faced, cold, and uncomfortable, the passengers stared up at Sealby through the fog. In a steady voice he told them they were in no immediate danger, but to be on the safe side he wanted to transfer them all to *Florida*. Collectively they turned to the fuzzy apparition with the caved-in bow that lay a few hundred feet away. "I expect you will be cool and not excited," Sealby reminded them. "Take your time getting into the lifeboats!" He made it plain that women and children were to go first, followed by those in the most expensive staterooms and finally the others. The crew would be the last to leave the vessel.

In the meantime, the action was growing heavy in Jack Binns's radio shack. After *Baltic* had answered the CQD, other signals from other ships came straggling in — the French liner, *La Lorraine*, the S.S. *Furnessia*, S.S. *Lucania*, the Revenue Cutters *Gresham* and *Seneca*, all within an easy day's sail, if it hadn't been for the fog. *Baltic* was the closest, and soon Binns was in direct wireless contact.

He repeated *Republic's* last known position and condition, reported that her passengers were being transferred to *Florida*, and warned that the fog was unabated — visibility still almost zero.

Binns didn't mention that he was numb with cold and fatigue. The raw, icy fog had been blowing in on him all morning through the open side of the radio shack, and without ship's power there had been no way for him to keep warm. Still, he stayed by his key, forcing his fingers to tap out message after message, keeping *Republic* in touch with the world.

A strong signal came through at noon from *Baltic* — only ten miles away from *Republic's* estimated position! But Binns knew the fog could make the two ships seem worlds apart. Until they actually saw *Baltic*, they couldn't be sure where she was.

Then a message came from Captain Sealby. The transfer of *Republic's* passengers to *Florida* had been completed in just a little over two hours. While Binns was tapping out the news, Captain Ruspini on *Florida* was realizing he had new problems. The decks of his medium-sized ship were suddenly very crowded; people had little space to sit or lie down. *Republic's* passengers were not properly dressed for the biting January weather, and there was some grumbling from the *Florida* passengers. It was this last that concerned him most. If *Florida's* passengers got it into their heads that their own safety was being threatened by the new arrivals, he wasn't sure he could keep things calm for a number of reasons. There simply were too many people aboard his ship. He had to keep within sight of *Republic* — to lose her in the fog could be disastrous. Then too, thirty feet of his own bow had been crushed; there was only one collision bulkhead between the sea and the below-deck compartments.

Suddenly, up forward, a bulging knot of passengers were shouting and waving their arms. What had happened? He was about to order his Chief Officer to investigate when a sailor came panting up the ladder and onto the bridge. "What happened?" Ruspini demanded.

"It's over, Captain. One of our passengers . . . scared . . . a knife . . . disarmed," the sailor stammered.

Several people from *Republic* had been threatened by *Florida* passengers afraid that the extra load would sink their ship. In the brief spell of panic, there had been a couple of ugly scenes.

"Injuries?" Ruspini asked.

"None, Captain." Ruspini turned away, relieved, staring once again into the unremitting fog. It promised to be a long day.

Booooomm! came a muffled explosion from *Republic*. High over the ship red sparks mushroomed and slowly filtered out of sight in the fog. Boooooomm!

In *Republic's* radio shack, Jack Binns had been in contact with several other ships, including *Baltic*. They were all around, somewhere in the fog. In an effort to get some circulation going, he began to take the radio messages received up to the bridge himself instead of sending them by messenger. He had been at the key for more than eight hours, and he needed to move around.

"Let's signal by rocket," Sealby said, directing Binns to inform the other ships.

And in a few moments . . . boooooommm!, and then again.

On *Baltic* Captain Ranson was becoming frustrated. Here it was the middle of the afternoon, they had been steaming a zig-zag course for hours all around *Republic's* estimated position, and somehow they hadn't been able to locate her. Even the rockets *Republic* radioed they were setting off couldn't be heard!

She's got to be there, Ranson thought, but where? We'll fire our rockets too, he decided. "Radio the *Republic*," he ordered.

But all through the afternoon and into the early evening the searchers came up empty. *Baltic* stuck to her zig-zag course across *Republic's* estimated position, setting off periodic rockets and waiting for a response. Other ships did the same, but as each hour dragged by no one could report anything.

On *Republic*, Sealby avoided using rockets because all the other ships were now using them. He decided to ring the ship's bell instead.

As the January darkness mingled with the fog, Sealby couldn't help feeling added concern. His ship was definitely down by the stern, and he suspected sea water seepage through the rivets and bolts of the rear bulkhead to the engine room. He had to face the stark reality — was his ship going to stay afloat? It had been more than twelve hours since the ramming, and *Republic* was definitely in a bad way.

What was that? Everyone strained an ear to the fog. A faint muffled explosion somewhere out there — the first contact! In the radio shack, Binns received *Baltic's* short message about rocket firing. He notified Sealby, who immediately gave him a message to send. "CAPTAIN *BALTIC*: THERE IS A BOMB BEARING NORTHEAST FROM ME. KEEP FIRING."

There weren't enough boats for everyone, and the panic would create a terrible situation.

For a few moments there was nothing more. On *Republic's* bridge Sealby and his Chief Officer strained to listen. It was pitch black now, and except for the few emergency lights on *Republic* and the hazy glare from *Florida* a few hundred feet away, there was nothing else visible. The minutes dragged by, and the elation Sealby had felt at the first sound slowly ebbed.

Then . . . boooooommm! . . . somewhere in the fog, still muffled, but closer, Sealby was sure of that. "Keep sounding that bell!" he ordered, and the sharp clanging was stepped up.

"Send this!" he scribbled out a message and had it run to Jack Binns. In a couple of moments Binns was tapping out: "YOU ARE GETTING LOUDER. KEEP STEERING EAST-SOUTHEAST. LISTEN FOR OUR SHIP'S BELL."

On *Florida* Captain Ruspini was growing quite concerned. He had had a large piece of white canvas placed over the crushed-in bow and lashed down to help keep out the seawater, but his ship was dangerously overcrowded, and who knew how long the collision bulkhead might hold? He should be making for port. Suppose *Florida* began taking on water, too? Suppose he had to order *abandon ship*? There weren't enough boats for everyone, and the panic would create a terrible situation. Rescue was nearby, he knew that, and his ship just didn't belong here anymore.

He motioned to his Chief Officer. "We had better notify *Republic*." Within minutes a message was being relayed to Siasconset. "*FLORIDA* IN BAD SHAPE, LEAVING FOR NEW YORK, IN NEED OF ASSISTANCE. *BALTIC* IS NEARING *REPUBLIC* WHICH, STILL AFLOAT, IS DIRECTING *BALTIC'S* STEERING."

On *Republic* Sealby concentrated on locating *Baltic*, urging his signal man to ring the ship's bell and listening for the answering rocket explosion. The blackness seemed impenetrable. Then Boooooomm! Not far away. "There!" someone shouted, pointing to a brief, hazy glow high above them.

"Send this." Sealby scribbled another message for Jack Binns to relay to *Baltic*. "YOU ARE VERY CLOSE NOW. RIGHT A-BEAM. COME CAREFULLY. YOU ARE ON OUR PORT SIDE. HAVE JUST SEEN YOUR ROCKET. YOU ARE VERY CLOSE TO US."

On *Baltic* Captain Ranson nodded with satisfaction at the latest message from *Republic*. Close — they were so close, but the fog was like a curtain all around. He and his men were very, very tired; they had been searching for almost twelve hours — and they had been only sixty-four miles away when they had started! Twelve hours to cover sixty-four miles — they must have actually sailed three times that! "Careful now" Ranson told himself, barely moving his ship forward. "Look alive!" he instructed his lookouts.

Another few seconds, and then — "Off the starboard beam, Captain, a light!"

Everyone rushed to look. It was a light all right, a single, solitary green light, looming out of the dark hulk that was *Republic*. The two ships were no more than a hundred feet apart.

"All engines stop," Ranson ordered. Peering through the haze, he saw a much larger glow beyond *Republic*. That must be *Florida*.

It was. Though *Florida* had announced her intention to leave for New York, Captain Ruspini had decided to wait a little while longer to see if *Baltic* did turn up.

On *Republic*, Sealby and his small crew were overjoyed when *Baltic* broke through the fog. *Republic* seemed to be dipping ever lower into the water, and a decision had to be made about her. And something had to be done about the overcrowded conditions on *Florida*, too. Finally, the captains decided that because *Florida* seemed to be taking on water in her number-one hold, all the passengers would be safer if transferred to *Baltic*. All 1,650 passengers from both ships, that is!

Republic's and *Baltic's* lifeboats were best equipped for the job, and an hour before midnight in the pitch black North Atlantic with only *Florida's* and *Baltic's* searchlights to guide them, the first passengers from *Florida* sat huddled in *Republic's* lifeboats as strong armed crewmen rowed them across the water.

On *Florida's* bridge Captain Ruspini looked at his watch and realized that eighteen hours had gone by since the collision, the longest hours in his life. He felt a fresh breeze and was startled. The fog had lain on them so long, keeping the water still and calm, he'd forgotten that things do change. He marked the direction of the breeze — from the east — and felt a growing concern. The seas would grow rougher, making passenger transfer more difficult. It was bad enough having all these people scared, shocked, cold, miserable. But put them in small lifeboats, pitching through building seas at night, in the fog, there could be disaster.

Captain William I. Sealby of the Republic *(left) and Captain J.B. Ranson of the* Baltic *(right), who brought* Republic's *passengers safely to New York.*

His Chief Officer appeared, concerned. "Some more trouble with the passengers." He reported that *Republic's* first-class passengers had demanded to go into the lifeboats first, before any of *Florida's* passengers, claiming this as their privilege. This angered some of *Florida's* passengers, who felt that on their ship everyone was equal. The *Republic* people tried to push through anyway, and there had been shoving and nasty words. A knife or two had been drawn. "It's been worked out, I think," the Chief Officer added.

Investigation showed that *Republic's* passengers had stood firmly by the gangway, allowing none but their own to pass. To remove them would have required force and probably resulted in injuries. It was more important to get on with the transfer.

Out on the water lifeboats bobbed in and out of the searchlights' glare, oars splashing through the wintry ocean, on their way to *Baltic* with *Republic's* first-class passengers. Ruspini shrugged. "It's done."

By 6:40 A.M. Sunday, twenty-five hours after the collision, *Baltic* could wire New York: "ALL PASSENGERS OF *REPUBLIC* TRANSFERRED TO *BAL-*

TIC. NOW COMPLETING TRANSFER OF PASSENGERS FROM FLORIDA WHICH IS IN A DANGEROUS CONDITION." Three and a half hours later, all the passengers were aboard *Baltic*, the fog had lifted, and *Florida* and *Baltic* were on their way to safe harbor.

*   *   *   *   *

As the fog lifted, suddenly other ships appeared all around. *Republic's* condition was deteriorating rapidly: she was sinking about one foot per hour. Sealby and a skeleton crew remained aboard, including Jack Binns. It was decided to try and tow her close to shore so she could be beached and at least something be salvaged. The Revenue Cutter *Gresham*, less than half the size of *Republic*, fixed a heavy line to her bow and the S.S. *Furnessia* put a heavy line on her stern and acted as rudder. Groaning and straining in the early afternoon the cumbersome procession started out, *Republic* with her stern now deep in the water. They made about a mile an hour through the afternoon, while *Republic* continued to slip deeper and deeper into the sea. Only a single, dim light from *Republic's* bridge in the early January darkness showed she was still afloat.

At 6:40 P.M., the stern line from *Furnessia* parted without warning, and two hours later, a sharp order from *Gresham's* deck officer sent a sailor to cut the *Republic's* bow line. *Republic* slid beneath the surface, coming to rest in 450 feet of water.

The last person to leave her was Captain Sealby, who had sent Jack Binns and other crew members off *Republic* several hours before. As his ship shuddered in her death throes, Sealby went to the flying bridge and finally scaled the mast, watching the waters creep over the majestic liner up toward him. With just a few feet of mast left, Sealby finally gave up his ship and jumped into the icy North Atlantic, grabbing onto a floating hatch cover from which he was rescued a few moments later.

In New York, Sealby and Jack Binns would receive a hero's welcome. Vaudeville wanted them to come on stage, to recount the long, dramatic story. But they refused. Sealby sought no glory for doing what he considered to be his duty, and Jack Binns found satisfaction enough that now wireless communication had surely proven itself.

Who was at fault? No one could ever say with certainty. Within days of the collision, both shipping lines put out statements, each claiming that their people had been observing proper procedures. Indeed, from the way the collision happened, it was impossible to point a sure finger. Some are willing to leave it at this: the Nantucket fog was so heavy and widespread that a major ship disaster was inevitable. *Republic* and *Florida* just happened to be in the wrong place at the wrong time.

Singular Rescue of the USS S-5

Because of the Alanthus, *thirty-eight men who would otherwise have died were alive....*

By Irwin Ross

One bright August day in 1920, the Navy's finest submarine, the big S-5, departed from Boston harbor on a routine training cruise to Baltimore. As she sailed along proudly, flags flying, she passed the wooden Liberty ship *Alanthus*, whose captain, Edward Johnson, leaned dejectedly at the rail. Once he had sailed the *Alanthus* to Norfolk and back, he contemplated gloomily, he would no longer be a captain. His ship would join the fleet of war-built vessels now retired from active service. Moreover, his crew was missing two deck-hands and a radioman. The *Alanthus* left on her last voyage shortly after the S-5 sailed by.

The S-5 romped down the coast. As she prepared for a routine test dive, alarms honked, and seamen hurried to their stations. As soon as the dive began, Commander Charles Cooke, her captain, knew something was wrong. The dive was abnormally steep. He heard frantic cries and the sound of rushing water and ran for the control room. The air valve had been left open! A torrent of water was spouting from a ventilation duct.

"Torpedo room's flooding!" shouted a sailor. Water roared into the forward part of the boat. Men climbed grease-covered torpedoes to try to reach the valve on the ceiling, but fell back under the rush of water. At last they retreated and closed off the torpedo room.

Cooke tried to bring the boat to the surface. But the water in the bow dragged her down at an ever-increasing angle. With a shock the S-5 hit bottom, bounced, and rammed into the sea floor. The depth gauges read 165 feet. The flooding had been stopped, but now the question was — how deep were they buried?

Grimly, Cooke gave orders: jettison all ballast; force air into the torpedo room. An hour later, the S-5 was still stuck fast. There wasn't enough air for many more maneuvers. This time they'd blow all tanks and put the motors full back.

The boat shivered as the props whirled. They overloaded the circuits; blue sparks leaped from the control panel. The S-5 lurched and her stern arced upward, the bow still stuck. A cascade of tools, equipment, and men fell downward from compartment to compartment.

When the upward movement stopped, men hung from door handles or valve wheels. Commander Cooke scrambled to his feet. Amazingly, no one seemed to be seriously injured. But suddenly he received a report that battery acid was spilling and mixing with sea water, forming poisonous chlorine gas.

"Seal off the battery room!" ordered Cooke. "And put on gas masks!" The men in the battery room couldn't reach the hatch overhead. Hastily, Cooke ordered curtains ripped down and used them to hoist the men up through the hatch. The crew retreated up and through the boat, their lungs laboring as the gas followed. They huddled in two small compartments. Cooke knew they were in 165 feet of water, and that the S-5 was 231 feet long. If they were perpendicular, their stern would be above the sea. But they were tipped. He climbed upward, pounding on the walls as he went.

Twenty feet from the stern, there was still the sound of metal under water. Only one place left, the small tiller room. He dreaded tapping on the hull there. But when he did, it sounded as if it were above water.

Cooke called for a drill and turned it slowly against the steel. There was a wooden plug on hand in case water, not air, came through the hole. He braced himself as the bit suddenly broke through. He gave a shout, "We're clear! We're out of the water!"

Since it was night, nobody could see them. But they'd try cutting a bigger hole. This would let water in if the boat shifted position — a gamble they'd have to take. They had to have air.

An electric drill was passed up. They plugged it into the still-functioning electrical system. The sailor who held it crumpled to the floor; current was shorting through the wet casing. Another man took it and held it against the steel, though his muscles knotted as the electricity shot through him. The men took turns, each holding the drill as long as pain would permit.

When the batteries went dead, they used hand drills. By dawn they had cut a hole roughly six inches by five inches through the hull. Now began the agonizing wait for rescue. Cooke waved a dirty undershirt out the hole. The sun began to make a furnace of the S-5. The temperature hit a blistering 135°. Cooke frantically waved the undershirt but he knew the terrifying truth: they were miles off the shipping lanes. It would be a miracle if a ship came close enough to see them. He ordered emergency rations broken out.

Aboard the *Alanthus*, plowing through the seas some fifty-five miles off the Delaware coast, the mate suddenly noticed something bobbing on the water.

"Looks like a buoy, sir," he said.

"Wouldn't be a buoy this far out," Captain Johnson said.

As he peered through the glasses, his puzzlement grew. The rules of the sea said that obstacles to navigation should be investigated and reported. He ordered the *Alanthus* to put about and head for the object five miles away.

As they drew closer, the captain could see a flag of some kind on the thing. Suddenly, he shouted, "It's a submarine!" He kept studying the mysterious craft, as he maneuvered close to it. The rag was still waving — and not because of the wind.

They lowered a skiff. Johnson and four crewmen rowed to the submarine. The rolling seas slapped the small boat against its steel sides. The skiff might be crushed between the *Alanthus* and the sub, but Johnson knew he had to get a line around that sub. If there were men aboard her, he couldn't risk her sinking.

When the cables from the *Alanthus* were fastened, the oily rag still waved. He went up to the hole and peered inside.

A white face looked out at him!

"Who — what sub is this?" Johnson gasped.

"U.S. Submarine S-5. Commander Cooke speaking."

"Are your men alive?" Johnson called.

Commander Cooke's voice came back weakly. "All hands alive, so far . . . but we're dying . . . chlorine gas . . . need air . . . radio the Navy."

But Johnson knew the *Alanthus* was missing a radio operator. He could head for port, but their cable might be the only thing that would keep the sub in position. Towing was out; the S-5 might break up if they moved her. No, they'd stay right here and hope that a ship would see their distress signals.

They ran a hose, and pumps aboard the *Alanthus* sent a stream of life-giving air into the sub. Another hose delivered water. The hideous temperature in the sub dropped a little, Cooke reported.

The hoses had hardly been run when Johnson went to work enlarging the hole in the S-5. He had no electric drills, only a few hand tools to cut through heavy steel.

Hour after hour, the strange catch tugging on the cables, they worked from a weaving float. It seemed as if the pitiful tools made no progress. At this rate, it would take a week to make a hole big enough for escape.

The September sun was sinking when they saw a column of smoke approaching. Captain Johnson dropped his tools and rowed for the newcomer. A few minutes later, he was aboard the Panama liner *General Goethals*, explaining to her Captain Simson that the *Alanthus* had a submarine on the end of its cables.

Now an S.O.S. could be sent. The answer was not encouraging at all. It would be several hours before the first Naval rescue ship could get there! The ship's doctor of the *Goethals* shook his head. The men in the *S-5* might not last much longer.

Captain Johnson went into conference with William Grace, the chief engineer of the *Goethals*. Now, while Johnson stood by to keep the generators working, it was Grace's turn to fight those stubborn steel plates. Grace tried to keep up the spirits of the men inside the sub, but the responses became weaker. About midnight Grace called to the men inside and got no reply. He signaled for the men to stop the drills and called again. No answer. At 1:20 A.M., more than an hour since they had heard any response from the men of the *S-5*, Grace crowded his men onto the small treacherous platform to pry at the steel. "Heave!" he shouted.

Men leaned on the prybars. The metal groaned; there was a tearing sound. It grew louder. The plate came free! Foul air blasted from the sub, and then came a voice. Commander Cooke! The fresh air had revived him.

Swiftly, the rescuers carried the grimy, groaning men into slings that lifted them to the *Alanthus*. Captain Johnson kept count: thirty-five . . . thirty-six . . . thirty-seven. One left. At 2:45 A.M., Commander Cooke emerged. Every man was out alive!

As dawn broke, an armada of destroyers, tugs, even a battleship, was drawn up about the *Alanthus*. The little wooden ship was crowded with high brass. Lost among the gold braid, Johnson suggested that since he already had the line on the *S-5*, he might be allowed to tow her in. No, they'd give that job to the battleship. The *S-5* was secured to the *Ohio*. But the *Ohio* had towed the *S-5* only a short distance when the empty submarine sank irretrievably to the bottom.

Captain Johnson stood by while men were transferred to waiting Navy ships. One by one, they shook hands with him until only Commander Cooke remained. There was no need for words between the two men.

From every ship in the Great Navy flotilla came a whistle of salute as the *Alanthus* steamed proudly past. Her voyage toward oblivion no longer seemed so forlorn to Captain Johnson. Because of the *Alanthus*, thirty-eight men who would have died were alive.

On October 5, 1920, Captain Johnson was awarded a gold watch by the Secretary of the Navy "in token of appreciation of valuable services rendered in the rescue of the crew of the USS *S-5*."

The Night the Sea Took the
Ocean Ranger

For Newfoundlanders like Bruce Porter, glimpsing the Ocean Ranger *for the first time through the darkness of a July night was like coming upon an object beyond imagination. Standing in the ocean on great stilt-like legs, ablaze with tiers of lights that glowed through swirling sea mists, the huge drilling rig towered over the little supply ship that had steamed out from St. John's like a monolithic giant from another planet.*

BY EVAN MCLEOD WYLIE

In 1979 waves of excitement ran through the Canadian Maritime Provinces when it became known that a huge oil field, one of the richest found anywhere in the world in the past decade, had been discovered beneath the ocean bed off the famed Grand Banks. The oil field, known as the Hibernia Discovery, was located 166 nautical miles east of St. John's. It was estimated to contain about 1.8 billion barrels of recoverable oil and about 1.5 trillion cubic feet of gas. There would be formidable engineering challenges in the development of this oil field because of drifting icebergs and the fact that the Grand Banks lie in the path of some of the worst winter weather in the North Atlantic, but the oil industry felt confident that it could overcome them.

To the new discovery was sent the mightiest rig of all. Designed in New Orleans and built in Japan at a cost of $125 million, the *Ocean Ranger* was the world's largest semisubmersible offshore oil rig. Larger than two football fields, it was 408 feet long and 300 feet wide. From its submerged pontoon hulls to the tip of the drilling derrick, it was thirty stories high. The huge upper structure, seventy feet above the water, was a honeycomb of power plants, machine shops, offices, radio communication center, navigation bridge, and storage spaces. Beneath a heliport were three decks of living quarters. When operating at sea, the rig, which seemed gigantic even to men from other offshore drilling platforms, carried a crew of up to a hundred, including a drilling team, roustabouts, engineers, electricians, electronic specialists, geologists, and office workers.

The *Ranger* had begun its career prospecting for oil in the Gulf of Alaska. By 1979, it had been towed around Cape Horn and was operating out of Davisville, Rhode Island, the new base for offshore rigs drilling in the North Atlantic on Georges Bank and in the Baltimore Canyon. In November, 1980, it arrived off the coast of Newfoundland and, along with two smaller rigs, was assigned to conduct exploratory drilling on the Hibernia oil field.

Newfoundlanders, with a floundering economy beset by inflation and depressed mining, timbering, and fishing industries and the lowest per capita income in Canada, welcomed the offshore oil industry. Men from St. John's and outlying bay villages sought work on the oil rigs or in the scores of new companies on shore that sprang up to support them.

Newcomers quickly found themselves swept up in the drama of life aboard the *Ranger*. Floodlights transformed night into day. Supply ships steamed out from St. John's to cluster about the great legs in all kinds of weather. When spare parts were needed in a hurry, helicopters groped their way to the rig through pea-soup fog, descending suddenly out of the thick mists like huge spiders from their webs. Around the clock the drill platform reverberated with the clash of drill pipes and shouts of the drill crew. From the open upper deck below rose the muffled roar of diesels, the whine of winches, and the resounding thuds of cargo slings and pallets.

But inside the the double doors that led to the living quarters and offices, all was air-conditioned, soundproofed, and weather-proofed. Gleaming passageways led to staterooms with cheerful decor, offices, a library, "rec" room, and mess hall.

"Everything," one worker recalled, "was trim and immaculate. There was a spit-and-polish atmosphere that was almost military. We took pride in this and felt a part of it because *Ranger* was queen of them all."

Working shifts were twelve hours long, and the men spent a "hitch" of twenty-one days at sea alternated with twenty-one days ashore, but the pay was high and living conditions excellent. No alcoholic beverages were permitted aboard the rig, but the mess hall, graced with background stereo music, stayed open twenty-four hours a day to provide breakfast, luncheon, and two hearty main meals that featured shrimp cocktail, soup, roast beef, broiled steak, and Southern-style barbecued ribs and chicken. For dessert, there was ice cream and freshly baked pies and cakes. An all-night snack bar offered hamburgers, sandwiches, coffee, and sodas. Television was beyond reach, but feature films were shown every night in the rec room.

The *Ranger's* drilling crew was composed mainly of seasoned oil-field workers from the Deep South. As the rig moved into the North Atlantic, they were joined by New Englanders and Canadians, who teased the Southerners about their tendency to fight off chilly ocean breezes by wearing snowmobile suits in the summer months.

During the summer, the rig was so frequently enveloped in fog as to give its crew the sensation of being suspended in space. When the mists blew away, there were pleasant star-filled nights and pastel sunrises. Still, there was little to suggest a vessel at sea. The 15,000-ton rig was so huge that it took a large sea to lift its massive bulk, and even then the heave of the deck was almost imperceptible.

"Aboard the *Ranger*," said Bruce Porter, "you had a sense of strength and omnipotence. From the main deck the sea far below seemed calm, although actually the supply ships down there might be bobbing about like water birds on the waves."

These supply ships, 214 feet long, were not insubstantial. Yet it is no wonder that the crews of these craft, struggling to handle cargoes on the pitching, rolling decks as their captains maneuvered against the strong currents that swirled around the legs, held a different view of the *Ranger*, calling it the Monster or the Ocean Danger.

The men who built and operated the *Ranger* firmly believed that no serious mishap could occur. Like the *Titanic*, which went to the bottom barely a hundred miles away from the rig's position, the *Ranger* was considered unsinkable. Designed to ride out storms with winds of 115 miles per hour and 110-foot waves, it could even continue drilling safely in fifty-knot winds and thirty-foot seas.

To Pat Doyle, who had sailed the world's oceans on ships large and small, the *Ranger* seemed as safe as a steel island. "I was out there for fourteen months," he said, "and we never gave the weather much thought. Even when seas tossed spray as high as the main deck, the prospect of a catastrophe never occurred to us. I never got into a lifeboat."

Bruce Porter had been hired as a roustabout, to be trained later as a ballast-control-room operator. The ballast-control room was located down in the after-starboard leg of the rig below the lower deck. To reach it, he went through a hatchway, descended a circular staircase within the hollow column, and emerged into a blue and gray circular chamber furnished with a desk, telephones, and a video display unit with roll, pitch, heave, wind, and wave information. In front of the desk was a control panel studded with switches and gauges to control the pumps and valves on the ballast tanks which were located in the submerged pontoon hulls eighty feet below the surface of the sea. Color-coded lights flashed and glowed to indicate whether water was flowing in or out, and gauges noted when the tanks were empty or full. At first, he merely visited the control room in his spare time, becoming acquainted with the operators on duty, observing, and learning by asking questions. In September, Porter began spending two or three hours out of his work shift in the control room. His instructor was Don Rathbun, a lean, handsome, blue-eyed Rhode Islander who had been on offshore rigs for five years. He was enthusiastic about the work, pleased with his promotion to control-room operator, and conscientious about the job. He and Porter became good friends.

At times, as seas built up, breaking waves surged thunderously between the columns and girders, reaching up toward the lower deck.

As he spent more time down in the control room Porter became aware that it offered a unique opportunity to observe the rig and the ocean. In the circular chamber there were four glass portlights, eighteen inches in diameter, sealed and composed of thick, tempered glass, providing an extraordinary view of the underside of the rig and the sea thirty-two feet below.

Porter discovered that he could actually enjoy the ocean storms. When the wind shrieked across the rig with such force that men were not allowed on the main deck unescorted, he found that if he descended to the ballast-control room he could be snug and warm while gazing through the portlights at the raging seas below.

At times, as seas built up, breaking waves surged thunderously between the columns and girders, reaching up toward the lower deck. The first time a wall of green water rose as high as the control room and slammed against the portlights, Porter dodged back in alarm, but was relieved when nothing came of it.

An engineer explained to him that the rig had been designed to permit the seas to slip between its legs. By not presenting a solid front, it dissipated their strength. But remembering the action of the waves as he saw them from his post in the control room, Porter wondered. "I can recall the way the sea sometimes seemed to seize the *Ranger* in its grip and make it shudder and tremble. The behavior of the rig as we could see it from the portlights conflicted with the observations of the engineers and their graphs and calculations. But we accepted it and did not feel threatened. When seawater occasionally leaked in around the rims of the portlights, we blotted it up with paper towels and went about our business."

The fog-white days of summer faded into the blustery storms of autumn. Curtains of snow enveloped the rig, and frigid winds blasted down from Labrador and the Arctic, but drilling went on as usual, biting steadily deeper into the ocean floor. On Christmas Eve, operations were temporarily halted by a howling northwest gale that sheathed the rig in ice and flung spray as high as the main deck. But, as dining steward Pat Doyle said proudly, "*Ranger* didn't budge an inch," and inside the living quarters men played ping-pong in their shirt-sleeves.

Still, at times it seemed that these oil men, concentrating on their drilling operations, were oblivious or indifferent to the sea around them. Kent Thompson, commander of the rig, was a veteran oil driller known as the Tool Pusher. There was also a marine captain aboard, but unless the rig was actually moving, the captain was subordinate to the Tool Pusher.

Time for matters other than drilling was given grudgingly. Captain Karl Nehring, a ship's master with thirty-five years' experience who served aboard the *Ranger* until January, 1982, later testified that "Abandon Ship" drills were held once a week by a safety coordinator, but Nehring was not satisfied with them because noise levels on the upper decks were so high that it was impossible to issue proper instructions. He began his own lifeboat training course, but when it came time to instruct the men from the drilling platform, the Tool Pusher told him the men could not be spared for the thirty-minute course.

At that point, Nehring stated, the lifeboat training program fell apart, and he lost heart. There were supposed to be seven certified lifeboatmen available on the rig at all times, but whenever Nehring checked, there never seemed to be more than three or four including himself.

Nehring became increasingly frustrated, and on December 31, 1981, after diesel oil from a supply ship leaked into the ocean and the rig manager refused him permission to radio a report on the oil spill to the Coast Guard, he resigned.

"A Tool Pusher should not be in charge on a seagoing rig," Nehring said later. "You can't put a Kentucky hillbilly in charge of a ship."

Despite the crucial role that the ballast-control room played in keeping the rig afloat, its operators were not required to pass qualification tests nor did they receive any formal training. The captains, nominally in charge of the control room, spent little time there, and no attempt was made to provide masters with indoctrination of systematic instruction.

In February Bruce Porter, whose on-the-job training had won him a promotion to junior control-room operator, was directed by a new captain to go down to the pump room in the submerged pontoon.

As he was descending by elevator, he noticed that the *Ranger* had begun to tilt at an alarming angle. Hastening back up to the control room, he found that loudspeakers had already ordered the crew to lifeboat stations. The shaken and infuriated Tool Pusher, wearing a lifejacket, had routed Don Rathbun out of bed to correct the mistake. The new captain had flooded the wrong ballast tanks!

On February 11, Bruce Porter completed his first hitch of the new year and came ashore by helicopter. Pat Doyle had left earlier, at the urging of his wife, to take a shore job after fourteen months at sea on the *Ranger*. Before they left, both bade farewell to fellow crewmen who had become their good friends. Among them were Bill Dugas and George Gandy from Louisiana, who were retiring to spend more time with their families and grandchildren. Don Rathbun also was expecting to leave shortly for a new job on a new giant rig, the *Ocean Odyssey*.

As a seagoing drilling rig operating under the U.S. flag, the *Ranger* was subject to inspection by the Coast Guard every two years. Its certificate had expired December 26, 1981, but ODECO (Ocean Drilling and Exploration Company), which operated the rig, did not get around to notifying the Coast Guard of the inspection due until late January. The Coast Guard, because of Washington budgetary restrictions, had no procedure for keeping close tabs on the rigs.

At its last inspection, the Coast Guard had given ODECO two years to replace unapproved lifeboats and provide davit-launched life rafts, but in January the rig's operators were still delaying the inspection date while they added two lifeboats. On Friday, February 12, they had installed the third lifeboat, but the fourth boat was still lashed to the deck, unequipped and unavailable for use. Two Coast Guard inspectors were due to arrive on the rig Monday, but they would never see the *Ranger*.

Early Saturday, as the *Ranger* and two smaller rigs nearby the Grand Banks rode easily in a slight sea swell, a severe winter storm was forming off the coast of South Carolina. If it followed the usual winter storm track, it would strike New England and Newfoundland by Sunday.

By noon on Saturday, the U.S. National Weather Service was warning of a dangerous storm with winds of fifty to eighty knots and waves as high as twenty-five to thirty-five feet. Gale warnings began flying from Cape Hatteras to the Canadian Maritimes. The warnings created little concern aboard the *Ranger*. It had already weathered a winter of heavy storms, and no special precautions were taken either on the rig or by its shore managers in St. John's.

By 1 P.M. on Sunday, the weather service was warning: *This dangerous storm will move east and slow down. This is one of the most intense storms seen so far this season and should be avoided by all ships if possible.*

Snow now swirled around the offshore rigs and the wind was rising. At 1:30 P.M., the *Ranger* reported to its shore office that it was still drilling at eighteen feet per hour. Nineteen miles to the north, the rig *Zapata Ugland* had decided to cease operations. During the afternoon, as winds rose to sixty-two knots and seas mounted to twenty-seven feet, they sheared off their drill pipe, "hung off the hole," and deballasted the rig to float five feet higher above the waves. At 4:30 P.M., the *Ranger* was still drilling, although it was making preparations to "hang off."

Just before 7 P.M., *Ranger's* drilling foreman reported to St. John's that they had sheared off the drill pipe with underwater hydraulic rams and sealed the well. With winds at hurricane force, they were getting twenty-foot "heaves" off the main deck with spray reaching up into the spider deck to the drill floor. He added that they had no problems.

But actually an extraordinary chain of events was unfolding on the *Ranger* which would lead inexorably to tragedy.

Between 4:30 P.M. and 7 P.M., men on *Sedco 706*, a smaller rig located nine miles east of *Ranger*, overheard portable walkie-talkie radio conversations between *Ranger's* Tool Pusher and the men in its ballast-control room. "There's a wet panel in the control room," they heard an operator report. "We're working on it and getting shocks off it."

In a second conversation, the control room was reporting to the Tool Pusher, "Everything fine. Mopping up glass and water."

At 7:45 P.M., *Sedco 706*, which had just been struck by a monstrous wave that damaged its upper deck, overheard the voice of Nick Dyke, *Ranger's* junior control-room operator on his portable radio. "We have water and glass on the floor. All valves are opening on the port side . . . water on the floor . . . gas detection panel knocked out . . . public address system out . . . getting electrical shocks. . . ."

But at 8:44 P.M., the *Ranger* advised St. John's that "a wave has taken a window out of the control room. Mopping up; no problems."

At 9 P.M., as one of the supply ships fighting to stay on station reported seas at fifty to sixty feet and winds up to a hundred knots, *Sedco 706* overheard *Ranger* control-room operator Don Rathbun announce over his radio: "We need an electrician down here. We have shocks from the control panel. Valves opening on their own."

At 10 P.M., *Ranger* assured the St. John's supervisor that all equipment was functioning normally; the radio-telephone conversation concluded with agreement by both parties that the rigs were riding out the storm with no problems, and they would talk again in the morning.

Nothing more was heard from *Ranger* until nearly an hour after midnight, when the radio silence was broken abruptly.

Monday, February 15, 1982

12:52 A.M. *Ranger* to *Sedco 706*: MAYDAY! MAYDAY! We have a severe list and require immediate assistance.

1:00 A.M. *Ranger* to St. John's: Call the Coast Guard!

1:05 A.M. *Ranger* to *Seaforth Highlander*: Can you come in a little closer, please? We have a problem here on the rig; we have a list. All countermeasures negative. Come as close as you can.

Seaforth Highlander to *Ranger*: I'm on my way.

Ranger to *Sedco 706*: Send out a MAYDAY on us immediately. If you call us back and don't get an answer, we have already taken to lifeboats.

1:09 A.M. *Ranger* to Coast Guard Air-Sea Rescue Center in New

York: We are experiencing a severe list in middle of severe storm. Request assistance as soon as possible.

Ranger to St. John's: We have a MAYDAY. We must evacuate. Need helicopters.

1:15 A.M. *Ranger* to other rigs: Send boats! MAYDAY! MAYDAY!

1:30 A.M. *Ranger* to *Sedco 706*: Going to lifeboat stations.

Jorgensen saw a large hole in the lifeboat's bow and the men inside bailing frantically.

The supply ships, crews already bruised and exhausted from the pounding they had taken trying to remain near the rigs during the weekend storm, headed out toward the stricken rig. *Nordertor* was twenty miles to the north. *Boltentor* was coming from eight miles to the east, and *Seaforth Highlander* was seven miles to the south.

Through darkness and driving snow, *Seaforth Highlander* battled its way toward the *Ranger*. Captain Ronald Duncan, *Highlander*'s skipper said later, "The run-in was a nightmare. The seas were enormous — fifty to sixty feet on our beam. I was concerned that we might roll over."

1:31 A.M. The Canadian Air Force Rescue Unit at Gander had been summoned, but blizzard conditions at Gander and St. John's made it impossible for helicopters to get off the ground.

1:50 A.M. *Seaforth Highlander* was in sight of the *Ranger*. Numerous small white lights were observed in the water. A red distress flare arced skyward. Then another. Captain Duncan switched on his floodlights and ordered all hands on deck. Led by First Mate Rolf Jorgensen, they clung to stanchions to avoid being swept overboard by the raging seas. A covered lifeboat was sighted on the crest of a mountainous wave. Seas were bursting over the afterdeck of the *Highlander* as Duncan maneuvered close in. The lifeboat was under power, and there was a man in the stern steering turret. Jorgensen saw a large hole in the lifeboat's bow and the men inside bailing frantically.

The lifeboat crossed *Highlander*'s stern and came up along the port side only a few feet away. The man in the stern turret was shouting, but his words were lost in the fury of the storm.

Seaman Bert Woolridge tossed a line to the lifeboat, and the man in the turret made it fast. Other deckhands were trying to get a bowline fast, but their numbed fingers fumbled the line. The lifeboat was very close now, bumping against *Highlander*. Then a sea carried it six feet away.

Men with hard hats emerged from the lifeboat wearing work vests or lifejackets. Apparently fearful of being crushed between *Highlander*'s steel hull and the lifeboat, they balanced on its port side, standing on the gunwales and clinging to the handrails.

As the men on *Highlander* watched in horror, the lifeboat began to roll slowly over, capsizing to port. Despite desperate efforts to hang on, the men on the gunwales tumbled one by one into the icy seas. The lifeboat rolled completely over to float bottom-up. The stern line attached to *Highlander* snapped.

Only twelve feet away, men were screaming in the water. On his hands and knees, Mate Jorgensen reached out to one, but the man slipped from his grasp. A huge wave broke across the afterdeck of *Highlander*, slamming Jorgensen and Dennis Chaytor into the bulkheads. Dazed and bruised they crawled back to try to help the men in the water. Eight or nine clung to the capsized lifeboat, wearing lifejackets with lights. For a minute or two, the lifeboat was alongside. Then as it drifted along the port side, the men still clinging to it lost their grip. The life raft, thrown down on Duncan's orders, inflated properly beside the men in the water, but they were too weak or too frozen to grasp either the raft or the lines thrown to them.

A tremendous sea carried *Highlander* away from the lifeboat, one man still spread-eagled across its overturned hill. Duncan steamed upwind, then drifted down to the lifeboat, but by that time the men in the water were floating with their heads under and arms outstretched. In the wild seas *Highlander* could not maneuver to pick them up, or the many other bodies now floating lifeless in the water.

2:30 A.M. Coming in from the east, *Boltentor* saw *Ranger* listing heavily, showing only two small lights. Approaching to within five hundred feet, Boltentor steamed around the rig, playing its searchlight over the decks. The sea had the great steel structure in its grip. Waves were breaking over the main deck and flooding into the anchor chain lockers in the hollow legs. There was no sign of life and no radio contact. In a few minutes, *Boltentor* was summoned by *Highlander* to assist in the attempt to rescue survivors. *Boltentor's* crew sighted thirty to forty lighted lifejackets in the water, but searchlights revealed only dead bodies suspended in straps, and in the violence of the storm the ship was unable to get close enough to pick them up.

3 A.M. *Nordertor*, approaching from the north, had the *Ranger* on its radar. Suddenly, when he was about six miles away, *Nordertor's* captain saw the pale blip on the green radar screen vanish. In a moment it was replaced by two smaller blips in the same area, images of the pontoon hulls of the rig. The *Ocean Ranger* had capsized, toppling into the sea and turning completely upside down. The time was 3:15 A.M. on Monday.

4:30 A.M. Two helicopters from St. John's reached the scene. They sighted numerous lights in the water, but they were passenger helicopters and not equipped for sea rescues.

7 A.M. *Nordertor* encountered an overturned lifeboat with a life-ring from *Seaforth Highlander* still attached to it. As they attempted to take the boat aboard, seven or eight bodies spilled from a large hole in the bow, and the captain saw as many as twenty more still trapped inside. In the attempt to recover the boat, the line caught in *Nordertor's* propeller and snapped. The lifeboat drifted away, never to be seen again.

From dawn Monday until dusk on March 1, the intensive air-sea search continued. Of the twenty-two bodies eventually recovered, death was attributed to hypothermia due to loss of body heat in the icy water. The remainder of the crew of eighty-four aboard the *Ranger* that weekend were presumed dead. The sunken rig lay completely upside down, about five hundred feet from the drilling site. Later, divers found the derrick and drill pipes scattered over the sea bottom, but the rig's structure appeared undamaged, except for two broken portlights in the control room.

Investigators concluded that waves exploding through those control room portlights had inundated the console containing the electrical switches for the pumps of the ballast tanks in the submerged pontoon hulls. As short circuits knocked out the switches or caused them to open the tank valves, water flooded into the forward ballast tanks, causing the fatal list of *Ranger*.

At the time of this writing (November, 1983), four separate investigations by U.S. and Canadian government agencies were ongoing. Speaking at one of the U.S. investigation hearings, Bruce Porter commented on the inadequacy of the *Ranger's* lifeboats: "The boys didn't have a chance. If they could have gotten away from the rig, they still didn't have a chance of being fished out of the sea, which is tragically ironic. We have put millions of dollars into this marvel of technology that can drill miles into the ocean floor, but we haven't yet devised a contraption that would take a few men and transfer them a few hundred yards to a boat that would save their lives if that rig were in trouble."

In this country, the loss of the *Ranger* touched families in a score of states from New England to Texas. Pat Doyle, who escaped death aboard the rig by a matter of weeks, said that for Newfoundlanders, "It was like a death in the family. There were men aboard that night who came not only from St. John's but from many of the tiny bay villages along the rocky coasts. In the week that followed, while the ships and planes still searched the seas, hoping to find even a single survivor, many family members were at their mailboxes collecting the Valentine greetings and birthday cards that had been mailed from *Ranger* just before it sank — the last messages ever received from fathers and husbands."

She Sailed Aboard
the *Titanic*

A 1981 interview of a survivor of the ill-fated maiden voyage of that great ship unwisely billed as "unsinkable" by the White Star Line.

By Scott Eyman

At the age of fifty-six, Mr. Arthur W. Newell of Lexington, Massachusetts, had finally attained that station of life to which he had long aspired. Born in Chelsea to poor parents, he had risen by dint of his unquestioned integrity and single-minded attention to detail to be Chairman of the Board of the Fourth National Bank of Lexington. A somewhat distant, austere man with a Vandyke beard, a student of the Bible, a mediocre-to-poor keyboard player, he had a tendency to bring the office home with him. When that happened, his wife and three daughters would form a quartet, and play classical music to relax him and bring him out of his shell.

In 1909, Newell had taken his family on a European trip, one of those leisurely three-month junkets that people had time and money for in those days. Late in 1911, he decided to repeat the adventure, but his wife, who had a delicate disposition, and a daughter, who shared her mother's temperament, begged off, having found the arduous embarkings and disembarkings infinitely wearing.

So it was that in February of 1912, Arthur Newell and daughters Madeline and Marjorie set sail for Europe. They traveled to the Pyramids (Marjorie Newell celebrated her twenty-third birthday in Cairo), and made exhaustive investigations of the Holy Land: Port Said, Jaffa, Bethlehem, and Jericho. After taking a ship to Marseilles and traveling thence up to Paris, the Newells arrived in Cherbourg, where they were to start the long voyage home.

There the daughters found one more surprise awaiting them, for A.W. Newell had booked first-class passage for himself and his daughters on the maiden voyage of the world's largest ship. She was eleven stories high, a sixth of a mile long, weighed over forty-six tons, and had a top speed of twenty-four to twenty-five knots. Their trip home would encompass another week or so of sumptuous luxury and a triumphant arrival in New York harbor before the glorious vacation would be over.

The Newell girls would certainly have something to tell their grandchildren — what it was like to sail on the world's greatest ship; to travel in the company of some of the world's richest men, like John Jacob Astor, or Isidor Straus of Macy's Department Store, or Benjamin Guggenheim. In short, Marjorie and Madeline Newell would have had the inestimable pleasure of having sailed on the White Star Line's crowning achievement, a jewel of the post-Edwardian age, the R.M.S. *Titanic*.

"It was a most beautiful ship," said *Titanic* survivor Marjorie Newell Robb, interviewed in her low-ceilinged 200-year-old house at Westport Point, Massachusetts.

"The *Titanic* was a massive affair in every way; four enormous smokestacks, carpets that you could sink in up to your knees, fine furniture that you could barely move, and very fine paneling and carving. Everything on the ship was of the finest quality.

"We were, I think, five days out of Cherbourg; I do know that it was Sunday night. We had finished a lavish dinner in the corner of the magnificent dining room and had gone up to one of the foyers. We just sat there for a while, feeling very refreshed and invigorated after this lovely trip. My father smiled and said, 'Do you think you can last till morning?' You see, we had rather large appetites, and he was kidding us about whether we'd need more food. While we sat there in the foyer, I distinctly remember that John Jacob Astor and his wife walked by, looking very affable and distinguished.

"As the evening wore on, my sister and I decided to retire, so we went to our rooms. I don't remember how long we'd been down in our rooms, but we suddenly felt and heard a great vibration; its size was just staggering."

It was 11:40 P.M. on April 14, 1912, latitude 41°46'N, longitude 50°14'W. The grinding, tearing sound that had awakened Marjorie Newell and her sister was made by an iceberg shearing a 300-foot gash in the *Titanic's* bow, helped along by the ship's rapid twenty-two-and-a-half-knot speed and the fact that a half-dozen warnings about drifting ice had been more or less ignored.

Marjorie Newell sat up in bed, won-

Mrs. Marjorie Newell Robb in 1981 with photographs of her father and mother.

dering what had happened. Far below, in the ship's boiler room, what seemed like the entire starboard side of the ship collapsed, the sea flooding in over the "watertight" bulkheads.

On the upper decks, little seemed to be wrong at first. The *Titanic* lay dead in the water, three of her four funnels blowing out steam with a large, thundering noise. Yet somehow Marjorie Newell's father knew something was terribly wrong.

"Very soon after the noise, there was a knock at the door. It was Father. 'Put on warm clothing and come quickly to the upper deck,' he said. We obeyed. We always obeyed Father."

Several minutes later, the Newell sisters arrived on the top deck. There was no moon that night, but through the thickish fog that surrounded the ship it could be seen that the sky was full of stars, and Marjorie Newell remarked that the water was perfectly smooth.

On the starboard well deck, near the foremast, lay several tons of ice that had been shaved off the iceberg by the collision.

"When we arrived on the top, there were really very few passengers about; I believe we were among the first. And it was quiet; everybody was so stunned and frightened that hardly anybody was speaking at all."

Slowly the decks began to fill with people wearing incongruous clothes: bathrobes, evening clothes, turtleneck sweaters, fur coats.

About twenty-five minutes after the crash, the ship's crew began preparing the wooden lifeboats, sixteen of them, eight to a side, as well as the four collapsible canvas lifeboats. If filled to capacity, the twenty boats would hold 1,178 people. (On that cold April night, there were 2,207 people on board the *Titanic*.)

Distress rockets began to be fired and the ship's "CQD," the forerunner of SOS, was picked up on the Cunard ship *Carpathia* at 12:25 A.M. The *Carpathia*, fifty-eight miles away, radioed that she was "coming hard."

By one o'clock in the morning, the bow of the *Titanic* was slowly moving deeper into the water and the ship had developed a nasty list to port. Passengers and crew alike moved over to the starboard side in an attempt to restore her balance. Slowly the wounded ship regained its equilibrium. Still there was no panic; rather, the busy, scurrying silence had taken on an intense, dreamlike quality. Marjorie Newell was about to leave the *Titanic* under considerably less glorious circumstances than her father had anticipated.

"I believe we were in the second boat to be lowered. The ship was listing rather badly, and we were at a great height. The boat we were on had only one boatman. There were no supplies, and everything was ill-prepared. My father said, 'It seems more dangerous for you to get in that boat than to stay here,' but he hustled us into the boat anyway. Father stood there just as stately and calm as if he were in his living room.

"Most of the people in the boat were women, and they were very frightened ..."

"We were lowered. Most of the people in the boat were women, and they were very frightened; nobody was saying anything. I thought to myself, 'You have to help where you can,' so I took hold of an oar and rowed and rowed. I was young then, and strong.

"We got a distance away, and we could see the ship was listing very badly; people were in the water, gasping and yelling for help; one rocket after another was going up."

At 1:55 A.M., the last distress rocket was fired, and all the lifeboats but one had been launched. By this time, the ship was at something approaching a twenty-five-degree angle, with the forecastle head very close to the water, and the remaining passengers and crew moving towards the stern of the ship. In her lifeboat, Marjorie Newell looked on with mingled horror and fascination.

"In a way, it was beautiful; every light on the ship was on, and each porthole was illuminated. And then, across the water, came this enormous, awful roar."

As the bow plunged deeper, the stern tilted higher. The sound resembling some monstrous metal beast in battle that came across the water to the waiting lifeboats was nothing less than everything on board the ship breaking loose. As Walter Lord describes it in *A Night to Remember*, "Twenty-nine boilers ... 800 cases of shelled walnuts ... 15,000 bottles of ale and stout ... tumbling trellises ... the fifty-phone switchboard" — everything went tumbling end over end.

Now, finally, the *Titanic* rose up, almost majestically, perpendicular to the water, sending people on board catapulting, skidding, sliding, and screaming into the water. The lights of the ship flickered once, flashed again, and finally went out.

And there, after a minute or two at a ninety-degree angle, the ghastly rumbling roar mixing with terrified screams, the hull outlined now only by the red and green running lights and the clean white light of the stars reflecting on the placid water, the *Titanic* began to go down, moving at a slant, picking up speed as she went. When the water closed over the flagstaff on the *Titanic's* stern, it was 2:20 A.M.

"I can remember, to this day, the noise the ship made as it went under," said Marjorie Newell, trying hard to maintain her composure. "You could actually feel the noise, the vibrations of the screams of the people, and the sounds of the ship.

"I don't really know what happened on board after we left. People have asked me if the ship's orchestra was playing 'Nearer My God to Thee' as the legend has it, but I don't think so. I know I didn't hear it, but that may be because we were far away by that time, as far away as we could get." (The band was playing "Autumn.")

As the morning broke, the *Carpathia* arrived, and the survivors, some 705 rowing, floating, sobbing, shocked men, women, and children, could at last see just where they were.

The lifeboats were scattered over four square miles of water. Surrounding them and separating them were dozens of small icebergs as well as three or four large ones 150 to 200 feet high. Off to the north and west, five miles away, there began a field of ice that stretched on forever. The spot where the *Titanic* had gone down was marked only by flotsam: crates, deck chairs, rugs, a few lifebelts, and one dead body, all rapidly being dispersed by the gentle waves.

Slowly, the survivors began boarding the *Carpathia*.

"Seeing all the icebergs around shocked us; it proved how dangerous our passage had been, and how irresponsible the *Titanic's* Captain Smith, who went down with his ship, had been. Anyway, we wanted to get aboard the *Carpathia* as fast as we could, so we could be reunited with our father. It never occurred to us that Father hadn't gotten off; we didn't realize how few had been saved.

"We climbed onto the ship and there was a silence like a funeral. The *Carpathia* by that time was loaded with *Titanic* survivors. People were lying all over the deck, just trying to find someplace to rest.

"Father wasn't there. But I was so proud of him, that he'd abided by the rule of the sea: women and children first. Some men didn't. I know I sat beside a man on the *Carpathia* who had shoved aside women and children to save his own life. Why, even John Jacob Astor got his wife on a boat, but never got off the ship himself."

Shortly after nine o'clock the *Carpathia* had picked up everybody left alive and turned towards New York. Arthur Newell, who just twelve hours before had paused to muse on his daughters' healthy appetites, was listed among the missing.

"We reached New York on Thursday and were hurried over to the old Manhattan Hotel where my mother and other sister were waiting. My mother had seen lists of those who had been saved, but she was hoping that there had been an oversight. I can see her now in the hotel corridor, her arms outstretched, giving a howl of despair when she saw that only her two daughters had been saved and not her husband.

"Mother turned down an offer of a settlement from the White Star Line. No, she never asked us for details and didn't want to talk about it. She forbade us ever to speak of that night. She wore black or white for the rest of her life. When she died, at the age of 103, she was still in mourning."

Two weeks after the *Titanic* disaster, the body of Arthur Newell washed up on a Newfoundland beach. Identified by distinctive jewelry and a pocket diary, he was buried in Lexington's Mount Olive cemetery.

So now, Marjorie Newell Robb, like Melville's Ishmael, is left to tell of the mighty ship. Considered unsinkable, it sank on its maiden voyage, taking with it all the interlocking assumptions about modern man and the perfectability of his works, the smug, hubristic self-assurance of the Gilded Age. For along with A.W. Newell and 1,502 others, the *Titanic* took with it an entire insulated way of life.

"The irony of it all is so striking," says Arthur Newell's last surviving daughter. "The unsinkable ship, all the money that those men had that was of no use to them at all. And the irony even touched my father. One of the ways we identified his body when it washed up was an onyx ring he always wore. One of my grandchildren wears it now. And on that ring, you see, is a carving of Neptune, King of the Sea."

Three Hundred Miles Out
I. A Plumb Lucky Dog

This article was published in the June 1957 issue of Yankee *magazine, under the title "The Psychic Dog."*

By A. B. Stockbridge

Although this story may seem incredible to those who are unfamiliar with the mysterious workings of the sea, old-timers along the Gloucester, Massachusetts, waterfront vouch for its truth. It happened near the turn of the century, back in the days of sail, when Gloucester had no close competitors as the world's leading fishing port. The circumstances under which this dog made his first appearance in fishing folklore are almost unbelievable, but true.

The scene for his dramatic entrance into the Gloucester picture was laid in the North Atlantic about three hundred miles from land.

On a beautiful day in early spring, one of the crack schooners was homeward bound, "loaded to the scuppers," after a long hard trip to the Grand Banks. Visibility was exceptionally good, and the sea was unusually smooth for those waters — but not a sail or a telltale column of smoke was in sight. One of the crew went to the lee rail to empty the slop bucket for the cook when his eye spotted a dark object in the water almost dead ahead. It is by no means out of the ordinary to encounter flotsam of every description on the high seas, and little attention is paid to it unless it is something to endanger shipping. For some reason though, this looked different from the usual run of debris, and he called it to the attention of some other members of the crew. Much speculation was advanced as to what it might be; one said it looked to him like the body of a colored man. The captain was notified, but when they were near enough to make identification positive it proved to be a large Newfoundland dog. He was not only alive but swimming vigorously toward them. The captain hove the vessel to, and they soon had the Newfoundland safely aboard. No one rescued at sea was ever more appreciative than that dog.

When they reached port, inquiries were started to find out how so fine an animal came to be in that unusual situation. They lasted for the lifetime of the dog. Newfoundland dogs are said to be as much at home in the water as on the land, but three hundred miles out for a casual swim is a little too much even for that noble breed. All ports of the maritime provinces of Canada and those of the New England coast denied any knowledge of the lone seafarer. No clue was ever found that shed any light on his origin. It remains a mystery to this day.

He became a great favorite along the Gloucester waterfront, but the vessel that rescued him was always his home, and he made every trip with her. No matter who the captain was or what type of fishing the vessel was engaged in, she was always among the "highliners," and the dog was given credit for bringing good luck. This went on for a number of years until one season when she was again "fitted out" for "banking."

As the sailing date approached, the dog showed signs of restlessness, and when the day arrived his agitation was apparent to everyone. No amount of coaxing could get him aboard. He showed his disapproval by loud barking, behavior very unusual for him. One of the crew shrugged his shoulders and said they would probably have a "broker" if the dog wouldn't go. But his refusal had more significance than that.

They sailed without him — the vessel rounded Eastern Point, disappeared into the offing, and hasn't been "seen nor heard tell of since."

II. The Explanation

What does appear to be the answer to the riddle of "A Plumb Lucky Dog" was furnished by Mr. Mosher in the following letter to Yankee, *published in its August 1957 issue.*

BY O. M. MOSHER

After reading Mr. Stockbridge's story of "The Psychic Dog," which appeared in the June '57 *Yankee*, I think I can furnish a clue to the origin of the dog. He may have been and probably was my dog. It would be about sixty years ago now, when I was a lad around four years old, that my father, then skipper of a trawl-fishing schooner sailing out of Mahone Bay on the east coast of Nova Scotia, brought a Newfoundland puppy home to me.

The dog had a black curly pelt with white patches. As he grew up we were inseparable, and before long he was bigger and heavier than I.

About the time he was fully grown, I ventured upon some young ice in a cove near our home and broke through into salt water over my depth, but was brought safely ashore by Prince, who immediately jumped in beside me and took hold of my sweater at the shoulder. (I still remember it was a very nice gray one that I liked very much.)

That winter, boys on their way to and from the one-room country school at Indian Point, our small community on the shore of Mahone Bay, would sometimes throw snowballs at the dog on the other side of the picket fence in front of our home. Prince probably thought it was a kind of game and that he was expected to retrieve them as when I threw sticks into the water for him to get.

Naturally, he would bark sometimes, and when he did it was like a lion talking. This alarmed the little girls who were also attending the school, and soon their mothers were expressing concern.

To ease the situation, my father permitted an uncle to take the dog with him aboard a schooner bound for the West Indies with a cargo of dried fish, to bring back salt from Turks Island.

Some weeks later, we received a letter from my uncle informing us that the dog had been lost overboard during a storm. They all had wanted to turn back and get the dog as they could see him following in the wake of the ship, but the captain thought it might endanger the vessel and crew to do so, as the schooner was old and heavily loaded.

I doubt if I could find out any more just where and when this occurred, because as far as I know, the folks who might know are all gone by now. (So is the new puppy I was given soon afterward.) But, as the courses these two schooners were taking would cross, it seems quite probable that this could be the same dog. He would have been still young and a sharp swimmer.

Maybe the old-timers around Gloucester will agree with me that it could have been the same dog.

At any rate I shall always be glad for having run into Mr. Stockbridge's story in *Yankee*, for I can feel now that my dog was not lost at sea after all, but found new friends and a good home.

Three "Blind" Lookouts

Reminiscent of the Essex *tale, but the villains here were humans, not a whale.*

BY HOWARD L. CRISE III

On the afternoon of June 23, 1849, the bark *Janet* was cruising the whaling grounds off the coast of Peru, 3°N 104°W, when "She blows! Blows! BLOWS!" boomed from the masthead. A fresh wind gusted, but with less than a hundred barrels of sperm in the hold and nearly eight months out of Westport, Massachusetts, Captain Charles B. Hosmer took little time making his decision. Three boats lowered and went their separate ways, each pulling swiftly through the heavy seas toward its quarry.

Within the hour, all boats had made fast to a whale, lanced the vitals, and hacked a hole in the tail gristle to pass the tow line through. Captain Hosmer's crew sat by their oarlocks ready to put about for the bark as Third Mate Francis Hawkins of Augusta, Maine, turned to resume his position of boat steerer. Suddenly, the boat pitched, Hawkins careened against the gunwale, and six men spilled into the deep along with all their whalecraft, including boat-bucket, lantern-keg, boat-keg, and compass — items that would be sorely missed during the ordeal just begun.

The men righted the boat and lashed the oars athwart her, she being filled with water and the sea continually breaking over her. They attached two red waifs to the collapsible mast and pivoted it upright. The other boats were glimpsed riding the waves one and a half miles off.

The surging waters that had swept away their boat-bucket would have made bailing a waste of energy had Hosmer given orders to do so. Gripping the gunwale as the swamped boat dipped into the trough of each seaswell, the Captain saw no cause for alarm; he knew that the huge carcass of their kill marked their position beyond all doubt. The greenhands were assured that it was standard procedure for the others to fulfill their primary mission before retrieving capsized shipmates.

Thus, Captain Hosmer, along with Hawkins and Seamen Edward Henry Charlez and Joseph Cortez of the Azores, James Fairman of Ohio, and Henry Thompson of Philadelphia watched patiently as the other boats took their whales alongside the distant *Janet*. They saw the boats raised to their davits and the ship's company secure the whales to either side of the bark. Finally, they craned their necks anticipating junction with the 194-ton vessel making directly for them under full sail.

But, when approximately a mile away, the *Janet* veered off on another course.

The above is based on Captain Hosmer's own account of the bizarre events leading up to being marooned. After the initial shock of watching certain rescue fade into inexplicable abandonment, his narrative of the subsequent three weeks reflects an agonizingly long nightmare.

The men clambered into the boat from atop the whale to bail, but their efforts were more frantic than concerted. They cut the harpoon line, jerry-rigged several pieces of torn sail, and clinging to the gunwales, steered toward the receding bark. By dusk, *Janet* was three miles away. During the night, they saw an intermittent light, but lacking their lantern-keg they could not signal in the dark.

Dawn revealed *Janet* in the same position. After breakfast aboard ship, the deck swarmed with hands cutting in the whales. Desperately needing the emergency rations of their boat-keg, the weakened men crawled onto the whale and signalled in vain. Bailing again proved useless. At midday, the wind grew favorable, and they resumed trying to regain the bark. However, their elusive goal moved farther away and disappeared in the murkiness of an early nightfall.

By the following afternoon, when the crew had finally managed to bail the boat dry, the Pacific had already claimed two. Soon, with no water for forty-eight hours, two others became delirious.

Hosmer determined Cocus Island, a thousand miles away, to be the closest accessible land. Also, the northeasterly course would carry them

into the rainy latitudes. To supplement the shredded sail, they improvised a wind-propeller out of boards from the boat's ceiling. Hosmer headed the boat for 5°27'N, 87°15'W, with only the South Sea rolling from behind and the North Star shining above by which to navigate.

On the seventh day, barely able to flex their fingers, they drew lots for one to die so that the rest might live. Soon after breakfast, a shower gave the three survivors their first water in a week.

On the eighth day, a seaman died from exposure. Hosmer and Cortez further restored their stamina. Three days later, they altered their course northward to seek rain.

During the course of the day, as a pelting tropical storm drenched them, they fell in with a school of gamboling porpoises, one of which leapt into the boat.

Several days later they began snaring terrestrial birds, and on July 13 Hosmer sighted land due east. His landing on the uninhabited isle, his destination for three weeks, ranked Hosmer behind only Captain Cook and the *Essex* whaleboats for record long-distance, open-boat journeys. The bloodfeasts necessitated during the voyage evidently had whetted the appetites of the two survivors, for they quickly caught a wild pig, ripped its jugular, and slaked their thirst.

... barely able to flex their fingers they drew lots for one to die ...

Two days later, a whaleboat from the *Leonidas* of New Bedford beached for wood and water. Thus, a whaler rescued them as unexpectedly as another had deserted them.

On August 21, Hosmer arrived in Paita, Peru, and recorded every detail in a letter to the *Whaleman's Shipping List*, but no accusations were stated or implied.

Was this incident attributable to a whim of fate?

According to James A. Crowell, previously First Mate and now Captain of the *Janet*, in a letter to Henry Wilcox, the owner's agent, dated August 1, 1849:

> At 3 P.M., I had my whale alongside, and soon the ship came to me, and when I got on board there was but one boat in sight, and that was five miles to the leeward of the ship. I went down to it with the ship, and found that it was the 2d mate's boat. He had seen Captain Hosmer two hours previously fast to a whale, and went to the leeward of him when last seen from his boat. We proceeded in the direction in which the Captain's boat had last been seen and lay too *(sic)* all night with all sails set, and with all our lights fixed. In the morning saw nothing of the boat. We cruised three days with all hands at the mast-heads, but unfortunately without meeting any trace of her. In the meantime, four of our hands were sick and we were under necessity of making the best of our way to this port (Paita).

It is easy enough to create mysteries in an armchair, but the fact is that it is virtually impossible not to sight anything within a ten-mile radius of the crow's nest — especially a whale. Boats were often lowered despite inclement weather, and frequently they would pursue or be towed by Leviathan many miles, and even beyond the horizon, with few ever lost at sea. The odds against locating a nearby marked boat, with the gargantuan mass of an adjacent dead sperm and ample daylight remaining, were nil.

The analogy of everyone at some time not being able to find glasses, keys, or wallet when known to be in a specific area is not a good one. First, human life is not involved. Further, given sufficient motivation, methodical search invariably results in finding the missing object.

In this case six lives were at stake, one of which was economically invaluable. The success of any voyage hinged upon the captain. Aside from maintaining discipline and morale, he provided a storehouse of information on the migratory habits and idiosyncrasies of the sperm, right, bowhead, and humpback whales. As Melville points out, for the captain to expose himself to the dangers of the chase was unjustifiable.

There were no repercussions from the macabre mishap. Crowell finished the voyage as captain and shipped again as master of a ship in 1855, while Hosmer took command for the same agent eleven months after his harrowing experience.

Still, a blatant discrepancy exists between the statements of Hosmer and Crowell. Only by understanding the fine distinction drawn between criminal negligence and malice aforethought during the era of wooden ships and iron men can a circumstantial judgement be made.

The *Janet* embarked for the Pacific and sperm on November 11, 1848. Four months later, she had doubled Cape Horn and was off the coast of Peru with thirty-five barrels of oil in her hold, meaning two or three whales at most. Each day's failure to raise whales undoubtedly created tension. Captain Hosmer probably paced constantly during the day and likely took lookout himself on occasion.

It is understandable, then, that when sperm were sighted on that dismal June afternoon he should pounce without hesitation and climb into a boat to personally ensure the capture of at least one of the shoal.

But what of the irreconcilable facts of the aftermath?

Hosmer reported being within sight of the *Janet* for 24 hours after capsizing; indeed, within one mile and minutes of being rescued.

Crowell asserted that three lookouts sighted no trace of the boat in three days. Did they not even espy the whale? Or, did the whale in fact comprise part of the 250 barrels that Crowell reported on reaching Paita on July 22? How tempting is it to become captain by looking the other way for a minute? Especially if one has popular support?

Was Hosmer an archetypal tyrant? Did Crowell bribe the others or swear them to secrecy on pain of death?

Speculation is endless. The truth lies somewhere between the captain, the mate, and the deep blue sea.

Mystery of the *Don*

Unsolved to this day. . . .

By Norman R. Tufts

On Maine's picturesque Bailey Island, thirty-five happy pic-nickers boarded the 44-foot motor cruiser *Don*, bound for a shore dinner on Monhegan Island. On that sunny morning of June 29, 1941, the horizon wore a soft collar of fog, but over-head the skies were blue, and the sea was calm.

Captain Johnson and his crewman started the *Don's* engine and let it idle as they cast off. Around 10 A.M., the cruiser pulled away from the landing at Dyer's Cove and moved slowly seaward. Many of the excur-sionists stayed up on the foredeck or sat on the cabin roof to enjoy the sunwashed scenery and fresh salt air. Then the *Don* lifted to the first gentle swells of the open sea, and they were under way at last, not slated to return until 7:30 that evening.

Envious onlookers watched until the cruiser and her thirty-seven people vanished in the hazy distance. It was a beautiful day for a picnic. Overhead the gulls wheeled, gleaming white in the morning sun that gilded the spires of close-packed spruces atop the ledges.

The long, slow, early summer day ripened into evening. Gulls began their customary leisurely flights to night stations. From a heavily wooded point, a whippoorwill sent his persistent call across the little bay as herons headed toward their island nesting sites. Although it was past time for the *Don* to land, no one was worried. Captain Johnson was intimately acquainted with this section of the Maine coast. Wind and tide could play few tricks that were new to him. His knowledge of the treach-erous reefs in the area was unsurpassed by any other skipper, for the *Don* was a reformed rum-runner. Roaming these restless waters in darkness was nothing new to the *Don* and her master. And according to Bailey Island fishermen, the recently overhauled cruiser was in fine condition, carried plenty of fuel, and ran easily at eight to ten knots.

During her career as a shady lady on the hooch run, the *Don* had been powered by huge twin engines, and her long, lean hull was designed for speed. But she had recently been converted to a single engine. The only criticism voiced by professional fishermen was that she was not beamy enough for maximum seaworthiness — but this was hardly a problem for a skipper like Captain Johnson on a calm sea.

By dark, there was still no sign of the *Don*. The weather was becoming unsettled, with fog making in here and there. Along the murky horizon, lightning flickered ominously. The very air was charged. The night wind, while gentle, was fitful and restless as it sighed through the black spruces that rimmed the waiting land. But anyone who had ever had to round up picnickers ashore on an island as beautiful as Monhegan knew how difficult it could be to adhere to any set time schedule. Indeed a late arrival could almost be predicted.

By Monday's dawn, anxiety had sharpened. Fog that had hung unmoving on the horizon during the day had slipped in during the night, enveloping the shore with what one fisherman described as "a dungeon of fog." A few small boats slowly felt about in the gloom, searching

cautiously over the dark opaque sea. They found only each other. Faint hope stirred, for seldom was a vessel lost without leaving life jackets, gear, or some kind of debris afloat. Maybe the *Don* had taken shelter in an island's lee or near an isolated stretch of shore. In that swirling vapor, she would have been invisible a boat length away. If only the fog would lift, search planes could take to the air.

Once again, darkness came with no *Don*. Throughout that long night, Halfway Rock's foghorn groaned in the streaming blackness. When watery daylight came, the horn still moaned, an invisible presence in the unrelenting gray vapor. More small boats prepared for sea.

Then Claude Johnson found the first body. A chill swept the island as the siren howled from Mrs. Helen Murray's rooftop. It was a signal for help. At the Bailey Island Post Office, grim fishermen organized the search. Soon scores of small craft were carefully feeling their way to sea.

In Boothbay Harbor, Sea and Shore Fisheries' sturdy 53-footer *Maine* started up her powerful diesels and edged out into the murk, where Captain Meservey and his crew steered a course-and-clock run toward Halfway Rock. Periodically her engines idled until a buoy could be picked up and identified in the smothering vapor. Out there somewhere were motor lifeboats from Coast Guard stations at Popham and Damariscove, like the *Maine*, slowly probing their blind way through the ledge-infested waters. Lonely sentinel bell buoys, nudged to cadenced voice by the oily swells, could be heard ten minutes before they were reached. In the opaque, moisture-laden air, their strangely muffled clangs seemed off-key, other-worldly. At regular intervals, the horn at Halfway Rock sent its guttural warning forth, sea and swirling mists trembling as a unit.

Except for the muted rumble of engines, the only other sounds were the soft shush of gently rolling seas against a hull, and occasional murmurs from the searchers. Even the gulls were shore-bound. The only light came from directly overhead, pale, unreal, casting no shadow.

The *Maine* successfully passed The Sisters, low-lying rock knives. The brooding mass that was Seguin vanished quickly in the gloom astern. When the *Maine* stood to off Jaquish Island, near Bailey, a lobsterman loomed up with two men aboard. They reported nothing found. Then, eerie and unplanned, as though on signal, another boat materialized. She was the *Marion* out of Bailey Island. Her skipper, Bill Munsey, told the *Maine's* commander that he and his crew had pulled aboard the bodies of two women. A small cruiser suddenly appeared, circling, to be followed almost immediately by the Coast Guard power lifeboat from Popham. As abruptly as it had formed, the little flotilla broke up, each vessel simply swallowed in the gray half-night.

At Bailey Island's Mackerel Cove, one by one, the boats loomed from the dark sea, some to report nothing, others to leave off grim cargoes.

For six endless days and nights, the hoarse moan of the foghorn fought the stagnant, unrelenting fog that locked the coast in its clammy embrace. In the gray twilight spectral islands — each wet black rock and lonely cove (some uncharted) — were located and searched. Each find only served to deepen the mystery of the *Don*.

Captain Johnson's body washed into Smith Cove. A fisherman friend of mine who helped to pull the dead man aboard said: "He wore an expression of terror on his face as if something had scared him to death. His arms were crossed over his body, he was tied to a keg with three fathoms of line, and all he had on was his shoes and underwear!" The keg was from the *Don* and bore her name and home port. At Dyer's Cove, the late Captain Johnson's dog paced the fog-shrouded landing, lifted his muzzle, and howled repeatedly.

A teenage boy noted for being an exceptionally strong swimmer was found dead on the shore of Ragged Island. His was the second of the only two male bodies found among the thirteen victims recovered.

In September of 1969, I wrote Mrs. Alice Fuller on Monhegan to see if she could find anyone who could resolve the question of whether or not the *Don* had reached the island. The answer came back promptly. Fishermen who had been on the island in 1941 and clearly remembered the disaster stated that the vessel did not reach Monhegan. It was their opinion that she was lost somewhere off Bailey Island in a sudden, disastrous explosion that gave no time for anyone to get into life jackets or lower life rafts.

Other odd and sometimes contradictory data were found. U.S. Weather Bureau spokesmen said that a severe electrical storm had occurred, and that the boat likely passed through the storm center. But the Seguin Lighthouse keeper believed he had sighted the missing craft at seven o'clock, on course for Bailey Island, with weather clear and sea calm until after 1 A.M. From Seguin Island to Damariscove, the going was (and is) often treacherous, but the *Don* usually covered that distance in about thirty minutes. Thus she was already much behind schedule before she reached Seguin — if the sighted vessel actually was the *Don*.

Three Portland yachtsmen reported seeing a boat resembling the *Don* near Ragged Island at or about eleven o'clock on Sunday night. This was interesting information, as watches on several of the victims' wrists had stopped at 11:45. A State Fisheries warden claimed the *Don* "reeked of gasoline fumes" when he boarded her on Saturday, June 28. Other officials claimed she was overloaded, and Lieut. T. J. Sampson of the Coast Guard said, "There was no doubt that there was fire and an explosion."

The body of one woman bore marks resembling burns on both legs and one hip. Another had a bruise on her forehead. The Brunswick Medical Examiner explained that all ten bodies he had examined had been in the water at least twenty-four hours, and the marks that resembled burns were, instead, "skin crawling" caused by exposure to water. His verdict was death due to accidental drowning.

On the night of the tragedy, a lone sardiner heard an engine that sounded as though it were racing wildly in reverse, followed by abrupt silence. An oil slick that appeared off Mark Island ledge later proved to have resulted from waste dropped into the water by a boatman cleaning his engine.

Bodies were found from an area west of Small Point westward to Biddeford Pool . . .

Bodies were found from an area west of Small Point westward to Biddeford Pool, where the last victim was picked up by a dragger two miles offshore. This was the last body of which I can find record, and it had been carried some twenty-six miles from the suspected site of the tragedy.

Twenty-eight years after the *Don* disappeared, I asked a veteran Bailey Island fisherman if he remembered her. He looked out over the sea, sparkling in the bright sun. Then he replied, "Yes, I remember her well."

"Would you mind answering some questions about her?"

He looked straight at me. "Why? And what do you want to know?"

I explained that a friend of mine had been lost with the *Don*, and I had known some of the fishermen who had joined in the fog-shrouded search and had helped to recover some of the drowned. Too, I was intrigued by the mystery still surrounding the cruiser's disappearance. My questions were: Over the years that had passed since then, had any new evidence been found? What did he feel had happened to the *Don* and her thirty-seven people on that fateful night?

He nodded and thought for a moment. "Well, as you know, the Coast Guard still claims there was an explosion and fire. But there were no burns on the dead, no charred wreckage such as you get when a boat blows up and burns. I firmly believe she ran smack into a ledge — some of those ledges stick right out of deep water there, so she could hit and sink awful fast. Then the dragger crew heard a raging engine that night, right where we think she went down. If her skipper had come up on those ledges all of a sudden, like in fog, and him being a mite off course from squalls and currents, say, he'd have reversed her wide open trying to clear the rocks. Then, too, that would tie in with a find one of our draggers made — in 1967, I believe it was — right out there in a sandy gulch that runs along there. They picked up some old shoes and a pair of badly corroded binoculars. At the time, they didn't think much about it, so they tossed 'em back. But as far as I'm concerned, the *Don* struck a ledge, maybe stove in her bow so that no loose planks floated free, and she sank like a stone."

Someone suggested that the cruiser struck a mine, but no explosion was reported, nor was any debris found. Another idea was that a German submarine (not uncommon off our coasts in 1941) might have escorted the *Don* off to sea and sunk her to prevent her reporting a sighting, but this seems far-fetched.

As of now, we know only that the *Don* vanished with all thirty-seven of the people aboard, probably on the night of June 29, 1941. Time but deepens the mystery of her fate.

Showdown off Cherbourg

"Old Beeswax" Semmes had captained the Confederate cruiser Alabama *to world fame, sinking fifty-five Yankee vessels in the Civil War at sea. For two years Bostonian John Winslow held the* Kearsarge *in dogged pursuit. On June 19, 1864, the two brave crews played out the final act as thousands of spectators looked on.*

BY JOHN M. TAYLOR

On June 11, 1864, the residents of the French port of Cherbourg were intrigued to see a sleek, black-hulled cruiser steaming slowly past the breakwater. The surprise visitor was perhaps the most famous ship afloat — the Confederate raider *Alabama,* a British-built warship that had destroyed fifty-five Yankee merchantmen in the Civil War at sea. The Union Navy, embarrassed by the *Alabama's* depredations, had no higher priority than to bring the Rebel "pirate" to bay.

Skipper of the *Alabama* was Maryland-born Raphael Semmes, a career Navy man whose pointed moustache had brought him the nickname "Old Beeswax." The combative Semmes would have preferred fighting the Union Navy to harassing Northern shipping. When acting as a commerce raider he fought by the rules; there had been virtually no loss of life aboard the Yankee merchantmen he had overtaken and destroyed. Now the *Alabama* was a tired ship. After twenty-two months at sea Semmes could no longer postpone a refit, and he hoped that France would prove a politically hospitable host to the *Alabama,* a "weary foxhound, limping back after a long chase."

Some three hundred miles northeast, at the Dutch port of Flushing, Captain John Winslow of the U.S.S. *Kearsarge* received electrifying news: the notorious *Alabama* had been seen to enter port at Cherbourg. The 55-year-old Winslow, who had spent two years pursuing the *Alabama* from the Baltic to the Azores, wasted no time in getting under way, and by the morning of June 14 the *Kearsarge* was off Cherbourg. Winslow and Semmes had been messmates in the old Navy; now they were enemies and each was spoiling for a fight.

The *Kearsarge* and the *Alabama* were almost equal in size and fighting power. Both were screw steamers of about the same tonnage, and while equipped for sail, depended primarily on two coal-fired engines. *Alabama* carried a crew of 149 and mounted eight guns; *Kearsarge* had a complement of 163 and mounted seven guns. The outcome of the battle would depend heavily on the skill of the commanders and the degree to which each had maintained his ship in fighting trim.

One of the men aboard the *Kearsarge* was 20-year-old William Alsdorf, a native of Hamburg, Germany, who had signed aboard the Union cruiser in Spain. We do not know a great deal about William Alsdorf. Navy records show him to have been 5'6" with dark hair and hazel eyes. In contrast to Captain Winslow, a Massachusetts man of strong antislavery views, the German-born Alsdorf may have had only a limited understanding of the war in which he found himself. But he knew an exciting battle when he saw one, and five months after the *Kearsarge* took on the *Alabama*, William set down his version of what transpired, a narrative here published for the first time.

> We found the *Alabama* inside the Harbour of Cherbourg, France. We steamed up to her with our signal flags flying from stem to stern as a challenge for the *Alabama* to come out and meet us. . . . [On June 14] a boat flying a white flag came to our vessel bearing Lieutenant Kell of the *Alabama*. He presented the challenge for Our Capt. Winslow to our first officer Thornton at the gangway. . . . On receiving the challenge Thornton went to Capt. Winslow's stateroom and presented the challenge to him . . . Capt. Winslow, after reading the challenge, told the Lieutenant of the Alabama that he would meet Capt. Semmes with pleasure. On hearing this [Kell] saluted Capt. Winslow and returned to his boat and rowed back to the *Alabama*. Capt. Winslow stood for a few minutes with a very stern expression. On dismissing our Lieutenant he retired to his stateroom: as he retired he gave orders to unlimber guns, get ammunition ready, and be in order for immediate action. . . .
>
> After dinner Capt. Winslow came on deck and gave orders to the bosun mate to call all hands on deck for a general inspection and muster after the inspection. Capt. Winslow expressed feelings of great satisfaction at the condition of the guns, equipment and crew. Then Capt. Winslow took from his pocket the [*Alabama's*] letter and commenced to read . . . After he read the challenge he said, "We will wait for him, but do not underrate Capt. Semmes. He will do all he can to gain the victory. As for his crew I know nothing about them. Let every man be watchful and ready for action

Captain Raphael Semmes (right) standing by the Alabama's *110-pounder rifled gun, Lieutenant J.M. Kell looking on. Capetown, South Africa, August, 1863.*

at any moment." We then gave three cheers for Capt. Winslow and three cheers for the *Kearsarge*.

We cruised within the three-mile limit, keeping a close watch on the *Alabama*, as we suspected that the *Alabama* might leave the harbor at night. The next day [15th of June] the French admiral, on board a large iron-clad vessel, came alongside and hailed us, stating from the bow of his vessel that we should keep within three miles off the harbor or shore, otherwise he would fire into us. Our Capt. Winslow promised to avoid any breach of the international law. We cruised up and down outside the breakwater, running close at night and keeping outside the three miles at daytime. At intervals we noticed a steam yacht called the *Deerhound* flying the English flag, cruising outside the breakwater and harbor... In the meantime our opponent, the *Alabama*, was busy completing repairs, taking on coal, supplies, and ammunition in order to be ready for a trip.

Considering the *Alabama's* need of an overhaul, Semmes may appear to have been unduly eager to take on the *Kearsarge*. In point of fact, he had little choice. If he were to remain in Cherbourg, the Yankees would send so many fighting ships that the *Alabama* would probably be blockaded for the remainder of the war. Far better a fair fight in which the *Alabama* might bring new glory to the fledgling Confederate Navy!

One difference between the two ships, however, was unknown to Semmes. The enterprising Winslow had made imaginative use of his ship's chains (Alsdorf uses the term "side cable"), draping them along vulnerable parts of the hull and concealing them behind wood paneling.

> During the time we watched for the appearance of the *Alabama*, we overhauled the rigging and side cable, which was [wired] and fastened to the side of our vessel in order to protect the machinery and boilers. While the men were active in fastening the cable on our side, one of the crew fell overboard and nearly drowned, but one of the boat crew got him and swam to the boat with him exhausted.
>
> The following day [17th], one of our boats was ordered to go on shore with our officers to reconnoiter, and found the *Deerhound* also in the harbor near the *Alabama*, at anchor with her boats lowered, taking on board several men and going to the *Alabama* which now was fastened to the wharf. [These] afterwards proved to be first class picked British naval reserve men to fight the Confederates' battle on the *Alabama*. But most of those were wounded and two died on board after surrender . . .

Captain Winslow, in a letter written after the battle with the *Alabama*, noted reports that there had been dealings between the *Alabama* and the *Deerhound* in Cherbourg harbor, but there has never been evidence of official British assistance to the *Alabama*. Alsdorf picks up his narrative on the day of the battle.

> On Sun. the 19th, about 9 A.M. A beautiful morning — the atmosphere a little hazy and just enough breeze to make whitecaps on the waves. [We had finished] our morning routine, our crew were all dressed in clean blue muster clothes, and our decks were white as snow. The bell had just tolled for service, and our captain was ready to commence the reading from the church service. His first sentence was just finished when the captain of the first top look-out hailed "Ship ahoy!" . . .
>
> Every one of us looked toward the port and our service ceased immediately. Our officer of the deck espied a vessel with a Brazilian flag leaving the port. Next the large French iron vessel and after it the *Alabama*. On seeing the *Alabama*

> *One difference between the two ships, however, was unknown to Semmes.*

our captain ordered hard to starboard [and told] the engineers, "Give it to her." We swung around due north . . . We heard the crew of the *Alabama* cheering. [Later we learned] that Capt. Semmes was making a speech stating that the cable fastened to our sides was nothing, as a shot would smash those cables and would enter in our machinery and sink us; that we were frightened and now running away.

The clash between the *Kearsarge* and the *Alabama* was, among other things, pure theater. It seemed that everyone in France wanted to view what would prove to be the last single-ship duel of the era of wooden ships. Excursion trains brought the curious to Cherbourg, and throngs of small craft hovered outside the breakwater for a closer view of the hostilities. As Alsdorf indicates, Semmes did in fact make a speech to his crew, reminding them that "the name of your ship has become a household word throughout the civilized world," and asking rhetorically, "Shall that name be tarnished by defeat?" His men shouted back, "Never!" But it is doubtful whether Raphael Semmes ever thought that the *Kearsarge* was running away; Winslow sought only to avoid any infringement of French waters. And Semmes knew nothing of the *Kearsarge's* protective chain.

As soon as we saw the *Alabama* approaching, every man sprang to his station. The guns were unlimbered ready for action long before the long roll of drum and fife [called] us to quarters. As we were running out to sea the captain gave us orders to fill the water tanks, sand the decks, and batten down the hatches. When we were near [7 miles] from shore, our captain commanded, "Hard to starboard." We heaved around until we were headed straight for our opponent.

Our boys were anxiously watching the movements of the *Alabama* as we were within 1,200 yards of our opponent. She gave us a volley of seven guns, and one shot struck the waterline within 10 feet of our starboard bow. The next shot struck the water and burst, and the pieces flew over the forecastle and cut off some of the rigging. The other shots did not do much harm. We were going at the fullest speed toward the *Alabama*. As we were unable to fire any of our guns, the Captain shouted, "Lay down, boys," as the *Alabama* had a raking bullseye on us, and if one of his 100-pound rifle balls would sweep our deck it would be a great loss of life.

Our boys stepped down for a little while, looking through the portholes at the *Alabama* and the shots striking the water and bursting and some going over our heads. Many of us thought Capt. Winslow intended to run into her. But he intended to run at her stern to give her raking shots in return. The captain of the *Alabama* . . . sheared around to starboard, parallel to our starboard side, firing his starboard battery of guns at us, thereby going in a circle. As soon as Semmes came around, enabling us to gear our side guns on him . . . the boys shot off their guns. The Marines on the forecastle deck let go their 30-pound rifle and we trained our guns for a shot at the *Alabama*.

Winslow had hoped to run under the *Alabama's* stern and there deliver a broadside, but Semmes turned away to prevent this. The result was an engagement in which the two antagonists fought in a circular track, each with his starboard side engaged, at a distance of from one-quarter to one-half mile. A Union sailor was reminded of "two flies crawling around on the rim of a saucer."

Our battery of five guns came into action . . . Whilst we were thus engaged a shell struck amidships and exploded, setting the side on fire. The fire alarm sounded and the fire squad soon extinguished the fire. Next I saw Jack Dempsey come along with one arm dangling loose at his side. He threw his other arm toward the *Alabama* and said, "Take this one, too," as he disappeared between decks, and Doctor Brown took charge of him. Presently Billy Gorwin came crawling along on his hands as he was shot in the lower part of his body . . . I was a loader on the 2nd division of the 11-inch Dahlgren gun, and while we were loading the gun, having a few minutes time, I sprang to him to assist him to the hatchway of the berth decks, but he vehemently asked me to let him alone. I then sprang back to my gun and tended to my lever. Our gunners could not fire on account of [being too close] to the *Alabama*. Lt. Weaver of our gun got excited and hollered, "Fire, Fire, Fire!" "Hell," came the answer, "do you want me to blow off the anchor?" . . . and our shot when he found his range . . . went through the *Alabama's* side and we saw the coal fly through the air midships. [Another shot] struck midship and exploded on the *Alabama's* starboard side, bursting open her deck; large pieces of timber and coal flew in great quantity.

Captain John A. Winslow (third from left) and Kearsarge *officers stood on deck for this group portrait by Mathew Brady.*

The *Alabama's* captain would later confirm the essence of Alsdorf's account. "The firing now became very hot," Semmes wrote, "and the enemy's shot soon began to tell on our hull, knocking down, killing, and disabling a number of men . . . in different parts of the ship." According to some accounts, Semmes offered a reward to the gun crew that could silence the two 11-inch Dahlgrens — one of them Alsdorf's — that were wreaking such havoc aboard his ship.

Quite apart from the *Kearsarge's* protective chains, the two antagonists offered contrasts in marksmanship. The *Kearsarge* fired a total of 173 rounds. Onlookers estimated that the *Alabama* fired about twice that many, but of the 28 shots that struck the Union vessel — many in the rigging — only two or three caused significant damage. Of the *Kearsarge's* three casualties, only one, William Gorwin, would die of his wounds.

> Both of our ships were completely enveloped in smoke, but as we were fighting in a circle we soon ran out of it, and then the shells flew thick and fast. After one hour's fighting the *Alabama's* fire slackened, and she tried to make sail and run for shore. As her fires were out and her engine useless, she began sinking. Her ensign . . . was shot down early in the engagement. They now fired their lee gun to leeward in token of surrender which we acknowledged. Our Captain ordered [us] to cease firing but to stand by our guns.

After we ceased firing . . . two shells came booming at us. Capt. Winslow shouted, "Give it to them, boys — they are playing us a trick!" Lieutenant Thornton ordered us to load our gun with canister and grape. We gave her another broadside, a raking shot which did great damage.

Then we noticed someone at the *Alabama's* stern holding a white flag as a sign of second surrender. They lowered a boat at the stern that came along with a Lieutenant Wilson . . . Our Lieutenant Thornton asked him if he surrendered. He stated, "I have no orders to that effect but to ask you to take these wounded men on board." He desired to pick up those men struggling in the water and deliver them to us on board. In the meantime the *Deerhound* came along our bow, and Capt. Winslow at the forecastle of our vessel spoke to the captain. "Will you please, in the name of humanity, pick up those men from drowning?" I.I. [*sic*, aye, aye] came the answer, and the *Deerhound* lowered her boats and picked up all they could find struggling in the water.

Nothing in the action would prove more controversial than the action of the English yacht, which shortly sailed off to Britain with the rescued Semmes, his first officer, and thirty-eight other "pirates" saved from the English Channel.

Lieutenant Wilson returned with his boat loaded with saved men. He surrendered and presented his sword to Lieutenant Thornton, who would not receive it and stated, "Never mind, keep your sword." The only gentleman among the pirate officers was Lieutenant Wilson. As soon as the *Deerhound* had our prisoners safe on board she steamed rapidly away for England with 40 prisoners, Capt. Semmes and 14 officers among them. Capt. Semmes and his officers had thrown their swords into the sea when they abandoned their sinking ship.

After every man from the *Alabama* was rescued and things on board put aright, Capt. Winslow called all hands to muster. He read a prayer and said, "We have won the battle without loss of life, and God must be on our side. Our boats, with the aid of two French pilot boats, picked up 65 men and five officers . . . You are requested to give them some of your clothing and report any expense to me. These men have surrendered and I want you to treat them as brothers and shipmates. Your dinner will soon be served; share it with them." The grog tub was brought up on deck and they helped us to splice the main brace.

The next day we steamed to the Port of Cherbourg and moored our vessel to the wharf where the *Alabama* had been located. We kept a few officers on board but discharged [i.e., paroled] all the crew of the *Alabama* as we had no room for these men. We sent our wounded on shore to the hospital and the next day left for London, England, and made some repairs. Then we were ordered home, and left after two days. We hurried to intercept the *Florida* [another Confederate raider], but not finding her steamed home to Boston whence we were marched through Boston with music and then discharged.

The two commanders in the *Kearsarge-Alabama* duel both survived the war. Raphael Semmes, whose escape to England further strained relations between the United States and Britain, returned to the Confederacy and commanded an army brigade in the closing months of the war. John Winslow was slow in getting recognition for his feat in destroying the *Alabama*; the Navy Department, in the best bureaucratic tradition, complained that Winslow's report on the battle was insufficiently detailed, and insisted that he submit a revised version! Nevertheless, his victory over the *Alabama* brought about Winslow's promotion to commodore. After the war he became an admiral, and for a time commanded America's small Pacific Fleet. He died at his home in Boston in 1873.

As for William Alsdorf, he settled in the United States and took up the vocation of a cabinetmaker. He married, moved to St. Louis, and in 1883 became an American citizen. When his wife died, William moved to New Mexico, where he became a miner. He married a local schoolteacher and once again outlived his spouse. He died in Orogrande, New Mexico, in 1935, at the advanced age of ninety-one. In all likelihood he was the last surviving participant in the battle between the *Kearsarge* and the *Alabama*, and the narrative that he so painstakingly penned after the battle was doubtless read aloud around many a campfire in the American West.

North Atlantic Nightmare

One of the most extraordinary marine disasters in American history, this marked the moment in the Twentieth Century when Americans came to grips with a major and growing threat to the ecology of the United States and the world.

By Evan McLeod Wylie

"MAYDAY! MAYDAY! MAYDAY! ARGO MERCHANT X AGROUND AND IN DANGER OF CAPSIZING X ENGINE ROOM FLOODED X 38 PERSONS ABOARD AND CARGO OF FUEL OIL X POSITION NINE AND ONE HALF MILES SOUTHEAST OF NANTUCKET."

One minute after 7 A.M., December 15, 1976, this message provided the world the first inkling of a desperate struggle underway in the Atlantic off the New England coast.

A wintry gray dawn was breaking over Cape Cod and the islands of Martha's Vineyard and Nantucket. At gale-whipped Coast Guard stations radiomen who had spent the night listening intently for distress calls from vessels fighting heavy seas were looking forward to the end of their watch. At Chatham, on the outer Cape, in a station on a bluff overlooking the ocean, radioman John Webster sat straight up as he heard very faintly an excited voice with a strong foreign accent repeating, "MAYDAY-MAYDAY-MAYDAY" and caught the words "length of vessel 641 feet."

Webster was startled. He had never heard a distress call from such a large ship.

"REPEAT YOUR POSITION. PLEASE REPEAT YOUR POSITION."

Chatham and the Coast Guard Station at Brant Point on Nantucket which had also heard the MAYDAY were replying, trying to pinpoint the ship's location. At Woods Hole, where the Coast Guard's Search and Rescue Center coordinates all responses to marine emergencies between Maine and Long Island, a radioman called to Petty Officer William Row-

As they watched, the bow section wrenched free and pivoted slowly, jackknifing alongside the stern, twisting skyward. Breakers triumphantly engulfed the wreck.

land, "We've got something going. Chatham and Brant Point are talking to a tanker in trouble."

Rowland, manning a console of radios, telephones, and electronic search equipment, flipped a switch. Through heavy static he heard a jumble of conversations as both Chatham and Brant Point tried to talk to the tanker. Quickly he directed Chatham to clear the channel for Brant Point, which was receiving a closer and stronger signal.

With one hand he picked up a phone which enabled him to listen in on Brant Point's communications with the *Argo Merchant*. With the other he poised a pencil over the chart, to find the ship's radioed position. "It didn't check out." As Rowland noted later, "Nine miles south of Nantucket is so full of sandbars you could go aground in a rowboat. He was out there on the shoals all right, but not where he thought he was. We'd have to find him."

He seized another phone and sent out a stream of urgent messages. Within minutes, ships, planes, helicopters, and men were on the move.

At sea, tne Coast Guard cutter *Vigilant*, cruising south of Martha's Vineyard, and a larger cutter, *Sherman*, on fishing patrol off Georges Bank, swung around and signalled their engine rooms for full speed. At the Coast Guard Air Station on Otis Air Force Base on Cape Cod, horns began blaring to clear the field for take-off. Huge hangar doors rolled open and helicopters, their crews scrambling aboard, were towed outside. By 7:29 A.M., the first helicopter, piloted by Lieutenant Bryan Wallace, was airborne, and whirling away toward the shoals, headed southeast over Nantucket Sound.

Wallace, a veteran pilot and participant in many ocean search and rescue missions, was skeptical about the Mayday distress call. "It was hard to believe that a large ship could have gotten into such a position. It sounded like what we call 'a bum scoop' — a hoax or a false alarm."

Flying southeast over the wave-tossed ocean, Wallace's incredulity increased as they passed the point nine miles south of Nantucket, scanned the sea, and saw nothing. But then, twenty-seven miles south of the island, amidst the white breakers of Fishing Rip Shoal, he spotted a huge tanker. She appeared to be heavily laden, hard aground, and her crew members were waving from the stern.

"We have the ship in sight," Wallace radioed. "Hey, this guy is big! Somebody better call the Atlantic Strike Team."

Other helicopters and planes were soon on the scene. It was quickly established that the tanker was in no immediate danger of capsizing or sinking. Wallace noted, "She wasn't deep enough on that shoal to capsize. The water was only twenty-six feet deep. They'd run her up on that shoal the way you'd run a boat up on the beach."

No oil could be seen leaking from the hull, but the *Argo's* engine room was flooding, and the cutters steaming at top speed were more than two hours away. On *Vigilant*, a damage-control party, garbed in rubber survival suits and armed with portable pumps and coils of hose, was quickly mustered on the flight deck. Helicopters from Otis AFB dropped down to pick them up, and then sped on ahead of the cutter to drop men on the tanker's stern.

From the fantail, the party followed a narrow inside passageway, jerked open a door, and stepped onto an open steel balcony. Below them lay the cavernous space of the engine room, sixty feet high from keel to overhead, cluttered with a maze of ducts and piping. Descending steep steel ladders, *Vigilant's* men reached the main deck of the engine room. They could go no farther. Below lay a lake of strong-smelling black goo. Already it had engulfed the ship's engines and boiler rooms. There was no more steam for heat or propulsion. The only remaining electrical power was being supplied by an emergency generator which roared away up near the stack.

Kneeling on the gratings and taking soundings, the damage-control party found that the black lake was thirteen feet deep. Twelve feet of the mixture was seawater. Atop the water floated a foot-thick blanket of strong-smelling oil. It was readily identifiable as No. 6 crude oil that must be leaking from the *Argo's* cargo tanks. Normally maintained at a pumping temperature of 120 degrees, it was congealing into a heavy, sticky mass as it mingled with the icy cold seawater also leaking invisibly into the engine room.

In a frantic effort to free the vessel, the captain had run his engines full speed astern for twenty-six minutes. The resulting vibrations had ruptured water lines and valves, permitting the sea to pour into the engine room, and oil to escape into it from the cargo tanks.

Using broomsticks and poles, the Coast Guardsmen forced the suction ends of their pump lines down through the oil. Scrambling up and down the steep ladders, they rigged their portable pumps in a series to lift the water forty-five feet to main deck level. Within thirty minutes, streams of oily water were pouring out of portholes.

To Coast Guardsmen tending pumps and hose lines in the flooding engine room, circling above the tanker in planes and helicopters, or gathering in front of wall-sized sea charts in Boston, New York, and Washington, D.C., it was obvious that they were in the midst of a deadly race against time, the sea, and the weather. *Argo Merchant* lay helpless in open ocean, exposed to gales from every quarter, in one of the most dangerous parts of the U.S. coast, the notorious Nantucket Shoals, a ship's graveyard area twenty-five miles wide by forty miles long. Here, far out to sea, ridges of sand and gravel are so shallow and exposed that waves burst over them, sending fountains of spray twenty feet in the air. The region is rife with powerful, turbulent currents. Year-round the weather is poor, and in winter frequently so violent that even veteran sailors become seasick. Aground on the shoals and laden with seven and a half million gallons of heavy No. 6 crude oil, *Argo Merchant* was a time bomb threatening the New England coast and some of the richest fishing grounds in the world.

The seas on the shoals that morning ranged around twelve feet. As they struck the *Argo* on her port side, the huge vessel shuddered and surged with the impact. Hard aground amidships, she floated free at the bow and stern. As the seas pounded her savagely, the men in the engine room felt the stern alternately rising beneath their feet and striking bottom with a jarring, hull-shaking thud, while the growing weight of oil and water in the engine room was placing overwhelming stress on the steel keel and bottom plates.

By noon *Vigilant* and *Sherman* had arrived, maneuvering cautiously in the treacherous shoal waters. A damage-control party from *Sherman* with more pumps was put aboard the tanker by helicopters which had begun to evacuate the *Argo* crew, hoisting them one by one from the stern. Before leaving, the crew had thrown open their galley to the Coast Guardsmen. Soaked with sweat and besmeared with oil, the damage-control parties took turns working the pump lines and crouching in a shelter lee on the stern, munching sandwiches of Greek bread, canned beef, cheese, and sardines.

"The water lines were ruptured so we had no drinking water," said one man. "We were thirsty and getting dehydrated in those rubber survival suits until somebody found a case of Greek beer."

The seas had moderated. The sun shone brightly. The motley array of pumps seemed to be stemming the flooding. Spirits rose. If only there were time for more powerful equipment to reach the scene, the tanker might be saved.

But by mid-afternoon word came up from the engine room that the pumps were failing . Designed to pump sea water, they were fouling with the heavy oil mixture. One by one they sputtered, lost suction, and quit.

Once again the lake in the engine room began rising, and soon it was just beneath the gratings of the main level of the engine room, posing a new threat. Although the emergency generator supplying electrical power for the interior of the tanker was high up near the stack, swarms of cables were connected with a main switchboard located down below. At 5 P.M., the switchboard was flooded. Cables short-circuited, lights flickered, and the *Argo* was plunged into darkness.

The damage-control men deep down in the engine room found themselves enveloped in inky blackness and surrounded by ghostly creaking and moaning. "It was like sitting in a coffin," said one. "The ship was making weird, creepy noises. The cargo tanks were breathing with whining and whistling sounds as pipelines gave way. We couldn't tell what would happen next."

Fearful that their men might become lost or slip and fall into the lake of oil and water, leaders ordered them to couple up in a "buddy" system. With the aid of flashlights, they retreated up the steep ladders, taking with them their clogged and damaged pumps, and groped their way through the corridors to the open fantail.

The first round of the battle to save Argo Merchant *was over, won by the sea.*

"It was like moving around in a strange house which was covered with oil in the middle of the night in the midst of an earthquake," another man recalled.

Helicopters which had been roosting on the nearby cutters rose and hovered overhead. One by one, the exhausted, oil-soaked men were hoisted off and returned to their ships. The first round of the battle to save *Argo Merchant* was over, won by the sea. However, even as they departed, a new round was commencing — a fresh assault by men and equipment.

At 8 A.M. that morning, soon after the grounded tanker was located, a summons had gone out to the headquarters of the Coast Guard's Atlantic Strike Team in Elizabeth City, North Carolina — one of three strike teams comprising a national force specially trained and equipped to move swiftly against oil spills, chemicals, and any other hazardous substances that may threaten U.S. waterways, the Great Lakes, or the American coastline. Each team of twenty men could respond with tons of heavy equipment to any pollution emergency within a few hours. Living "on-call" like firemen, the teams were constantly in the air en route to disasters occurring from Alaska to Florida. At the request of foreign governments, they had also fought tanker emergencies and oil spills as far away as Singapore and the southern tip of South America.

By 10:30 A.M., the strike team's advance party was on its way to Cape Cod aboard a large C-130 cargo plane laden with heavy pumps, booms, boats, and skimmers. Throughout the day, more equipment and men were shuttled northward. Vessels stood by to transport them out to the *Argo*, but seas were building and the wind was rising, making any transfer to the tanker impossible.

At 7:30 P.M., a Coast Guard helicopter lifted off from Otis AFB and flew southeast toward the shoals. Crouched in a jump seat was the leader of the strike team, Lt. Commander Barry Chambers, clad in jumpsuit, boots, and white hardhat fitted with a two-way radio.

The helicopter flew south until it picked up a cluster of bobbing lights from cutters *Vigilant* and *Sherman*, stationed near the *Argo Merchant*. Switching on searchlights, the pilots began circling and scanning the sea until they focused on the massive tanker hull.

"There she is," the pilot said. "We'll drop you on the stern."

Chambers rose, flipping up his jump seat. Behind him, the helicopter crew chief slid open a side hatch. A light steel basket was attached to a steel cable connected to a winch atop the helicopter. Chambers ducked inside the basket and sat hunched up with his knees against his chin and his head tucked low. The helicopter dropped down and moved in toward the stern of the tanker. The basket with Chambers inside was swung out and dangled. An icy blast of wind and turbulence from the whirling helicopter blades sent the basket spinning. It swung back and forth over the black ocean, narrowly missing the tanker's stack and the wires of the ship's radio antenna.

"Ten more feet," Chambers said into his mike. The hoist cable was slacked off, lowering the basket.

"Steady," Chambers said. He reached out and seized a stanchion on the tanker's stern, swung out of the basket, and landed on the *Argo Merchant* deck. In rapid succession, two more strike team members, Chuck McKnight and Keith Darby, were lowered from the helicopter with bags of tools, cutting torches, and air tanks.

"Take the engine room," Chambers said to them. "I'll check the bridge." Because of their specialized training, the three had no difficulty in finding their way around the dark, heaving ship. Moving through deserted corridors, Chambers emerged on an open catwalk and, dodging sheets of spray, ran forward to the main deckhouse. Hastening up staircases and through a chilly, dimly lit lounge where the remaining handful of *Argo's* crew lay bundled up in blankets, he mounted to the bridge and noted the compass heading of the ship and her degree of list so as to be able to detect any further shifting or sinking into the shoal. Hurrying back to the engine room, he descended the steel ladders and joined McKnight and Darby, who were measuring the depth of the lake of oil and water.

"How deep?" he asked.

"Twenty feet," McKnight replied. "About two feet of oil on top."

"We've got to start pumping tonight," Chambers said. Making radio contact with *Vigilant's* captain, he said, "Tell Otis I want my ADAPTS pump out here right away."

The team relied heavily on an ADAPTS system — a combination of powerful submersible pump and diesel engine capable of pumping a thousand gallons of oil a minute, or if necessary, a mixture of oil and water. Unlike the small emergency pumps used by the earlier damage-control parties, the ADAPTS system could take the gooey mass of seawater and oil without fouling. The strike team had brought three of these systems with them from Elizabeth City, each 5,000-pound unit secured to a pallet which could be lifted by a ship's crane or heavy helicopter. Too big to be loaded inside a helicopter, the pallet could be suspended beneath it by a sling. Never before had an attempt been made to deliver an ADAPTS system to a tanker in the open ocean in the middle of the night.

At the Coast Guard Air Station at Otis AFB, tractors hauled the ADAPTS to an open apron. A large helicopter rose and hovered over the pallet to which it was secured by a steel cable harness. With engines roaring, the helicopter lifted the heavy load and headed out to sea. Aboard *Argo Merchant*, Chambers and his men prepared for the arrival of their ADAPTS. There was a snap and a roar as acetylene torches were ignited, and then blue flashes and streams of yellow sparks as they burned away ship railings, stanchions, and wireless antenna so that the huge pumping system could be eased down onto the open main deck, with easy access to the engine room. By 11:30 P.M., the helicopter, bulky load lit by floodlights, had reached the tanker, and issuing instructions by radio, Chambers and his men got the load lowered and lashed down on the open main deck. Stripping off the waterproof casing, they set about rigging six-inch hoses in the engine room and firing up the diesel engine.

At midnight, Chambers discovered that *Argo Merchant* was settling further into the shoal. The list to starboard had increased — the portholes of the crew's quarters would soon be underwater. Unless they were closed tightly, the entire after-deckhouse would flood, and the sea would pour down into the engine room. But when Chambers and his men sought entrance to the crew's cabins through the dark, oil-slicked corridors, they discovered that the evacuated crew members had left their cabins locked, so that the portholes were inaccessible. The strike team attacked the cabin doors with fire axes and crowbars. Between midnight and 3 A.M., they battered and pried their way into fifteen cabins only to find that the portholes themselves resisted closing, having been painted and repainted for years, and never dogged down properly. It took the team another hour of hammering to get the portholes shut and sealed.

The ADAPTS pump had been going full blast, pulling torrents of oil and water out of the engine room. At 4 A.M., Chambers was heartened to see that the huge pump was holding its own against the flooding. Indeed the level of the lake in the engine room was dropping at a rate of eight inches an hour.

The mass of congealing oil floating on the surface still held some heat from the cargo tanks, and this now made the engine room the warmest place on the ship. Sitting in the darkness on a steel grating, Chambers and McKnight were taking a pre-dawn break from their labors when Chambers swept the beam of his flashlight over the bulkhead that towered above them and saw trickles of oil around the rivets.

Not good news, he realized. It meant that oil from the cargo tanks was flooding the pump room. The bulkhead was "bleeding"; they were sitting under a dam that might burst.

As dawn broke over the ocean, the wind slackened and the battering seas were reduced to long swells. On shore, mobilization of men and equipment had continued throughout the night, and reinforcements were on their way. From Woods Hole the Coast Guard buoy tender *Bittersweet* sailed with two more ADAPTS pumping systems and more members of the strike team. Barges were being towed from Rhode Island, and the seagoing tug *Sheila Moran* was en route from New York.

If the pumps could stop the flooding, and the barges could be brought alongside the *Argo Merchant*, it might be possible to off-load part of the cargo of oil and haul the tanker off the shoals.

Never before had such a large, heavily laden tanker been aground in the open Atlantic and never before had there been an attempt to maneuver barges, tugs, and ships under such extremely difficult and dangerous conditions, but Chambers felt that the effort had to be made. "When a fire department has a big one," he said, "they don't stand around and ask, 'Gee, should we try to put this out?' You've got to go in and fight."

Bittersweet was on the scene by early afternoon. With a remarkable display of seamanship, the tender moved in alongside the *Argo*, and the two new ADAPTS systems were lifted by a boom and swung aboard the tanker. In heaving seas, more strike-team members leaped across the gap between the tender and the tanker to join the battle.

One of the ADAPTS soon was adding to the effort to pump out the engine room. The other was set to work to pump out No. 5 cargo tank to lessen the pressure on the bulkhead that was threatening to collapse. Generators and banks of baseball-stadium floodlights were rigged to illuminate the decks of the tanker throughout the night. In the *Argo* dining room, Chambers spread blueprints of the ship's hull on the table and conferred with a salvage expert about the swiftest way to proceed.

But as the afternoon light faded, a severe winter storm bore down on the shoals. As the wind rose, mountainous seas hurled themselves against the tanker, surging across the open deck and swirling around the men who were struggling with heavy hose lines.

Geysers of black oil began spurting out of ullage caps and vents on the main deck. The bottom plates of the tanker's hull were opening up. As the sea forced itself into the cargo tanks, enormous pressures were building up in the hull. "Lines were screaming and whistling. Oil was shooting up all over the place," one member of the strike team remembered.

Down below in the engine room, the flood of oil and water now was rising faster than the ADAPTS system could pump it out. Eerily creaking and groaning as steel twisted and parted, the hull was surrendering to the sea. As they abandoned the engine room, strike team members found the decks in the passageways buckling. Overhead steel girders were ramming through the walls.

Searchlights stabbed through the darkness. The tug *Sheila Moran* had arrived from New York. Despite the storm, the tug's captain radioed to Chambers that he was prepared to try to put hawsers aboard and attempt to pull the tanker off the shoal, but Chambers replied that he would prefer the tug just stand by.

". . . if we went under there was no way they could have launched a boat in those seas to save us."

Later he explained, "There wasn't a prayer that he could have moved us, but if he had, I felt we might be worse off. We had lost the engine room. The bulkheads were ready to pop. In deeper water we might capsize or drift into a more hazardous position. There were sixteen of us still aboard, and it seemed quite likely that the ship might break up during the night. *Vigilant* and *Sherman* were out there, too, but if we went under, no way could they have launched a boat in those seas to save us."

Chambers recalled finding grim humor in the protestations of the *Argo Merchant* captain. "There he was with his ship on the shoals, and everybody's life including his own in danger, but the sight of that tug scared him even more. He was afraid if they put a line aboard they'd have a salvage claim which would get him into deeper trouble with the ship's owners — as if that were possible."

At 9:10 P.M., the storm-lashed Coast Guard Air Station at Otis AFB on Cape Cod received an urgent message from the *Vigilant*:

"ADVISED BY COMMANDER CHAMBERS *ARGO MERCHANT* TAKING ON WATER ALL COMPARTMENTS THROUGHOUT THE SHIP. BULKHEADS AND DECKS BUCKLING, IMMEDIATE EVACUATION REQUESTED."

In a few minutes pilots Wallace and Prindle and their crew boarded their large helicopter. A tractor towed them out of the hangar. The helicopter rocked and swayed, buffeted by winds and by sheets of rain that reduced visibility to near zero. At 9:25 P.M., they lifted off and headed out to sea where they found themselves in a driving snowstorm.

Flying with their gaze fixed on the radar screen, they listened as a smaller helicopter launched from *Sherman* succeeded in plucking seven men off the *Argo*. Visibility was so poor that the helicopter nearly landed on the tug *Sheila Moran*, wallowing nearby in the heavy seas, and came just short of skidding off the icy flight deck of *Sherman* into the ocean.

"We stayed up in the clouds to keep from icing up," Wallace reported. "We knew we were in for a rough pickup because of the gusting winds, rain, and snow. When we had the *Argo* in sight on our radar, we dropped down to about a hundred feet above the sea, switched on our floodlights, and eased in toward the stern. We could see waves breaking over the starboard side of the tanker and sweeping across the main deck. There was a small group of people gathered up on the weather deck."

Hovering in the fury of the storm, Wallace and Prindle inched in until the stack of the tanker was just below them. Using the stack as a holding point, Wallace radioed to Chambers, "Stand by to come aboard."

Down from the helicopter went the steel basket with a long line trailing from it. Strike team members seized the line and guided it down.

By radio Chambers signalled, "Haul away."

Up, one by one, came a stream of men — civilians, the last of the *Argo's* crew, and members of the strike team.

"We knew they were coming aboard," Prindle recalled, "because even up forward in the cockpit we could smell the oil. They were all drenched with it."

Next to last to leave the *Argo Merchant* was her captain, clutching a suitcase and a burlap sack from which emanated the plaintive wails of the ship's cat. Last to depart was Chambers, still sending a stream of radio reports to *Vigilant* to be relayed to Boston and Washington. A midnight Coast Guard dispatch summed it up:

"Advised *Argo* flooding rapidly in all spaces. Bulkheads and decks buckling. Evacuation of sixteen people on board completed. Chambers reports vessel fairly well grounded. Starboard side unworkable due to seas breaking over deck. Ports awash in after deckhouse. Starboard side flooding in staterooms. Vessel has 6-10 degree list. Pump room bulkhead buckling due to hogging. Some cargo tanks now open to sea. *Sheila Moran* and *Vigilant* maintaining watch with searchlights."

Throughout the night and into the next day the storm battered the abandoned tanker. That afternoon, strike team members Chuck McKnight and Keith Darby, who had spent the night on the *Sherman*, were again ferried to the *Argo* by helicopter. The stern had sunk so far that it was necessary to lower them to the main deck forward of the bridge. Rigging lifelines to protect themselves, the men ventured aft and found that the sea had engulfed the engine room and staterooms. The heavy ADAPTS pumping systems were afloat and awash. Oil spurting from ruptured deck lines and vents befouled the tanker from stem to stern. Steel beams projected into passageways as if fired from a cannon. "She was crumpling like a sardine can," McKnight remarked. At 4:30 P.M. Friday, they were hoisted aboard the helicopter and flown to Otis AFB, where Chambers awaited their report.

It was clear to all that despite the monumental effort and risk to life, the sea and the weather had won round two. All hope of refloating the *Argo Merchant* was now abandoned. "If we couldn't save the ship, we could still try to save the oil and prevent the spill," Chambers said.

Tugs and barges now were standing by in New Bedford and on Martha's Vineyard. To bring them safely alongside the tanker, "Yokohama fenders," immense rubber cylinders nine feet in diameter and eighteen feet long, had been flown up from Elizabeth City and would be rigged on the side of the *Argo Merchant*. Since the fenders were too large to be transported to the shoals by boat, an Army Skycrane helicopter was flown into Otis from Virginia. The fenders were slung beneath the Skycrane and the Army pilots, not used to maneuvering at sea, were escorted out to the *Argo* by Coast Guard helicopters.

To anchor the barges, destroyer mooring buoys were loaded aboard the buoy tenders *Bittersweet* and *Spar* at Woods Hole. Each mooring buoy would be anchored to the bottom by an 8,000-pound fluke anchor and a 12,000-pound concrete block. The bow anchors of the *Argo* would also be set out by the tug *Sheila Moran*.

By Sunday afternoon the Yokohama fenders had been lowered into place. During the night the winds rose again on the shoals. Huge seas picked up the giant fenders as if they were scraps of lumber and tossed them up on the main deck. Again the Skycrane was dispatched to the scene so that the strike team could re-rig the fenders.

All day Monday Chambers and his men worked furiously to prepare for off-loading the *Argo's* cargo of oil, which they hoped could begin the next morning. Oil now coated the decks of the tanker to a depth of several inches, and men were constantly slipping, sliding, and falling. To release the port bow anchor, Keith Darby was lowered by ropes tied to his ankles through an 18-inch hawser pipe. Dangling over the icy sea, he cut the shackles to free the anchor. The tug *Sheila Moran* moved in and, after several failures, succeeded in implanting the port anchor 150 feet from the ship. But the tug's heavy hawsers snapped repeatedly as a similar effort was made to set out the starboard anchor.

On shore, as the press and public became aware of the Coast Guard's last-ditch fight to prevent an oil spill, a clamor arose to bomb the tanker or set her afire with incendiary devices.

"Why don't they burn her?" was asked repeatedly.

"Because," explained Chambers, "you can't burn No. 6 fuel oil unless it's heated to a liquid and surrounded by plenty of oxygen. The *Argo's* oil had cooled and thickened to the consistency of chocolate pudding. And most of it is inside the cargo tanks. There is no way we can set it afire and keep the fire going."

The *Calico Jack*, a 165-foot vessel used to service off-shore oil rigs, was due in Woods Hole with a steam generator to heat the oil so that it could be pumped into barges. All that was needed to commence the effort was a respite from the North Atlantic winter weather.

No respite was to come. By Monday afternoon the barometer was dropping, new gale warnings were flying, and seas were building on the shoals. Work aboard the tanker was a nightmare. The ship lurched and shuddered as huge seas bore down upon her and burst thunderously against the port side, while currents dragged on the keel. At dusk, Chambers and the last of his men were hoisted off by helicopter. As they flew. toward shore, weather forecasters reported that winds were swinging to northwest, gusting from forty to sixty knots.

The final moments of the drama were at hand.

By midnight, winds on the shoals approached hurricane violence. Blinding flurries of sleet and snow blotted out all visibility. The cutter *Vigilant* and the tug *Sheila Moran*, stationed two miles from the *Argo*, plunged and rolled through a screaming gale. Both vessels were coated with a heavy mantle of ice. Their crews, bruised and battered, clung to stanchions or lay seasick on the deck. Every three hours, the tug moved in closer to focus its powerful searchlights on the tanker to see if she was surviving the storm.

At dawn, Commander Edward Cruikshank took *Vigilant* in for a closer look. The bow of the *Argo* had risen, and the stern had sunk deeper into the shoals. At 8:30 A.M., Cruikshank and his operations officer went out to the wing of the cutter's bridge. Before their eyes, *Argo Merchant* was sagging; she could take no more. As they watched, the bow section wrenched free and pivoted slowly, jackknifing alongside the stern, twisting skyward. Breakers triumphantly engulfed the wreck. The sea boiled with brown foam as seven and a half million gallons of oil began to spill.

The desperate battle was over. Now the threat became a ghastly reality. Oil, gushing from the *Argo's* broken hull, formed a black river in the ocean, sixty-five miles long and thirty-five miles wide. During the week it spread across three thousand square miles of ocean and became the most gigantic oil spill in American history.

Oceanographic research ships and Coast Guard vessels steamed into the spill to conduct tests and collect samples of seawater and ocean bottom, nosing among blobby black pancakes of oil which in some places were five feet thick. Search planes and earth satellites tracked and filmed it. Nightly on TV, millions stared with horrified fascination at the malevolent stain upon the sea.

Scientists declared that it was impossible to predict the spill's movements or calculate the impact on all that lay in its path. If it drifted eastward, it could invade the famed fisheries of Georges Bank, smothering the spawning grounds and destroying the plankton on which fish feed. If it moved south, it might envelop the eastern tip of Long Island. Or it might enter the Gulf Stream and be carried to the shores of Europe.

If it moved north, the oil would blacken the beaches, coves, harbors, and wetlands of the New England coast, wreaking havoc on the environment. Already the first victims of the spill were appearing on the beaches of the islands and the Cape. The bodies of hundreds of ducks, gulls, and loons washed ashore. Scores more, so soaked with oil that they could no longer fly, stood shivering and picking at their feathers in the chill winter winds.

Over Christmas, anxiety and suspense mounted as the edge of the giant island of oil crept to within twenty-three miles of Nantucket. A wind shift to the east would put it ashore in a few hours. An army of scientists, servicemen, and state and federal motorized equipment was mobilized. Squads of men in jeeps and on foot patrolled the beaches of the islands and Cape Cod. At Woods Hole, long lines of trucks and trailers laden with oil booms, skimmers, shovels, rakes, and chemicals stood by to be ferried to the islands.

But the wind shift did not come. The same howling northwest winter gales that had raged over the *Argo Merchant* now worked to spare New England as they drove the spill out to sea. As bells tolled in the New Year, the spill dispersed out to sea, breaking up into smaller blobs of oil, mixing with the seawater, vanishing toward the ocean bottom, leaving an aftermath whose effects were unknown and which scientists would be studying and debating for years to come.

DID THE *ARGO* TRY TO "SHOOT THE SHOALS"?

Argo Merchant was due in Salem, Massachusetts, at 5 P.M., to catch the high tide. If it missed the tide, it would have to lay outside the harbor for twelve hours before it could discharge its oil. In the shipping business, such delays are costly. Maritime experts have wondered whether the *Argo's* captain was deliberately and recklessly cutting across Nantucket Shoals to reach Salem by 5 P.M. when he ran aground.

Veteran fishermen whose draggers and "long-liners" frequent the shoals believe he was. "He was 'cutting the guzzle,' " says a Cape Cod captain. "We see them doing it all the time. They come barreling through the shoals at about thirty knots, tearing up our fishing gear, and making us dodge to keep from being run down."

Ordeal on Goose Rocks

*A day sail in a chartered boat. Suddenly strong
winds, steep waves, and, without lifelines or
safety harness, the inevitable ...*

By Lionel W. Taylor

"This beats working anytime," I said to my wife as I floated on my stomach watching *Sitzmark*, my 27-foot sailing charter, hover like a mirage on a shimmering blue mirror thirty feet away. Her sails hung lifelessly on a mast whose present duty was only to serve as an oversize drying pole in the breathless still of a completely calm Long Island Sound. Tossing a couple of lines overboard so we could climb back aboard, we had left *Sitzmark* earlier, to cool ourselves off in the tepid water. The fog, which had accompanied us since soon after leaving the sand pits of Port Jefferson, Long Island, surrounded us like a soft cottony womb shutting us off from the rest of our watery world. Far off we could hear an occasional fog horn of a passing power boat feeling her way to New York or one of the many intervening harbors. We had been up since seven that morning intending to get underway early for the twenty-one-mile crossing from Long Island to Branford, Connecticut. Soon after leaving the Mt. Misery shoal buoy astern, we could see a wall of what appeared to be low-lying clouds approaching from the eastern horizon. We were soon surrounded by a dense wet fog. The light wind that was blowing wavered a bit, switched direction once or twice, and then died away, leaving the fog in control. That's when we decided to have our swim. But now we were sailing again. A slight stirring of the fog and a feathery rippling on the water got us back aboard quickly, hoping this was the advance guard of a rising afternoon sea breeze. Wisps of thinning fog went drifting by, pursued by a series of wind puffs. Soon a bow wave was gurgling merrily under *Sitzmark's* white stem. "I wonder where we are," I said to my wife as I slipped a pair of trousers over my damp bathing suit. "There's a strong easterly set in this part of the Sound that could have a greater effect on our course than I'd planned. At the rate we're moving now, it won't be long until we know."

We must have been no more than a quarter the way across the Sound, however, because the afternoon wore on without a landfall. The breeze slowly increased until white horses were galloping almost everywhere on the watery plateau that surrounded us. It was a glorious sail. The sun was getting low in the western horizon when Fay called out, "There it is!"

The Connecticut shore appeared on our starboard bow, jagged vertical lines marking headlands, church steeples, and radio towers, still too far away to identify, filled in the horizon.

"Keep a sharp lookout to port for Negro Heads buoy," I called. "It marks the entrance to the Branford channel."

As we approached the shore, the waves became short and steep in the shallow water. My father-in-law's dinghy, which my wife had insisted on bringing, was acting like a recalcitrant puppy on a leash. Her towline would become alternately slack, as she slid down a wave, then taut as she dug her stern into a deep following trough.

The coastline was coming up quickly. In fact, I could see waves breaking on some rocks dead ahead, but still some distance away. Nothing about the surroundings looked familiar. We must have missed Negro Heads buoy because by this time we were well within the entrance to a large bay bounded by a steep headland on the eastern side.

"There's no headland to starboard of the Branford channel — just a series of small islands called the Thimbles," I mused. "See if we can see a red Number-Two buoy to starboard. Wherever we are there has to be a channel to safer water ahead." My wife quickly brought an end to that idea, as she called to tell me there were two red buoys just off to starboard, and breakers dead ahead where the channel should have been.

"Ready about," I said. "We're going back into deeper water until I find out where we are."

With *Sitzmark* beating out of the bay, we got a taste of how strong the wind and how steep the seas had become. Immediately after coming about, *Sitzmark* stood on her beam's end. The boat partially righted herself as I let the mainsheet run. The wind was blowing half a gale, and sheets of spray flew back into the cockpit as *Sitzmark* fell off a comber with a crash into a deep wave trough below. The dinghy behind us was swinging madly from side to side, half full of water.

"We've got to get some sail off the boat to stop this pounding," I shouted. My wife only nodded woodenly and looked apprehensively at the plunging foredeck, now under water, now pointed high in the air.

By dint of her deep keel, *Sitzmark* was slowly clawing her way off the perilous lee shore, and the breakers were receding in the distance behind us. I didn't want to let on to my wife that I was hopelessly lost. I couldn't for the life of me match the water-smeared lines and numbers on the chart with the rapidly receding shoreline. We were nowhere near Branford, of that I was sure. The real question was how far east had we been set during the prolonged calm.

Then things happened so fast I didn't get a chance to study the chart further. A sudden loud report came from the stern.

"We've just lost the dinghy," I groaned. The painter had snapped a foot below where it passed over *Sitzmark's* transom.

Since the dinghy was not mine, I felt it mandatory, despite conditions, to try to get her back. Although she drifted downwind like a grounded weather balloon in an Artic gale, *Sitzmark* could outsail that drift. In steepening seas, I maneuvered under her lee and let the dinghy drift downwind to me, the freed sail and sheets pounding and thrashing as if all the furies of hell were shaking them. After a few hair-raising near misses, Fay leaned over the windward rail and picked up the severed painter. Knotting and doubling up on the line, I got the dinghy back in tow.

We came about again and started our long thrash back to windward and safety. Waves seemed to be coming from every direction, as if we were sailing in a bathtub.

"What a dummy I've been," I thought. A passage in the cruising guide came back to me, " . . . it is a regular saucer bowl and in hard southwesters is apt to roll the sticks out of you."

This was Joshua Cove and the headland off to port was Sachem Head. We couldn't have found a worse lee shore! Looking back I thought I could see masts bobbing behind a point of rock upon which waves were breaking heavily. Should we go back now and try to find the entrance in the failing light and heavy seas?

A loud report from the stern made the decision for me. The dinghy was adrift again.

So, back we went, chasing a darting, swooping will-o'-the-wisp. In attempting to get close, I hit the dinghy broadside, splintering a few topside planks, as a sudden gust of wind pushed her on to *Sitzmark's* stem.

"That's it. I've had it. Let her go," I said reluctantly.

Convinced of the dire need to reduce sail, Fay crept forward to lower the jib that had been overpowering us since the blow began. She bravely climbed on to the trampoline that was *Sitzmark's* foredeck, now under water, now heaving skyward. Without lifelines or a safety harness, the inevitable happened. As my wife reached back for the jib halyard cleat on the mast, the boat suddenly reeled to an exceptionally steep sea. With a

cry, she tumbled backwards overboard. Because she was wearing a life-jacket, she came up quickly close aboard. I let the mainsheet run and pulled the tiller toward me hard, pushing the bow in my wife's direction, but turning the rising stern away from her head. Seconds later, I threw the bitter end of the slack mainsheet over the lee rail as she drifted by.

The good Lord was with us. She caught the line and hung on, dragging along behind a decelerating *Sitzmark*.

I got Fay aboard more easily than I expected. As a big wave approached from the stern and raised her to almost deck level, my wife automatically fended the transom off with her feet like a rappeller does the side of a cliff. I gave a quick tug on the inboard bight of the mainsheet, and suddenly there she was — sitting astride the transom like a popped champagne cork.

I looked around, with Fay exhausted and shaken in the flooded cockpit. The dinghy was just a dot to leeward, and we were drifting downwind fast onto an outcropping of rock not fifty yards away. As I wrestled with *Sitzmark's* tiller to come about, I knew with a sinking sensation that she didn't have the time or room to claw her way off as she had before. Successive seas struck the boat broadside, driving her the remaining distance to the rocks. With a heavy lurch to starboard, *Sitzmark* was aground. We were almost thrown out of the cockpit by the impact. *Sitzmark's* keel grated over the unseen rocks below. Then she slowly righted herself, as her keel bumped clear into the deeper water between the jagged heads.

I grabbed my wife under the arms and lifted her to her feet. She was almost deadweight, with little strength left to help herself. Her eyes were glazed, and she was shaking with the cold.

"We'll step off the stern into the water with the next grounding. When you come up, walk that way (I pointed to the east) until you're into deep water. I'll be right behind you."

"No, no," she cried, trying to pull away from me. "Cold . . . cold," she shuddered.

"Yes, I know," I said firmly, "but we must go. We can't stay here. *Sitzmark* is going to break up, and we'll drown." *Sitzmark's* keel bounced hard, once, twice. She was hard aground. As another wave approached, I dropped Fay off the stern and followed with *Sitzmark's* unshipped mainsheet clutched in my hand. The cold water was over my head as the next big comber lifted *Sitzmark's* stern. The boat rumbled by, carried higher on the rocks. I was thrown like a rag doll against the barnacle-infested rocks, badly scraping the side of my head and my left arm.

I came up in a welter of foam, and in my ears was the sound of surf and *Sitzmark* pounding heavily on her starboard side behind me. Fay was on her feet ahead of me wading unsteadily toward the eastern end of the reef and deep water. After the next wave surfed by, we came up together, clear of the rocks and floating in deep water.

Sitzmark had gone aground on Goose Rocks, a small outcrop about three-quarters of a mile southwest of Sachem Head Harbor. It was marked at the time by a red bell buoy anchored some 300 yards to the south in deep water.

Before Fay and I waded into deeper water, I heard the clanging of a bell buoy off to my right (that I hadn't noticed an hour before!). Deciding that shore was too far away for us to swim toward, I took a bearing on the buoy before the summer twilight faded into darkness.

"We can't stay here. Sitzmark is going to break up, and we'll drown."

The incoming tide was getting ready to turn, so the 300-yard swim from Goose Rocks to the buoy was accomplished with little difficulty in the slack but still rough water. Having to swim that distance contributed further to Fay's exhaustion, but the exercise seemed to revive and cheer her considerably.

Arriving at the foot of the buoy, I coiled *Sitzmark's* mainsheet in my left hand while holding the boat's boom claw (a U-shaped attachment sometimes used for securing a sheet to a boat's main boom) in my right. I backed off from the shadowy, clanging monster. Treading water as hard as I could, I got my right arm out of the water far enough to heave the claw at the buoy, hoping to entangle it in the superstructure. In the dark, I could hear the clanking sound of fiberglass seeking a toehold in the steel. When the noise stopped, I gave the line a pull; the claw splashed as it slid off the deck of the buoy, and the line went slack.

I recoiled the sheet and tried again. This time it held. Although we now had something to hold on to, the benefits were marginal. During the period of slack water, we were able to drop the line and swim around to keep warm. With the changing of the tide, however, the strong ebb flow forced us to hang on to our umbilical cord to avoid being swept away. An hour later, we were both chattering with the cold.

I tried getting my wife up on the the tilting buoy's deck, fearing the effects of hypothermia if we remained in the cold water much longer. After a couple of bruising slips on the green weed growing on the bobbing buoy's waterline, we gave up. I tried to keep up a cheerful chatter in the interim, but after a few feeble attempts at conversation, Fay lapsed into a morose silence.

Through it all the bell on the buoy kept up an incessant, nerve-shattering clanging. Although the wind backed and died, there was still a good sea running, and the buoy reacted in a horrible manner. It bucked and rolled, bumped and pitched, with the bell clapper whacking the stationary rim so savagely I was sure it would fall off.

Nerves taut, Fay shouted at me angrily through blue lips, "How much longer do you expect me to stay here? Why hasn't someone come to get us off? If only we hadn't gone on this silly cruise. . . ."

I tried to calm her by telling her that help would be arriving soon, knowing full well that if someone in a house on shore or on a boat on the Sound had seen our predicament, assistance should have arrived long before. I also knew I didn't have the strength to hang onto the buoy much longer or make the long swim to shore for help.

In this desperate moment, I heard the faint sound of a boat's engine coming from the entrance to Sachem Head Harbor. Pivoting around for a better look, I saw the bright green eye of a boat's starboard running light. It was some distance away on a course parallel to the headland and was headed out toward the Sound. We whooped and hollered, but she was too far away for our voices to be heard.

As the boat drew abreast the point, she suddenly turned around and headed in our direction until I could see both red and green running lights at the same time. I was never so glad to be on a collision course with a power vessel in all my life! We shouted and called until a light from the boat caught us in its beam. We were saved.

Later, as we sat in a cozy Sachem Head kitchen drinking steaming hot coffee supplied by the wife of our rescuer, we heard their story:

Yes, they had seen us in the late afternoon beating back and forth off Sachem Head. When we disappeared soon before dark, they assumed we had come into the harbor for the night, until my father-in-law's dinghy drifted onto their beach. With the condition of the wind and tide, they correctly assumed it belonged to the boat they had seen earlier.

However, it was the battered condition of the dinghy's planking that caused them to be concerned for our safety.

Goaded on by his wife's urgings, our host drove to the Sachem Head Yacht Club to ascertain if a visiting yacht had recently anchored in the harbor. When the club steward answered in the negative, they decided to take the club launch and investigate.

I had to grin as my wife reminded me, "I told you to take my father's dinghy on the cruise. I had a feeling it would come in handy."

Since then I have not disdained a woman's intuition.

Wolf Pack Attack

"We are surrounded by at least six U-boats, and are expecting an attack as it gets dark. Be prepared!"

BY OLIVER M. SALISBURY

I n September, 1942, I was assigned to a ship which I was to join in Philadelphia. After the going-away parties, my wife Norma, her sister Betty, and brother-in-law Natie went to the train with me. The parting was the usual hugs, kisses, tears, and handkerchief-waving as the train pulled away.

At the dock in Philadelphia where the ship was tied up, I saw hundreds of General Sherman tanks, all with Russian markings on them. I knew immediately my destination would be Murmansk, the northern port of the U.S.S.R., because these tanks were being loaded onto the SS *Charles Carroll*, my assigned ship.

The *Charles Carroll* was Liberty Ship Hull No. 2, the second one of those famous wartime ships to be launched. This was not her maiden voyage; she had already been out to India and back. In two or three days all the tanks had disappeared into the holds of the vessel, which carried in addition two huge railroad locomotives lashed to her deck. Their tremendous capacity for cargoes of a bulky nature and America's ability to run them out rapidly in great numbers made the liberty ships an important factor in winning World War II.

I met Captain George Evanson, an old-timer at sea though only about fifty years of age. He had commanded a Navy mine-sweeper in the North Sea in World War I. His greeting was somewhat ominous — "Sparks, I'm happy to have a veteran radio operator rather than a kid just out of school for this trip."

As the newly assigned officers and crew came aboard, it developed that most of them were survivors of the sinking of the SS *Express*. When the armed guard (Navy gun crew) came aboard, it turned out that they had also been reassigned from the ill-fated SS *Express*, which had been sunk by a Nazi U-boat off the West Coast of Africa. These men were on their first reassignment after surviving twenty-one days in a crowded lifeboat, followed by thirty days camped in the West African jungle, eating only birds, leaves, and fruit.

We sailed out through Chesapeake Bay on a dark night to rendez-vous with a convoy headed for Murmansk. Sometime during the next day I heard, "dit daa daa dit daa dit daa daa" crackle out from a coastal radio station, Morse signals for the *Charles Carroll's* secret wartime call letters, then a ciphered message. I hadn't expected to earn my keep quite so quickly. When decoded, the message to the captain read, "Your orders are cancelled. Report in to the Port of Boston for further orders."

Wartime procedure forbade breaking silence to acknowledge receipt of the message. You were just supposed to be on watch at that time and be alert enough to intercept it. Not to receive such a message could put your ship in the wrong place at the wrong time. Many stories about just that kind of thing were recited to us at the Radio Officers Convoy Procedure Briefings as examples of the cost of failure.

We docked at the Navy Yard in Boston, where the tanks were unloaded. We were to learn later that all convoys to Murmansk not already underway had been cancelled — the Nazis were annihilating

One of the first Liberty ships, photographed January 19, 1942, just before she departed on her maiden voyage.

them as they came into the North Sea. The German battleship *Tirpitz* was on the rampage and raising havoc.

A few days later we sailed again, this time loaded with ten thousand 100-gallon barrels of high-octane (aviation) gasoline for Great Britain. This was to fuel the start of the heavy bombardment of the German industrial cities.

Our convoy was not long in getting into action. The first night on the Atlantic, one ship rammed another. One sank and the other had to turn back. The air crackled with the SOS and rescue operations. Of course I didn't see any of it, but I heard it all in the radio room. It was a very black and foreboding night. Sort of set me up for what was to come.

In the first year of the war, there was only one radio operator to a merchant ship. We scheduled hours like two on and four off spread over twelve hours, and then the commodore ship, which carried several operators, could signal with flags or signal lamp for radio operators to get on watch and stand by, and they often did this. We were a slow, six-knot convoy consisting of forty-four merchant ships plus four Canadian corvettes as escort. We zigzagged on a route that took us far north into winter weather though it was only early October. The days aboard ship were humdrum, but the radio waves were exciting. I spent a lot of time in the radio room, even when not scheduled to be there. The Nazis were at the height of their submarine power, and we had not yet learned how to cope with the Wolf Pack attacks.

I heard the SSS followed by the ship's call letters (SSS was the submarine-sighting or enemy-action signal followed by the call letters of the ship) from a vessel in the convoy a day or two ahead of us getting torpedoed and sunk. It was not unusual to hear of fifteen or twenty ships being sunk in a single evening, and all day long isolated attacks were taking place. Ship's officers and crew members were constantly sticking their heads in the radio room door and asking, "What's going on, Sparks?"

I think they could tell by the expression on my face that I wasn't listening to an "Amos and Andy" comedy on the radio. I was very careful not to put out any information that could create panic and passed on to the Captain only information directed expressly to him. One night I logged twenty-three sinkings from another convoy, the last going into Murmansk, and I was glad our original orders had been changed. The enemy was attacking with bombers, submarines, fighter planes, and the *Tirpitz*.

Five or six days out, just at dusk, the Canadian escort corvette pulled alongside with a megaphone and called out, "We are surrounded by at least six U-boats and are expecting a Wolf Pack attack as it gets dark. Be prepared!" I thought they were very cool about it, like hunters expecting a duck flight, except that we were the ducks.

All hands were alerted and at battle stations. I was glad that the War Shipping Administration had seen fit to armor-plate the radio room. They had found that when the enemy submarines chose to do battle from the surface, as they sometimes did, the first shell would be aimed at the radio room, so that the presence of the submarine could not be announced to other ships. The armor plate was psychologically comforting to me.

Shortly after dusk the first ship was torpedoed. The snappy SSS followed by our convoy call letters and the ship's letters crackled out so loud I knew it was one of ours even before he gave his identifying signal. The poor fellow never finished his message before I heard a big explosion from the cargo of high-octane gasoline aboard his ship. That night several more ships and their heroic crews went the same way. There were no survivors. It was all the four little Canadian corvettes could do to try and protect the ships that were still afloat. To stop to pick up survivors would only have cost more ships and their precious cargoes.

There was a huge Norwegian whaling vessel in our convoy; it looked like twenty thousand gross tons and perhaps six hundred feet long. The Nazis were hot after her; they put a hole in her the first night and another the second night, but she kept her position in the convoy. The third night they disabled her so that she could not maintain her position, but during the next day we could still see her, straggling unescorted several miles behind. That evening, just at dusk, black smoke belching from her stacks, she rejoined the convoy. Sailors on the decks of all ships cheered. I made a light "dit" on the radio telegraph key, and others in the convoy followed with dits from every ship except, I am sure, the Commodore's. He must have been furious, but what good was radio silence when you were surrounded by enemy submarines? It had to make that operator on duty aboard the whaler feel good, just as the sailors' cheers from on deck conveyed the crews' congratulations.

The fourth night of the attack, the dogged Wolf Pack came in and finished her off. She was still in sight, the sailors said, when I heard her "torpedoed and sinking" message.

On the fifth night of the Wolf Pack attack, we were in a tremendous North Atlantic blizzard. I was going on watch at midnight and having coffee in the mess room with the second mate, Cecil Davies, who was also going on watch. I said, "Cecil, no one could be mean enough to sink a ship on a night like this." I was hoping for a night of respite from the continuing attacks. The mate gave me a skeptical look, gulped his hot coffee, and left for the bridge. He had been on the SS *Express*, and knew just what the enemy could do.

One minute later I turned on the receiver in the radio room just in time to hear the SSS crackle out from a ship in our convoy, and the following boom of the ship's explosion. We were running in thirty-foot seas with high winds and blinding snow; it was very cold, but apparently submarines traveling under the waves were not affected by surface weather. At least they were able to sink several more ships that miserable night.

He had been on the SS Express, and knew just what the enemy could do.

At dawn, I heard a tragic drama in code on the radio. It was a lifeboat radio sending a message to one of our escort corvettes. I copied it into my radio log: "We are forty-one men. High seas and bitter cold. In immediate danger of swamping. Can you attempt rescue? Signed, the Captain."

The corvette answered, "WE WILL GIVE IT A TRY. SIGNED, COMMANDER."

The corvette's radio operator sent out, "NOW WE SEE YOU. NOW WE DON'T." I put that in the log too.

The lifeboat's radio operator said, "WE SEE YOU THIRTY DEGREES TO YOUR PORT AT A HUNDRED YARDS."

This exchange of "now we see you, now we don't" went on for ten or fifteen minutes.

The corvette's operator said, "YOU DISAPPEAR IN A DEEP TROUGH AND THEN REAPPEAR SOMEWHERE ELSE. WE SEE YOU AS YOU CREST A WAVE."

The lifeboat's operator answered, "I KNOW, BUT IT'S HARD TO KEEP FROM SWAMPING."

After about thirty minutes of this the commander of the corvette sent a message to the captain of the lifeboat saying, "I AM SORRY, WE MUST ABANDON YOU AND RETURN TO THE CONVOY."

The captain of the lifeboat replied with a short message, which his radio operator had difficulty transmitting, saying, "I UNDERSTAND. THANKS FOR A HARD TRY."

I never heard their signals again. In the bitter cold and with those seas they wouldn't survive the day. I put my head on the table and wept.

But we weren't done yet. We had been through six days and six nights of the Wolf Pack attack, had lost fourteen ships and their crews, in the neighborhood of a thousand men, with no survivors. I was on duty in the radio room in the afternoon when a tremendous "boom!" was felt and heard. I said aloud, "This is it! We've been torpedoed!" I counted to five, waiting for the ship to explode.

Then I heard machine-gun fire, and the phone from the bridge rang. Adrenalin took over. It was the Captain on the phone saying, "Send an SSS. There is a submarine in the center of the convoy!"

I said, "Yes sir!" and sat down and sent the message. Quickly a radio message snapped back, "CEASE FIRE, YOU ARE FIRING AT OUR TOWING

SPAR." I rang the bridge, but got no answer. (They were handling the ship from the flying bridge.) I ran topside, and the gunnery officer was screaming into his phones, "Fire one! Fire two!" He was really raking the water with shell fire. With his headset on, he could not hear me and shoved me away. I grabbbed him and jerked off his headset, yelling in his ear, "Cease fire!" He was hysterical with excitement at this point, and one of the mates helped me hold him until we got through to him. I'll give him credit, his gun crew was accurate: the towing spar went floating by, shot to pieces.

As we had been traveling in heavy fog, to avoid collision some ships put out a towing spar which makes a wake or spray about 200 feet astern of the ship's propeller, thus alerting the ship behind to her location. One of the Navy armed guard, unfamiliar with this procedure, had thought it to be a periscope and sounded the alarm. In such situations, the word was act first and check out later, since later might never come.

When we reached Liverpool, we learned that the deck of the ship immediately ahead had been sprayed by our machine-gun fire, and that the steward had broken his arm getting below deck. Fortunately, we did not hit them with the five-inch cannon which had caused the big boom. From this experience and later ones, I learned that false alarms can be more frightening than a real emergency.

We finally got an old four-stack destroyer down from Greenland that drove off the Wolf Pack. This was one of the old World War I destroyers we had given to the British before we were in the war. Had it not been for that destroyer, the Wolf Pack no doubt would have completely destroyed us, and I wouldn't be writing this story thirty-five years later.

We came into the Mersey River and to Mersey Side Docks, Liverpool, England, just twenty-one days out of Boston — a long three weeks; a gruesome three weeks. I was amused at the conversations in the mess room. All agreed that we should go to church in a body and give thanks to God for our safe arrival. This was as we relaxed at the sight of land. However, I noted when we were safely tied up at the dock, and the men started going ashore, not a word was said about thanking God or going to church, but a great many questions were being asked of the bobby on the deck about the nearest tavern.

Perhaps that is where the Lord himself would have directed us. What we needed after that Atlantic crossing was cheerfulness and friendliness. And we knew we still had to go back across.

Mission Most Secret, and Thereafter

"One of the darkest pages in naval history, and the worst tragedy at sea in the history of the U.S. Navy."

By Evan McLeod Wylie

I t was about noon on a hot, clear day when a sailor from the *Indianapolis* came to young Dr. Haynes to report a stomach ache. He confessed that he knew what caused it. He had swum over to a nearby island and had drunk too much ice-cold tomato juice.

Dr. Haynes listened sympathetically. All the men of the heavy cruiser were his patients, and he held sick call every morning. But this day was different. Haynes and the sailor were alone out on the ocean. There was no island and no tomato juice. Both were the hallucinations of a man dying of thirst, as the sailor and Haynes floated and drifted beneath a searing sun in the crystal clear waters of the western Pacific. The nearest land was hundreds of miles away.

It was a bizarre scene, but no more strange and unlikely than all the other events that marked the last voyage of the *Indianapolis* in the summer of 1945.

It had begun about two weeks earlier, at 4 A.M. on Monday, July 16, when a convoy of Army trucks escorted by heavily armed guards rolled into the fog-shrouded naval base at San Francisco and halted alongside the shadowy bulk of the heavy cruiser *Indianapolis*. While most of the men aboard ship slept, a deck gang unloaded a long heavy wooden crate from one of the trucks. A crane lifted the crate to the hangar deck of the cruiser, where it was immediately surrounded by an armed guard of Marines. Two Army officers stood by while a small heavy cylinder was removed from another truck, carried up the gangway by two sailors, and taken to an empty officer's cabin. Shipfitters were summoned to weld steel straps to the deck of the cabin. The cylinder was placed within the straps and secured with a heavy padlock by the two Army officers, who thereupon locked themselves in the cabin.

With her strange cargo aboard, the *Indianapolis* made ready for sea, and at 8:30 A.M., the big cruiser slipped out of San Francisco Bay and headed west into the Pacific Ocean. Only a handful of wives and families lined the Golden Gate Bridge to wave farewell as the ship passed beneath them, because the ship's departure was so sudden that it had caught the crew of 1,200 officers and men by surprise.

A proud veteran of virtually every major Pacific campaign from New Guinea to Iwo Jima and Okinawa, and presently the flagship of the Fifth Fleet, the *Indianapolis* had returned to California in April after being damaged by Japanese suicide planes. While the ship underwent extensive repairs, there had been time for the crew to be reunited with wives and sweethearts and to enjoy colorful San Francisco. It was believed that the *Indianapolis* would not rejoin the Pacific fleet until the end of summer. But on July 12, orders had suddenly been received to prepare to put to sea immediately. Leaves were cancelled. Telegrams summoned hundreds of the crew back from visits to their hometowns. Men were still streaming aboard on Sunday night. Many had no idea it would be the last night that their ship would spend in the States.

Steaming at top speed, *Indianapolis* reached Hawaii in a record-breaking three days, paused only long enough in Pearl Harbor to take aboard fuel and provisions, and departed immediately on a course that would take the ship to the central Pacific.

Captain Charles B. McVay, the skipper for the heavy cruiser, was

This snapshot of a group of Indianapolis *crew members arrived in the United States after many of the men pictured had perished at sea.*

well aware by this time that rumors were widespread throughout the crew about their ship's mission and the mysterious cargo they were carrying. Officers and men alike invented reasons to visit the airplane hangar amidships for a glimpse of the long wooden crate surrounded by Marine guards. In the mess halls and wardrooms, there were endless speculations that the crate contained gold from Fort Knox to bribe Japanese politicians into ending the war, a secret rocket, or enough germs to wipe out the Japanese army. It was assumed that Captain McVay, who seldom left the bridge as he directed the dash across the Pacific, knew the answer, but actually McVay knew little more than any of his sailors. When he had received the sudden summons to prepare to go to sea, he had merely been told that the *Indianapolis* had been chosen for an extraordinary mission. A top-secret cargo was to be guarded at all costs, even after the life of his vessel. If the *Indianapolis* were to be sunk, the cargo was to saved — in a lifeboat if necessary. Speed was essential because *"every day you save will cut the cost of the war."*

While the crew were wondering about the large crate in the hangar, McVay was equally baffled by the small cylinder in the locked flag officer's cabin, guarded night and day by the two Army officers.

Dr. Lewis Haynes was also mystified by the behavior of one of the two Army men, who had been introduced to him as a doctor. Haynes invited him to visit the ship's hospital and chat about medical matters but the officer's response had been so vague and elusive that Haynes had told himself, "This guy is no doctor. He may be an FBI agent. And he is in on a big secret."

The secret was that the *Indianapolis* had been entrusted with the most momentous cargo of World War II. Within the crate reposing in the hangar and in the cylinder bolted and welded to the deck in the locked officer's cabin were the crucial parts to the world's first atomic bomb. Inside the crate was a 15-foot-long cannon designed to hold two pieces of uranium-235. Inside the mysterious cylinder was a lead-sheathed cartridge containing a five-pound piece of uranium, the end result of the massive, top-secret Manhattan Project. When the cartridge was fired six feet down the barrel of the miniature cannon, it would ram into another mass of uranium. The combined mass would erupt into a mammoth nuclear explosion.

At daybreak on the very morning that the *Indianapolis* had steamed out of San Francisco, the first test firing of an atomic bomb had taken place in Alamogordo, New Mexico, leaving stunned observers spellbound with awe and fear as they saw a "flash of light not of this world, a light of many suns in one."

A coded message regarding the successful test had been sent to President Truman, meeting in Potsdam, Germany, with Stalin and Churchill. While the *Indianapolis* sped across the Pacific, Truman waited for word that the Japanese wished to negotiate peace. If it did not come, the order would be given to drop the bomb carried by the *Indianapolis*.

On Thursday, July 26, the ship reached the Mariana Islands in the Central Pacific and anchored off Tinian, which had become the main base for the B-29s that were bombing Japan. Already at the island were the bomber crews who had been training secretly for a year for the special mission. They were as much a subject of mystery and speculation as the cargo on the *Indianapolis*. As soon as the cruiser anchored offshore, she was surrounded by a swarm of small craft. An amphibious LCT was brought alongside. The mysterious crate and cylinder were deposited on the LCT, which headed for shore.

His mission accomplished, Captain McVay took the ship to neighboring Guam, Navy headquarters in the Pacific, for further orders. He was directed to proceed to the Philippines for further training, preparatory to the invasion of Japan. It was a Friday. Any one of a thousand circumstances might have delayed the departure of the ship, by hours or another day. But fate decreed otherwise, and on Saturday, at 9:10 A.M., *Indianapolis* departed without escort for Leyte in the Philippines.

At that moment, the Japanese submarine I-58, commanded by Mochitsura Hashimoto, arrived at a spot in the Pacific Ocean that lay midway between Guam and Leyte. Hashimoto surfaced and found nothing. However, he knew this was a principal crossroads route between Guam and Leyte. He decided to linger awhile in hopes of sighting a target.

By Sunday, *Indianapolis* was nearly halfway to the Philippines, steaming at moderate speed in the long Pacific swells. During the morning, Dr. Haynes assisted the ship's chaplain, Lieutenant T. M. Conway, with hymns for the church services. Gathering on the fantail, members of the crew joined in such famed sailors' hymns as:

> Eternal Father! Strong to save/Whose arm has bound
> the restless wave,/Who bidst the mighty ocean deep/Its
> own appointed limits keep:/Oh, hear us, when we cry
> to Thee/For those in peril on the sea.

In the tranquility of the moment, all danger seemed far away. The war had moved northward to Okinawa and the coast of Japan. This corner of the western Pacific was deserted. That evening, though the moon rose at 10:30 P.M., it was not visible in the clouded sky through which stars shone only dimly. The night was so dark that Captain McVay had directed that the zigzag course steered as a defense against submarines could be discontinued, to be resumed at the discretion of the officer in charge of the bridge. Leaving orders to call him if in doubt, McVay retired to his nearby cabin at 11:15 P.M.

In the warm, humid darkness of the tropical night, *Indianapolis* steamed toward Leyte, the silence broken only by the muffled whine of the engine turbines and the murmur of the ventilation blowers. Except for the men on watch on the bridge, in engine rooms or damage-control centers, and scattered groups engaged in card games, bull sessions, and reading or writing letters, the ship slept. On the bridge, it was so dark that the men of the watch could not make out each other's faces. The ship's new engineering officer, Richard Redmayne, of Kittery Point, Maine, was looking forward to his relief, who would arrive when all watches changed at midnight.

Bringing his binoculars to bear on the eastern horizon, Hashimoto saw a dark silhouette outlined against the moonglow.

Toward 11:30 P.M. the sky brightened as the clouds broke open. The moon, rising higher in the sky, was now intermittently visible. On the Japanese submarine *I-58*, Hashimoto roused his crew. All Sunday the submarine had remained deeply submerged to avoid detection. Now Hashimoto took his ship to battle stations and rose silently to scan the horizon. As the sub reached the surface, the moon broke through the clouds again, and the officer on the bridge exclaimed, "Possible enemy ship!" Bringing his binoculars to bear on the eastern horizon, Hashimoto saw a dark silhouette outlined against the moonglow.

Quickly he ordered another dive. Then, once more safely beneath the sea, he raised his periscope. There in the path of the moonlight shining on the ocean was a vessel so large that Hashimoto decided instantly that she must be an enemy battleship or cruiser. She was steaming directly toward the submarine, almost on a collision course. If the moonlight held, the *I-58's* torpedoes could not miss. As silence gripped the submarine, Hashimoto remained glued to the periscope, making his final calculations, lining up his boat for the optimum range.

On the *Indianapolis*, watches were changing. Men were relieving those who had been on duty on the bridge and in the engine rooms. Lieutenant Redmayne left the bridge and went to his quarters. John Muldoon finished a letter to Kathy, his sweetheart back in Lynn, Massachusetts, and climbed into his bunk. Dr. Haynes, weary after a long day of medical duties, had gone to his small cabin in the forward part of the ship.

The time now was one minute past midnight and on the *I-58* Commander Hashimoto shouted "Fire!" In a matter of seconds, six torpedoes were speeding toward the *Indianapolis* at 48 miles per hour.

Suddenly — a tremendous blast near the bow of the *Indianapolis*, and a column of water rising higher than the ship's bridge, followed moments later by two other blasts in the vicinity of the forward gun turrets, accompanied by thundering explosions deep within the ship.

Thrown from his bed, Captain McVay picked himself up and rushed stark naked to the bridge. The men there had been hurled to the deck by the explosions. Fire was visible forward.

"Do you have any reports?" McVay asked the officer of the watch.

"No, sir," the officer replied. "We have lost all communications. I can't reach the engine rooms."

"I'll send down word to get out a distress signal," McVay replied. He gave the order and rushed back to his cabin for some clothing. By the time he returned to the bridge, the ship was listing and from deep within the hull came muffled wrenching, groaning noises.

"Forward compartments flooding fast," reported a damage-control officer. "Do you wish to abandon ship?"

"Not yet," McVay replied. "I think maybe we can hold her."

He dispatched another messenger to the radio shack to confirm that the distress signal had gotten off, but the man never returned.

Commander Joseph Flynn, Executive Officer, reached the bridge. "We're finished, Captain," he said. "I recommend we abandon ship."

"Okay," McVay said. "Pass the word."

The most important task left was to make sure that a radio message had been sent. McVay started down the ladder from the bridge to the radio room, but the ship was already starting to roll over. He fell to his knees and clung to a rope. As the ship turned completely on its side, he pulled himself up, climbed over a railing and walked down the hull. Waves came to meet him, washing around his feet.

As the ship shook with the reverberating roar of the explosions, John Muldoon leaped out of his bunk and dashed into the adjacent mess hall. A badly burned sailor was stumbling about with shreds of skin dangling from his arms. Pulling on dungarees, Muldoon headed for his battle station in the engine room, but men were pouring up the ladders crying, "We've lost steam pressure. There's a fire below."

Turning back, Muldoon joined a damage-control party. To a friend who was listening on earphones, he cried, "Benny, what's happening?"

"I don't know," the sailor replied. "The phones are dead. We can't raise anybody."

Now Muldoon felt the deck wobble as the ship lurched beneath his feet. He followed another friend nicknamed "Halfhitch" through the passageway toward the stern. The walls were collapsing. The fantail was a jumble of men trying to rig lifelines. An officer was shouting, "Don't leave the ship until you get orders!"

"There won't be any orders," Muldoon told him. "There are no communications." The deck tilted, and he slid towards the water.

Lieutenant Redmayne had made his way to his battle station in the after-engine room. Lights were still burning. Turbines hummed. But pressure in the lines was dropping, and there was no communication with the bridge or forward portion of the ship.

"I'll go topside to see what's going on," Redmayne said. He hurried up the ladder toward the main deck. As he neared its top, the ship suddenly lurched heavily to starboard. Redmayne found himself pitched up the ladder, out through a hatch, and into the sea. As he came to the surface he glimpsed lights still burning below decks as *Indianapolis* rolled over on her side.

Dr. Haynes was asleep when a violent explosion shook the starboard bow of the *Indianapolis*. He rose and stumbled out into a flame-filled corridor as another explosion erupted beneath him. The blast hurled him to the deck, and the heat seared his hands. The wardroom was dark and filled with choking smoke. Feeling that he was dying, he collapsed into a chair; someone fell on top of him. He fought his way clear and to a porthole, miraculously open, and thrust out his head. With his burned hands he pulled himself out of the porthole, clambered up to the main deck, and made his way to the emergency aid station in the airplane hangar. It was already filled with men, burned, blasted, dead, dying. His chief pharmacist's mate was there, and they both began administering shots of morphine. But within a few minutes, the ship was lurching to starboard. Haynes and a few others got lifejackets on everyone they could, and they crawled up the slanting deck to the port side, where they were swept into the sea by a wave of black oil.

The stern rose higher and higher until it towered over the men struggling in the water. Men could be seen standing on the blades of the giant propellers. Then, gathering momentum, the ship slid straight down to disappear beneath the surface of the ocean. With it went all those still trapped below decks in the engine rooms and crew's quarters, and those injured, dead, and dying from the blasts of the torpedoes.

It was 12:14 A.M., July 30.

John Muldoon was among those swept into the sea at the ship's stern. Seeing the great propellers of the cruiser rise out of the water to tower above him, he swam desperately away from the ship to escape the suction as the stern slid down into the depths of the sea. All through the night, he floated in a mass of choking black fuel oil mixed with jumbled debris, eventually finding himself in the company of three other men. By dawn's light, they could see others, and Muldoon heard the familiar voice of a ship's cook.

"Spinnelli," he cried, "have you got any chow over there?"

"Are you from the *Indianapolis*?" someone called.

"No," yelled Muldoon sarcastically, "we're on a swimming party."

"This is Quartermaster Allard," the voice replied, "The Captain is with us. Get over here."

Muldoon and his companions pushed and kicked their raft over to where five men were holding onto two rafts. Captain McVay, half-blind from the fuel oil, tossed him a rope.

"Throw a bowline around that raft," he told Muldoon, and then watched incredulously as Muldoon fumbled with a knot.

"Is that what you call a bowline?" he asked.

"I'm sorry, Captain," Muldoon replied. "I'm a machinist's mate. I haven't tied this knot since I was a recruit in boot camp four years ago."

Soon three rafts were lashed together and McVay, directing an inventory, found that he had ten cans of Spam, two tins of malted milk tablets, seventeen cans of biscuits, a first aid kit, a can of signaling flares and a signaling mirror. There was no water.

McVay felt that by rationing their supplies carefully, they could last for ten days. His wristwatch was still working, and he began to keep a log, using the stub of a pencil and scraps of paper. Watches were set. Allard tore up pieces of canvas to fashion caps for protection against the sun. As the rafts wallowed heavily in the troughs of deep ocean swells, McVay's party craned their necks and peered through oil-inflamed eyes for other signs of life. They found none, and thought they were the only survivors.

There were others. About a mile away to the southwest, Lieutenant Redmayne had a command of about a hundred men surrounding three small rafts and a floater. Farther east was the largest group — one to two hundred men in the water, in desperate straits. Without rafts, provisions, or water, they were simply struggling, swimming and floating in the sea.

As the sun rose on Monday morning, men who had been swimming alone and in tiny groups sighted other heads bobbing in the sea and heard distant calls for help. Those who were strong enough gathered together. Finding himself the senior surviving officer, Dr. Haynes took charge of a group of what he estimated to be between three and four hundred men, drenched in fuel oil, swimming, paddling, drifting, clinging to bits of wreckage. As a doctor, he was wild with frustration. All about him were badly burned and wounded men, but there was no first-aid equipment — *nothing* to relieve pain and suffering. For many of the burned and injured, it was to be their last day. Exposed to the pitiless glare of the tropical sun, without water or medical treatment, they grew steadily weaker until death overtook them.

One man in Haynes's group found a cork life ring. It was buoyant enough to support one badly injured sailor. A long line trailed from the ring, and Haynes directed them to station themselves along the line to keep themselves from drifting out of sight. Soon there were fifty or sixty men clinging to the line. Slowly it coiled by itself around the life ring, forming a natural protective circle. Freed from the fear of being alone in the sea, the men on the line dozed, supported each other, and clung to life and hope.

The sea was calm, but the intense glare of the sun on the great oil slick created a blinding photophobia. Even through closed eyes, it burned and blinded until men cried out that they could not see. Some, endowed with enormous strength and determination, tore strips of clothing from their bodies to shield their own and other's eyes.

For Dr. Haynes, the cries of "Doctor! Doctor!" never ceased. Again and again he would swim over to a sailor striving desperately to help, to use his medical knowledge to determine whether there was a spark of life left. When it was clear to him that there was

Captain Charles B. McVay describes the sinking to war correspondents.

none left, he would repeat the Lord's Prayer, remove the dead man's dog tags and lifejacket, then let him sink slowly away. Nothing in his life ever caused Dr. Haynes greater anguish than being unable to help these men who so desperately needed medical assistance.

Those who lived to see dawn break on Tuesday felt a surge of hope. This was the morning that the *Indianapolis* was due to reach Leyte in the Philippines. Radio messages announcing the arrival of the ship had been sent from Guam. When they failed to arrive, more messages would fly back and forth. Search planes would be dispatched. Their ship's course and speed were known. It would certainly be only a matter of hours before the debris and giant oil slick were discovered.

But, incredibly, the strangest chapter in the tragedy was now about to unfold. Even though the *Indianapolis* was overdue and unreported since it had left Guam, the Navy did not know that it had been lost. No planes or ships were being dispatched, because no one had any idea the ship was in trouble.

According to printed naval procedures for routing combatant ships, *"Arrival reports shall not be made."* If a combatant ship arrived at its expected port, it was not to be reported. If it did not arrive, it was not to be reported either. It was to be assumed that the ship had been diverted, delayed, etc. Thus, in Leyte and on Guam on Tuesday, no one took the slightest notice of the fact that the *Indianapolis* had not appeared or been heard from.

On Monday, Captain McVay had picked up one more raft and a lone sailor. With a command of four rafts and ten men, he doled out tiny portions of the rations at each sunset and scanned the skies for searchers. He, too, was sure that by Tuesday, his ship would be missed, but he felt that it might take days to find them. On Monday and Tuesday his men sighted high-flying aircraft. McVay used his mirror and flare pistol to signal to them, but the planes flew on. McVay cut the daily ration in half in hopes that they could last twenty days instead of ten. But without rain they would die from thirst long before then. Already their throats and lips were parched and blistered. Salt-water ulcers were appearing all over their bodies. John Muldoon spent much of his time staring at a four-foot shark that prowled among the rafts. During the daylight, the shark kept out of range of the paddles with which they tried to flail him, but at night they would feel him bumping and ripping at the rafts and were fearful that he might attract a whole school of sharks and barracuda. As one man slipped into delirium, the others fought off the growing fear that they were doomed to drift beneath the broiling sun until death overtook them.

By Tuesday afternoon, Dr. Haynes, with clinical detachment, was noting the steady physical deterioration of himself and those around him. Although the seawater was warm, it was at least fifteen degrees lower than the human body, and he and the others were shaken by severe chills. Loss of body fluids from vomiting the oil, together with severe shock and exhaustion, brought on high fever. His throat was inflamed, and he was burning with thirst, but still he hoarsely exhorted and implored, "Don't drink the water! It won't do you any good. It will kill you."

The salt in the seawater, he knew, would act like a powerful laxative. It would bring on diarrhea, more dehydration, and an ever-mounting craving for more fluids. But another day under the burning sun was too much for some of the men, and they quenched their thirst with deep drafts of sea water. Soon they became wild-eyed and frenzied. Other sailors who were still resisting the urge to drink were drowned in their struggles to save them.

As night fell on Tuesday, a voice arose, "There's a Jap here. He's trying to kill me."

"Get him! Get the Jap!" arose cries from all sides. Knives were drawn, and men slashed and stabbed at each other.

Haynes was attempting to subdue and calm a man, when he was thrust under water and held there by two others who attempted to drown him. As the fighting became more desperate, the group separated. Men who had clung together for their lives now swam and struggled to escape each other's attacks.

At last, Haynes found himself alone. A full moon rose in the sky. Whenever he glimpsed crazed men in the water, he swam away from them. But his strength was fading, and when late during the night he heard other voices, he called out feebly for help. A man swam over to him. It was his chief pharmacist's mate. He put his arm around him, "Easy, Doc. Hold on. I'll hold you up."

He towed Haynes to another group of survivors who were in a little less desperate straits. Putting his arm through Haynes's lifejacket, the pharmacist's mate supported him on his hip while he slept. In this fashion many who would have died hung on.

Wednesday was the day when the men in the water reached the limit of their endurance. Their kapok life preservers, soaked and water-logged, had lost most of their buoyancy, and only the men's heads remained above the choppy sea. With no fresh water since Sunday, their thirst was overwhelming; it became impossible for Haynes and others to dissuade them from drinking. Burning up with fever, dehydrated and delirious, they could no longer believe that the cool, clear water in which they were floating could harm them. Many cupped their hands and drank deeply. Soon hallucinations were common. A man dove down in the sea and reappeared, exclaiming, "I've found it! The ship is down there!" And to others he said, "There's water down there! I dove down and found a scuttlebutt in the after-diving compartment. It's working. There's good fresh water down there!"

A frenzy seized many men as they dived deep. Some surfaced shouting, "There's water! Fresh water! All you can drink! Down below!"

Even Dr. Haynes saw the ship shimmering in the water beneath him. He almost dove down toward it, but he knew that it must be a mass hallucination. He drifted as men dove and reappeared, shouting with glee. Some shed their life preservers in order to dive even deeper. They were never seen again; even those who regained the surface sank further into the delirium that preceded death.

Toward evening Haynes noticed a group of men had formed themselves into a long line in the sea and seemed to be waiting with patient expectancy for something to happen. When Haynes asked why they were lined up, one explained, "There's a hotel up there, Doc. We're waiting to get in. But it only has one room and one bed. We have to take our turns. Better get in line with us right away."

There was no hotel . . . no water . . . no hope. Only more dying. Another night closed in. For three days the ship's chaplain had swum from one group of men to another, praying with them, urging them to fight to survive, consoling those who could not make the effort. But this night the chaplain, too, became delirious. He lapsed into a feeble chant in English and Latin and struggled against the sailor who had been supporting him. Thrusting his arm through the chaplain's life jacket, Haynes held him with all his strength and then tried to reach the sailor to help him, too, but it was no use. The exhausted sailor drifted away, face down in the water, and disappeared in the moonlight. A little later the chaplain, too, ceased struggling.

As another day dawned, one group of men decided that they would swim to Leyte. The nearest land was 600 miles away. Haynes and others tried to dissuade them, but they swam away, never to be seen again. It seemed to make little difference, for it was clear that Thursday would be the last day of life for the men in the water. Semi-conscious, dying, they drifted in their water-logged life jackets, silently suffering, mutely sinking into oblivion.

It was midday on Thursday when Dr. Haynes heard the roar of a large airplane. He scarcely bothered to lift his head so sure was he that it was just another cruel delusion in the delirium into which he felt himself sinking. But as the roar of engines grew steadily louder, Haynes and others saw that it was indeed a real plane. Nothing in the tragic voyage of *Indianapolis* was stranger than the quirk of fate that brought this plane swooping out of the sky.

Lieutenant Wilbur C. Gwinn, commander of a Navy patrol bomber, was on a flight far north of the island of Peleliu when he left his seat in the cockpit and went to the rear tail blister of his airplane to help his crew untangle a trailing radio antenna wire. The plane had dropped down to 5,000 feet to get under an overcast that was forming, and Gwinn was unreeling the wire when he suddenly glimpsed an oil slick in the ocean. There was no reason to believe it could be coming from anything but a Japanese submarine. Gwinn made a dash back to the cockpit while the crew opened the bomb-bay doors and prepared for a bombing run. Diving down to 1,000 feet, Gwinn headed straight for the slick. In another ten seconds, the plane would have let go a string of bombs. But at the last moment, Gwinn and his co-pilot saw heads in the water. He zoomed up and swung around for another look. There were men down there, no doubt about it, floating in the oil and waving feebly.

Not knowing whether he had sighted Japanese or Americans, Gwinn dropped life rafts, sound buoys, and lifejackets. Then he pulled up and, using the long-range radio antenna, got off a message: "Sighted thirty men in water. Lat. 11°30' North, Long 133°30' east." As he climbed for more altitude, he radioed again: "Count seventy-five in water," and then a minute later "Count one hundred and fifty."

The greatest search-and-rescue operation of World War II was underway. More planes roared into the sky from Peleliu. Ships from hundreds of miles around were ordered to proceed to the scene at top speed. The Navy still had no idea who the men in the water might be or how they happened to get there. As far as the Navy was concerned, none of its ships was missing. And it would be many hours and far into the night before the nearest ship could reach the area.

At 4:30 P.M., Lieutenant R. Adrian Marks, circling overhead in a huge amphibian patrol bomber radioed back to Peleliu, "Counted between 100 and 200 survivors. Many without rafts."

Daylight was fading. What would happen to the men in the water before another day dawned? Winging low over the ocean, Marks found there were twelve-foot swells, enough to swamp his plane or crumple its hull like an egg shell. Nevertheless, he made a decision and radioed back to his base, "Will attempt open sea landing."

As Dr. Haynes and others watched, the PBY glided in toward them and cut its engines. The huge plane dropped into the sea, bounced high into the air, struck heavily again, and surged to a halt. The landing had cracked open the hull, but the pumps were still holding.

Lieutenant Wilbur C. Gwinn, who spotted the men in the oil slick from his plane.

With another plane circling above him and radioing directions, Lieutenant Marks taxied among the scattered survivors. Finding many too feeble to help themselves, two of the PBY's crewmen donned lifelines and dived into the water to pull them aboard. By the time darkness fell, the PBY had rescued fifty-six men. The flooded hull of the plane was filled to overflowing, with many men lashed to the wings. As a beacon to the rescue ships, Lieutenant Marks aimed the plane's searchlight straight up into the sky. Another glowed in the distant sky as Commander W. Graham Claytor of the *Cecil Doyle*, still fifty miles away, turned on his searchlights and came charging in, ignoring the risk from Japanese submarines.

At midnight, the *Doyle* pulled up near the PBY and sent over a boat to pick up a load of survivors. One of the men brought aboard asked to be taken to the bridge. It was Dr. Lewis Haynes. Through swollen, parched lips, he whispered to Claytor, "This is all that is left of the *Indianapolis*. We have been in the water four days."

The fate of the *Indianapolis* was finally known, but it was three more days before the magnitude of the disaster became clear. Of the 1,200 officers and men who had been aboard the cruiser when the torpedoes struck, only 316 survived. Dr. Haynes and others estimated that as many as eight hundred men had abandoned ship. Five hundred had died of injuries, exposure, and thirst before the rescuers arrived.

Meanwhile, World War II was moving toward the climax. As ships and planes combed the debris in the ocean for a flicker of life, the atomic bomb that the *Indianapolis* had brought across the Pacific was loaded aboard the B-29 *Enola Gay*. At 9 A.M. on August 7, the bomb was exploded over Hiroshima. Within a week Japan had surrendered. At the same time that President Truman in Washington was announcing that the war was over, the Navy was releasing the news of the sinking of its cruiser. In some cases, "Missing in Action" telegrams reached homes in which families had just begun to celebrate. Fate, which had picked the crew of the *Indianapolis* for the mission which would help shorten the war, had decreed that they would be among the last to die and that their ship would be the last major combat vessel lost.

In the aftermath of the tragedy, the Navy court-martialed Captain McVay for the loss of his ship — even though the orders he left on the bridge that night were entirely proper, and an American submarine officer testified at his trial that zigzagging would not have prevented the sinking. Later the sentence was recanted but McVay's career was finished, and he retired from the Navy not long afterward.

Dr. Haynes never lost his love for the sea. He remained in the Navy, serving aboard ships and at shore stations for twenty years, eventually becoming Director and Chief of Surgery at the U.S. Naval Hospital in Boston, Massachusetts. After his retirement as a captain, Haynes joined the staff of the Lahey Clinic in Boston, where he was interviewed for this story.

Over the years since the war, the survivors of the *Indianapolis* have gathered regularly for reunions. In 1978, the men and their families traveled from twenty-six states to Groton, Connecticut, to attend the commissioning of a new *Indianapolis* — a 360-foot, 900-ton nuclear submarine.

"I'll be standing up for my shipmates," said Muldoon, who, like the others, saw the new submarine as a living memorial to the courage of the men who died in the Pacific.